Priestess of Isis

Priestess of Isis

Edouard Schuré
Translated by F. Rothwell, B.A.

Ibis Press
An Imprint of Nicolas-Hays, Inc.
Berwick, Maine

Published in 2004 by
Ibis Press
An Imprint of Nicolas-Hays, Inc.
P. O. Box 1126
Berwick, ME 03901-1126
www.nicolashays.com

Distributed to the trade by
Red Wheel/Weiser, LLC
P. O. Box 612
York Beach, ME 03910-0612
www.redwheelweiser.com

Cover design by Kathryn Sky-Peck

Printed in the United States of America

BJ

CONTENTS

BOOK I

THE VEIL

BOOK II

THE RAY

BOOK III

DARKNESS

BOOK IV

LIGHT

BOOK I

THE VEIL

" In sleep the eye of the spirit opens."
                                  —Aeschylus.

THE PRIESTESS OF ISIS

CHAPTER I

HYMENÆE ! HYMENÆE !

Hymen! Hymenæe!

Chanted by virgin voices, the mysterious chorus sent forth into the distance its quivering vibrations to the sound of flutes, cymbals, and *sistra*. Borne on the wings of the wind, through mingled sounds and shouts, the hymn rose above the streets, undulating above the awnings, the terraces and hanging gardens, trembling in the warm air and disappearing in the limpid blue sky like the fluttering of tiny wings. Voices more sonorous and words more distinct quickly filled the open space where a crowd was collected, making holiday.

Hymen! Hymenæe! And the motley crowd of gladiators, freed men and slaves, women and children, assembled on the steps of the basilica, on seeing the marriage procession arrive, repeated in long-drawn shouts: *Hymen! Hymenæe!*

To witness the gay spectacle, both the scum and the pride of the town had taken position in the vast forum, flanked by four temples, the heart and crown of the gay Græco-Latin city, the Acropolis of Pompeii.

It was a long rectangle. At the southern end the three tribunals opened their shady porches where stood the curule chairs of white marble. On the left stood the temple of Apollo; on the right, the arcades of the Curia and the temple of Augustus. Porticoes, altars, and statues abounded. At the other end, to the north, on a terrace of sixteen steps, rose the temple of Jupiter. Rebuilt of lava, and covered with stucco after the last earthquake, this splendid monument dominated the whole country around. Its Corinthian columns, painted purple at the base and ornamented with red and black flutings, spread out into multi-coloured capitals, like foliage decked with fruit. The shields of the architrave shone in the sun between the triglyphs. On the pediment a group of many-coloured gods flashed forth from an azure background. A couple of eagles with extended wings brooded over the projecting pediment, whilst a bronze Victory crowned the whole building.

The solitary, majestic temple, resplendent with the pomp and power of imperial Rome, and adorned with the spoils of the enslaved genius of Greece, reigned over this city of pleasure.

Beneath the portico of the temple, on the top of the terrace, three men were conversing as they watched the swarming crowd below.

The first, dressed in a rose-coloured tunic and a blue cloak, with a wreath of myrtle on his brow and his blonde curly locks shining with oil, was gesticulating excitedly as he spoke to his neighbour, a tall, slender man, wearing a black mantle, with close-cut hair and emaciated face. The third stood a few steps distant, carelessly leaning against the corner column of the peristyle. The face of the young military tribune stood out with a look of proud elegance against the red background of the massive pillar. He wore a flowing white toga with broad purple bands and a light bronze crown imitating the leaves of the oak tree. In all that crowd of servile senators, cynical magistrates and priests bored to death, his countenance was the only one which seemed to reflect the soul of Rome. At a front view his broad, strong brow, firm mouth, projecting chin, and deep steady eyes beneath their contracted brows, all seemed to compose the mask of a Brutus. But on looking at the delicate profile, stern and hard as a Roman medal, with the domineering aquiline nose and tightly-pressed lips, one would have taken him for a youthful Tiberius of thirty. Was this man, with his flashing eyes beneath that ram-like brow, meditating liberty or tyranny? None of his friends—himself less than any other—could have told this.

"Well, Ombricius Rufus, tribune and primi-pilaris, what art thou thinking of, thou who hast just returned from the East, covered with glory and renown, crowned by Titus and under the protection of Vespasian? By virtue of thine inheritance from thy veteran uncle thou hast become one of us. What thinkest thou, the most valorous of Roman knights, of our city, the pearl of Campania?"

"Thou jestest, Simmias," replied Ombricius bitterly, "for neither my valour nor my glory is to be envied. True, I have obtained a crown, but I am in disgrace, and my uncle's inheritance, a wretched hovel and a small field, are not worth a Suburra tavern. As for this city of yours, it appears to me very small."

"Then what is thy desire?"

"I know not, though my ambition is too lofty to be content with so little. Thou art right, I have aimed at glory, but the fickle god-dess has betrayed and disgusted me. Shall I spend my life casting longing eyes on a Capitol I can never attain to?"

"Give pleasure a trial."

"Willingly would I do so, but such pleasure would have to be sufficiently great and powerful

to pour forgetfulness into my mind. Where
shall I find the nectar which will extin-
guish the fire eating out the very marrow of
my bones?"

"Look at this city beneath thy feet," said the
wealthy, loquacious Greek, with an oratorical
wave of the hand as though speaking from the
top of the Pnyx. "Look at Pompeii, with her
palaces, her baths and theatres; in comparison
with her, Rome is nothing more than an old vice-
wrinkled matron, and Parthenope a mere street
courtesan beside a Greek courtesan, who plays
on the cithara, sings like the Muses, and dances
like the Graces. She knows pleasure, literature,
and art, and here offers thee, as in a basket,
her actors, her musicians and her women. All
belongs to thee—branches, flowers, and fruit—
if thou wilt. Look and choose!"

"Then let it be so!" said Ombricius, leaving
the colume. As he spoke, he slapped Simmias
on the shoulder and exclaimed:

"This day I will make my choice between
glory and pleasure."

"Hercules between virtue and vice?" asked
Simmias, with a laugh.

"Not at all. Vice offered Hercules none but
the most commonplace delights; I must have
more. I want some sensation which will efface
the past, some pleasure to kill my ambition,
joy cloudless and unalloyed. To tell the truth,

I do not believe it exists, though if ever I do meet with it there is one sign by which I shall recognise it."

"What is that sign?"

"A smile of genuine happiness on a human face."

"Thou wilt see a hundred if thou seest one on this day of festival."

"I doubt it. Many a look and many a face have I fathomed, but never once have I encountered true joy—infinite, unadulterated, all-defying joy. Should I behold it to-day, I will bid farewell to the legions, to the forum, and to Cæsar, and become a convert to the religion of Epicurus. But then," added Ombricius, with a disdainful smile, "I am quite sure I shall not meet with this goddess!"

"A sophist's jest!" interrupted Calvus the Stoic. "Dost talk of glory and pleasure and forget philosophy, the only path leading to true happiness?"

"An orator's jest!" retorted Ombricius. "I too once believed in virtue; when a youth I loved my master Afranius, a Stoic like thyself, as though he were my own father. I drank in his lessons as though they were divine words of wisdom. By Nero's orders, he cut his own veins. What has resulted from such a life and death?"

"A noble example," said Calvus, raising his

bare arm from beneath his black mantle and pointing to heaven with his thin finger.

"We must not miss the most interesting moment of the day," interrupted Simmias. "The bride arrives; let us descend among the people."

Thereupon the three friends hastily quitted the peristyle of the temple, and soon the Greek's blue cloak, the philosopher's black mantle, and the purple-striped robe of the Roman knight mingled with the crowd collected at the farther end of the forum.

.   .   .   .   .   .

The whole of Pompeii was bent on seeing Helconius the prætor accompany his daughter Julia Helconia to the temple of Jupiter, there to offer up the sacrifice of fire, and then conduct her to the abode of her husband Helvidius.

Preceded by a chorus of musicians and dancing girls, the bride's chariot, to which were harnessed a pair of white horses adorned with leaves, emerged on to the square. The eyes of all were fixed on her. Dressed in a peplum of white wool and wearing an orange-coloured veil which completely covered and concealed her features, she, a mute idol, throned it over the noisy crowd and the joyous procession. On both sides of the chariot, two young men, wearing state mantles, waved aloft torches dipped in resin. Behind the chariot, patrician children were bearing osier baskets containing a distaff, an ivory shuttle and spindles—instruments used in women's work, and which the virgin was transferring to her future home. Then came a chorus of virgins, friends of the bride, followed by magistrates with angular, massive features, and each wearing a long trailing toga; old matrons, draped like vestal virgins; beautiful patrician ladies and young men with perfumed hair adorned with fillets.

The procession halted in the middle of the square, and the people arranged themselves in a large circle under the orders of the lictors. Immediately the flutes and cymbals sounded forth, and the chorus of virgins resumed their song. At the same time the dancing girls, crowned with ivy and evergreens, advanced in front of the bride's chariot, as the Hours go before the chariot of the Dawn, and, with rhythmic songs, made a circle all around. From her chariot the bride, stately as a goddess, tore a red scarf into fragments, which she scattered to the winds, to be carried off as charms by the eager throng.

The people were now silent. The bride came down from the chariot and the whole procession mounted in the direction of the temple. Ombricius, in sombre pensive mood, was thinking over the words of the hymn he had just heard, and wondered what was the meaning of that thrill of gladness caused by Love, the secret of the power of Eros.

From the distance he saw the bride mount the steps of the temple along with her father, at the head of the procession. Through the lofty door he saw the veil of fire, target of a thousand eyes, bury itself in the darkness of the sanctuary, and said to himself:

"Is this purple and orange veil the aim and end of all human effort, the crown of power and the fruit of life? Wherefore extol to the skies this ignorant virgin who, to-morrow, will be as all other women? Does happiness smile beneath that veil?"

Then he added ironically:

"O deceptive light of Love, wrapt round with the red veil of Desire, men fling themselves on to thee like maddened insects on to a flame, only to be burned and consumed through and through. Grief and sorrow, deception and disgust, crime and madness, this is what they find in the flames. O treacherous *flammeum*, impenetrable and all-devouring veil of fire!

Absorbed in thought, Ombricius buried himself in the crowd. Soon other feelings took possession of him. The people were strangers to him, as were also the magistrates and the bride herself, but the splendour of the rites, the dignified, graceful movements spoke of a sacred order, the eternal rhythm of things.

Instead of seeking after what was impossible, would it not be better humbly to submit to the law, form a link in the mighty chain, a docile note in the harmony of the universe?

At this moment a litter crossed the square; six Lydian slaves, with dark, savage faces, bore proudly on their shoulders the richly-adorned palanquin. Behind its half-closed curtains a faint glimpse could be caught of a superb woman's form dressed in violet. Indolently reclining on purple cushions, she was carrying a large ivory-handled fan of peacock's feathers. A golden comb, in the form of a diadem, crowned her shining black hair. Her dilated nostrils breathed in the odours scattered about in the air, whilst her eyes, rolling to and fro in their orbits, looked down on the crowd like those of a panther at rest. The haughty attitude and quiet look alike testified to a feeling of profound indifference.

Ombricius could not remove his eyes from that haughty, voluptuous form. The bearers were making a path through the crowd with loud cries, and jostling the young man, when the lady, with a turn of her supple neck, exposed to the gaze of Ombricius her charming bosom and imperially-poised head. Her eyes, dark and calm as those of a wild antelope, gave him a keen glance accompanied with a faint smile.

At the same time a Pæstum rose, thrown with stealthy hand, grazed the cheek of Ombricius and slipped into the fold of his toga.

"Knowest thou that woman?" said Ombricius Simmias, when the palanquin had disappeared in the street.

The wealthy Greek opened wide his eyes, and an eager expression came over his sensual mouth.

"Hedonia Metella, a rich Roman lady, a prætor's widow in search of a husband, the most dissolute and ambitious woman in Pompeii. She is worthy of thee, wily Ombricius, for you both seem possessed of an insatiable soul beneath an impassive mask."

Ombricius smiled in disdain, though his mind was troubled. Just now, at the sight of the veiled bride's procession, there had come back to memory the noblest impulses of his youth towards duty and virtue. But now, beneath the provocative glance of the proud patrician, a smouldering flame had enveloped his brain. Pleasure and ambition, between which he wished to choose, suddenly appeared before him in that powerful glance, seeming to attract him to a throne of unknown delights. Hence a new-born desire, more imperious than all the rest.

"Shall we go and see her?" said Simmias. "I know her."

"No!" said Ombricius, with terrified gesture.

Then he added in tones of sadness which astonished the frivolous Greek: "I would like to see the bridegroom the moment the bride removes her veil. Perhaps on his face I shall behold the happy smile I vainly seek!"

"Thou shalt see more than that," said Calvus the Stoic, who had now rejoined his friends. And, seizing the tribune's brawny arm with his thin hand, he added in low, mysterious tones: "After the priest of Jupiter has pronounced the marriage ceremony, a private festival will be celebrated by the newly-married couple. Only the closest friends of Helvidius are invited. Thou shalt form one of the party, for thou art worthy of the honour; I have spoken to him of thee."

"Then what must I do?"

"When the main body of the guests has departed, keep close to me. We shall stay behind with the friends I spoke of."

"And what shall I see then?"

"A marriage after the rite of Isis."

"The rite of Isis? What is that?"

"A mystery. We shall soon see."

"Who is to perform this ceremony?"

"The new Egyptian hierophant, who has been summoned to Pompeii by the decurions to reform the temple of Isis. They say he is an ascetic and a sage, named Memnones, who has been in Pompeii three months with his adopted daughter, Alcyone. So far no one has seen the face of the prophetess, for she is always veiled. Thou wilt see her this evening for the first time."

"Be it as thou sayest," said Ombricius; "I will follow my destiny. Two chosen virgins, the bride and the prophetess, will this day show me their unveiled faces and souls. If I discover therein neither happiness nor truth, then Jupiter and Isis are vain words. Come along!"

"I will leave you both to your mysteries," said Simmias. "This evening we will toast thee, Ombricius, and thou shalt declare thy choice before Myrrhina the actress and two girl flute-players. This evening, then, I shall expect thee at my house."

CHAPTER II

THE ELECT COUPLE

THE servants stationed in front of the house of Helvidius conducted Calvus and his companion into the vestibule, whose sole ornaments consisted of a statue of Minerva and a bronze chandelier. The two friends proceeded to the entrance hall, which was open to the sky and supported by Ionic columns. The place was crowded with people. Beneath the portico, on the left, were arranged the young men, whilst on the right stood the virgins who were to chant the nuptial song. The guests and members of the family crowded into the second room, which resembled the first and was called the peristyle. Under the guidance of a relative of Helvidius, the two new-comers made their way, not without difficulty, to a kind of semicircular retreat, with vaulted roof. This was the family sanctuary where the marriage ceremony had just begun.

In the centre, a brilliant flame was burning on a small marble altar, wreathed with flowers. Ivory statuettes of ancestors and terra-cotta images of the Lares, each standing on a pillar, formed a semicircle around. Behind the altar, the priest of Jupiter, an old man in a purple robe, threw on the fire grains of incense from a golden dish. The bride had drawn her veil slightly aside as the bridegroom held out to her the sacred cake, the *farreum*, which, after breaking into two, they ate as they looked steadfastly at the flame, the priest all the time uttering unintelligible words in old Latin. Then they drank in turn from a goblet containing wine mingled with honey, of which they poured a libation into the fire. Twice the fire crackled, shooting into the air a brighter flame. Then the bride and bridegroom, holding out their hands, looked fixedly at each other. The priest said in loud tones:

"In the name of Jupiter, the Lares, and the flame of the hearth, I declare you to be one. By the bread shared, the wine drunk, and the fire stirred you are now husband and wife. Julia Helconia, I declare thee to be the wife of Marcus Helvidius. His gods are thy gods, his house thy house, his relations thy relations, and his friends thy friends. By human and divine law are ye joined together."

Thereupon the husband lightly removed the veil from the brow of the bride and took both her hands in his. Looking into each other's eyes, they stood there motionless. The priest cast over the couple some lustral water and a few embers as he uttered the words :

"Jupiter, the god of oaths and of the hearth, alone can loosen those whom he hath joined together."

The whole assembly preserved a religious silence. With deep attention all had followed the sacred rite, as though every word the priest uttered had the power of a magical incantation.

Helvidius conducted his young wife to a side niche between the peristyle and the temple of the Lares. Two seats covered with lamb-skin had been placed there; on this domestic throne he seated her by his side. Julia Helconia, her bride's veil now cast aside, appeared with her hair collected on the top of her head, like all the vestals. She wore a wreath of vervain, the symbol of virgin purity, whilst her thick tresses were pierced by a golden arrow. the symbol of marital power. . . . An ineffable smile gave a softened expression to her noble features. Helvidius, with his beard and wavy hair, his fearless glance and broad expansive brow, resembled a torch-bearer saluting the goddess at the festivals of Eleusis.

Though admiring this couple, Ombricius could not restrain a feeling of envy; he suffered at the thought that such happiness was not his, and even more at feeling it inaccessible to his nature.

The priest of Jupiter departed. After innumerable congratulations and farewells the family had proceeded into the hall, where slaves discreetly passed to and fro, filling with wine the goblets of the guests. A dozen friends remained in the peristyle to attend the rite of Isis. The door of the hall was closed; night had come, and a single lamp, suspended from the ceiling by a brass chain, lit up the domestic temple.

At a signal from the master of the house, a slave opened a small door leading to the garden.

Then there was seen to enter a man of advanced age and austere mien, leading by the hand a stately, solemn-looking virgin, dressed like himself in the priestly garb of the temples of Egypt.

This was Memnones and his adopted daughter, Alcyone.

.   .   .   .   .   .

Memnones wore the linen robe of the priests of Isis and the leopard's skin flung over his right shoulder. The hierophant was tall of stature, gaunt and imposing. He was a man of projecting forehead and wide temples, his grey hair close-cut, straight nose, and pointed chin. In his right hand he held a *crux ansata* —a looped cross—the distinctive mark of the priests of Isis and Osiris. This key to the mysteries, the symbol of initiation, was made of a compound of gold and silver, a metal the

Greeks of Alexandria called *argyrochryseon*. The maiden he led by the hand formed the most striking and graceful contrast imaginable with her master.

She wore the costume of Isis, a pale yellow tunic with straight long folds, and on her head a blue *klaft*, whose folded wings, like a bird's, entirely concealed her hair. On her brow she wore a coiling serpent of gold, whilst from her pearl-coloured neck hung a tiny figure in black basalt. The face was that of a searching, un-tamed Psyche. The eyes, like veiled lamps, shone gently, seeming to seek something afar off, unseen by mortal gaze. In her hand she carried a few lotus flowers.

Alcyone sat down in front of the newly-married couple, to the left of the marriage chamber, in which could be seen a bed of ivory decked with roses.

The appearance of the priestess had surprised and fascinated Ombricius. He looked at her attentively. Quietly seated there, with arms crossed over her bosom and head flung back, she looked at the couple with long steadfast gaze. The slight quiver of her nostrils and the more frequent heaving of her bosom alone betrayed her emotion. Suddenly her eyelids began to quiver and finally closed ; Alcyone was sunk in profound slumber.

.   .   .   .   .   .

Then Memnones, standing before the family altar, holding the looped cross in his hand, spoke as follows, in slow, grave accents:

"At thy summons, Helvidius, I bring to thee and thy companion the benediction of Isis, of light and peace. Sublime truth can never be fathomed, though some of its rays have illumined the earth. Like a chaste virgin, glorious truth shines through the night of time. It sleeps in the temples, awakes at the voice of prophets, and speaks to its elect alone. Yours, therefore, its ray of splendour and joy, yours the message of Isis.

"You have just been joined together for earth and in earthly fashion; I am now ready, since you wish it, to unite you for heaven and in divine fashion. This is for you the day of trial; the hour is a decisive one. Are you indeed an elect, predestined couple? There are but few of these amongst millions of married couples and lovers. Or is your dream merely a mirage of terrestrial desire, the fleeting mist of your troubled senses, like that of countless couples who embrace but for a time? If you are ripe for the eternal marriage, ready not only for the works of the flesh but also for divine creations, the Voice from on high must speak to you, and your heart must reply thereto. The Voice from on high will speak, if it so desires, by the mouth of the prophetess. Give ear, therefore, and choose. The soul of the initiate is free, free as fire in air.

" First of all, listen to the message.

" Souls are the daughters of Osiris, the divine Spirit, and of Isis, the celestial light. Shining sparks, they were conceived by uncreated light fecundated by the creative Fire. Devoured with the desire of life, they come down on earth and incarnate in a thousand forms, then lightly rise to their natal heaven to descend once again, like the drops of rain which Ocean drinks in and the sun draws back. But whether in joy or sorrow, in songs or tears, in adoration or in blasphemy, they all aspire to return, radiant, to their initial source, the glorious, sacred night, where there is no longer a check to desire, a limit to knowledge, and where Isis and Osiris mingle together in a mighty ocean of sonorous and living light.

" The tracks of souls through the worlds are more diverse than the flight of swallows. Myriads float about in idle uncertainty, in a troubled limbo, an eternal shade. Thousands delight in evil, bury themselves in darkness and return to the elements. There is only a small number whose strength grows by struggle, whose feeble light condenses in the murky abyss. The latter, after innumerable efforts, life after life, rise to the pure fountain of immortal Dawn and plunge into the maternal Light, furrowed

with incessant flashes by the creative Fire.
Henceforth they share in divine power and the
government of the world.

"Souls, like bodies, are endowed with sex;
they are male or female according as they
resemble more closely their Father, the creative
Spirit, or their Mother, the living, plastic Light.
Destined to live and complete themselves in
couples, in order to reflect the perfect Being,
each seeks its inseparable companion, but
alas! . . . through how many wanderings! . . .
in the midst of what torture! . . . after how
many abortive attempts and lives of pain!

"There are but few perfect couples on earth!
Happy the man and the woman who, when they
meet, thrill throughout the depths of their being
as with a divine remembrance. Happy the
husband who has recognised and greeted the
immortal spouse! Sacred is their embrace!
Nothing can separate them or tear them asunder,
for they bear within themselves the torch of
wisdom, the science of love, the creative fire,
the power to feel, to understand, and to give
happiness.

"Do you, proud Helvidius and intrepid
Helconia, belong to these? Do you feel courageous enough to take the mighty oath? Will
you be bold enough to brave all the powers in
the name of the might of the soul, to dread not
the serpents of hatred, to consecrate your love

to the divine task, to be even here below the elect, loving couple?

"If it be so, join your hands over the looped cross, the sign of immortal life, without fear of being destroyed by the celestial fire we now invoke!"

. . . . . .

Pale with suppressed emotion, Helvidius and Helconia had risen from their seats, hand in hand. Their minds seemed decided on the performance of the solemn act, but in their attitude there was a lurking hesitation, as though the gesture they were about to make would hurl them from the banks of time into the abyss of eternity.

Just at this moment the eyes of Ombricius were attracted by a movement made by Alcyone.

Plunged in profound sleep, her head leaning against the wall, the young priestess had so far not stirred from her seat. Suddenly she sprang to her feet and raised her hands to her head. Though her eyes remained closed, an expression of terrible anguish came over her face. Her lips moved as though she were mumbling a string of disconnected words. Memnones noticed this, so he walked up to her, and touched her on the brow to drive away the terrifying vision. Violently she thrust him aside, and exclaimed imperiously:

"Leave me, all of you!"

The *klaft* which covered her head fell to the ground, whilst her wavy locks streamed in golden circlets over her shoulders. Her bare arms were thrust forward as though to clasp the limits of space. Her eyes, now open, assumed an expression of terror, the pupils being dilated and darkened by the ecstatic condition she was in. Another soul had entered the maiden; no longer was she the timid virgin; she was the Pythoness possessed by her god.

Memnones fell back.

Then, in panting, though musical and rhythmic accents, Alcyone began:

"Unhappy town! Pompeii! . . . Pompeii! . . . City of beautiful paintings and couches of luxury . . . of pleasure and forgetfulness, . . . wherein Rome delights herself, . . . where Crime and Voluptuousness lie together on purple cushions . . . meditating fresh deeds of evil, . . . what destiny is thine? . . . What fiery rod threatens thee? . . . What mantle of darkness wraps thee about? . . . Ah! thou dancest with laughter and triumph . . . like a Bacchante decked with vine-leaves, and wearing a dark veil over thine eyes. . . . Nothing can now deliver thee from thy fate. . . . Oh! the flaming streets . . . and then dark night . . . the earth quaking to its very foundations . . . the thunder above . . . and the thunder below, more terrible than the other! . . . And all

these fugitives . . . and all these dead! . . .
The ashes falling on arms and heads. . . . Ah!
I am choking!"

The prophetess, on the point of fainting away,
fell into the arms of Memnones. Her head
sank back like a broken ear of corn. With his
cross he touched her forehead. The cold metal
suddenly calmed her, and, gradually raising her
head, she clung to her master's arm and continued:

"Why bring me here, Memnones, to this
abyss of perdition? . . . So far, oh! so far
from the sacred Nile, that peaceful, meandering
stream! . . . Wherefore sacrifice me to thy
science, insatiable master, and fling me as a holo-
caust to this accursed city? . . . Look there, away
outside the city gates, on the path leading to
the tombs . . . the smoke is rising from my
nuptial couch . . . high as a pyramid . . . and
I am lying there, awaiting my husband. . . .
The incense burning at the foot of the couch
rises into the air like a blue serpent . . . mingling with the black smoke of the volcano."

As she uttered these enigmatical words,
Alcyone escaped from the arms of her master.
A radiant joy flooded her face, all transfigured
in ecstatic trance. Raising her arms, in the
attitude of a bird about to fly away into the air,
she sang rather than said:

"The Barque! . . . the Barque of Isis! . . .

It is floating through the immensity of the heavens. . . . Now it is coming towards us. . . . How light and beautiful it is ! . . . The goddess is seated at the stern, holding the rudder. . . . And standing by the prow . . . who is that stately oarsman ? . . . Is it thou . . . my Beloved . . . Anteros ? . . . He is signalling to me. . . . Yes, I am coming ! "

Overcome with emotion, Alcyone again almost swooned. Memnones checked her once more. Then, animated by sudden energy, she turned towards the married couple and in imperious accents said :

"You, the chosen couple, join hands over the cross. . . . Swear the great oath . . . and you shall mount into the Barque ! . . . Come ! "

Helvidius and his wife approached as though attracted by a magnet.

Their hands took hold of the looped cross, joining together over it. Above shone the symbol, seeming to cast pallid flashes of light around their hands.

In a deep, powerful voice Helvidius said :
" Thine for eternity ! "

Helconia added in accents gentle though firm :
" Where thou art, Helvidius, I will be, Helvidia."

Alcyone, convulsively clasping both their hands in hers, which had become strong as a vise, added solemnly :

"Love, Light, and Joy be your portion . . . mine be anguish, darkness, and death!"

Then, with head flung back, and arms raised aloft in despair, she exclaimed:

"The Barque ascends . . . it disappears. . . . Anteros bids me farewell. . . . He is leaving me! . . . Earth holds me once more!"

The final exclamation was accompanied by a heartrending sob. Upheld by Memnones, Alcyone sank down on to her seat, lifeless and cold. Her eyes had again closed, a state of deep lethargy succeeding the trance. Helvidius, with his wife and their friends, formed a circle round her, ready to lavish on her any needed attentions. Memnones refused all help, saying:

"Be not uneasy; all I need is a little lustral water. This I will gently sprinkle over her, and in a few minutes she will quietly awake, without the faintest remembrance of what she has said or of what has taken place."

.   .   .   .   .   .

In a whirl of conflicting emotions, Ombricius had followed the strange ceremony of the mystic marriage and the frenzied transports . . . stranger still . . . of Alcyone. Surprise and curiosity were followed by irony and stupor. In spite of a dull feeling of revolt, he had ended by submitting to the invincible fascination. He did not believe in gods or the immortality of the soul, nor had he any liking for priests, whom he looked upon as either impostors or fools. But how could he suspect the seeress and the splendour of her trance? At first it was the sudden transformation of her whole being that had attracted him. Afterwards the wonderful beauty of her attitudes, the outburst of her winged words had borne him away to unknown realms. He knew naught of the meaning of her oracles and visions, but then had he not seen the glow of another world on her shining countenance? Yes, that superhuman joy he had vainly sought, that smile of divine bliss he had seen flickering for a moment on that virgin's face, only to die away like a sunbeam in an ocean of tempest-driven clouds! Ah, how was he to penetrate that sanctuary, enter the door of that soul? What would he not have given at that moment for a single glance from Alcyone!

Spurred on by such thoughts, Ombricius returned to the entrance, and waited to see the priestess take her leave. She soon appeared, accompanied by Memnones, bareheaded, and again looking like a timid Psyche. The torches enhanced the alabaster pallor of her face, lighting into flame the twisted fringes of her golden locks. Superstitious maidens, standing near, touched her dress and kissed her hands. Without uttering a word, she gave them a distant, sorrowful smile.

Ombricius, in ambush behind the chandelier,

watched her as she passed, with an intense desire
to fathom the mystery of that soul. At a distance of three paces from the young man she
met his steadfast fixed glance. She halted
and shuddered with fear. Then the glance of
Ombricius assumed an expression of anguish,
and he clasped his hands in involuntary supplication. Straightway a softened look came
into Alcyone's eyes, and a smile of pity appeared
on her thin, arched lips. Her lotus wreath fell
to the ground. Straightway Ombricius, with
bowed head and eyes downcast, picked it up
and gave it into her hands.

Rising and taking a step backwards, he saw
that Alcyone was blushing, and had, in her turn,
cast down her eyes. With a protecting gesture
Memnones replaced the *klaft* on her head, giving
Ombricius a piercing glance as he did so. Then
the priest of Isis and his seeress slowly departed from the nuptial abode between rows of
kneeling slaves.

On returning home, Ombricius was too greatly
moved to call on Simmias. The shops were
closed, drunken cries would come at intervals
from the taverns on the way, whilst from the
gardens came uncertain voices or the dying
sounds of stringed instruments or flutes. Dull
with slumber and tired with pleasure, the town
was sleeping, whilst myriads of stars lit up the
immeasurable vault of heaven.

Filled with a superhuman emotion such as he had never before experienced, Ombricius reflected : "What has come over me ? Are my life and my thoughts about to change their course ? Has the universe suddenly grown larger ? Can there be another visible world behind this one ? Ah ! who will ever know this ? A dense, black veil conceals the secret of life. And lo ! a virgin has raised a corner of this veil . . . and a dazzling ray has shot forth ! . . . Where shall I meet this light again, if not in Alcyone's eyes ? But shall I ever see her again ? "

He crossed the empty forum, peopled in the silence of the night by the motionless statues of consuls and emperors. On reaching the vast arcade he cast his eyes over mountains, sea, and sky, as though imploring their aid in his dire distress. From the grey cone of Vesuvius, surmounted with a ruddy gleam, issued a thin stream of smoke. The two banks of the vast gulf stretched out like vaporous arms, scarce visible, away to the horizon. The stars twinkled with a deceptive light, and the entire universe, splendid and impenetrable, set the questioner at defiance, concealing beneath its magic beauty the sublime and terrible mystery of creation.

The veil had fallen back.

CHAPTER III

THE home of Ombricius, which he had inherited from his uncle, was a short distance out of Pompeii, in the middle of a field of vines and olives. A ruined house served as a dwelling for the farmer and the three slaves who tilled the soil.

He stirred up the fire and lit his terra-cotta lamp, which he placed on the table beside a scanty dish of pease which he had not touched at the morning meal. The preceding day and night had stirred up in him all the smouldering ashes of his past life. His first feeling was one of bitterness against his poverty, a wild revolt against the injustice of fortune.

What a troubled and tempest-tossed life his had been! His father was a veteran of Tiberius, a Roman knight owning property in Tusculum; his mother was a freed slave. His gloomy childhood was passed under the sanguinary reign of Nero, whilst his youth was polluted by the atmosphere of debauch and monstrous crime, at that time emanating from the throne of the Cæsars, and weighing over the whole world like a poisoned cloud. All the same this was the purest part of his life, the only one illumined by a ray of light. Destined to a public life, he attended the classes of rhetoric at Rome. His real master, however, was Afranius, an old Stoic philosopher, who lived in a solitary house on Mount Tusculum, where he gave lessons to a few pupils. In the presence of this poor man, whom Nero had exiled from Rome, and who lived on onions and dry bread in a peasant's hut, he had experienced the loftiest emotions of his youth, the purest yearning after virtue of a yet unsullied soul. The day on which Afranius had expounded to him and a few other youths the theory that the root-idea of Zeno's philosophy, the only good of the soul, lies in its freedom of will, that the sovereign boon is in the empire it exercises over itself, a new conception of man and of life had entered his mind. Later on, Afranius, addressing himself directly to the youth of sixteen, had exclaimed:

"Ombricius Rufus, if thou wilt be happy and free, if thou wilt have a great soul, renounce everything. Look aloft, and thou shalt be delivered from all servitude. Dare to raise thine eyes to God and say to Him: 'Do with me as Thou wilt!'"

On hearing these words, a thrill of robust

pride had come over Ombricius. On another occasion he had asked the master if he did not regret that Rome from which Nero had exiled him. Then Afranius had pointed away on the horizon to the seven hills of the Eternal City, which, from the heights of Tusculum, resembled tiny mounds, and said:

"If thou understandest the thoughts of Him who rules the universe, and bearest them everywhere in thyself, how canst thou pine for a few pebbles and beautiful stones?"

The young disciple was filled with amazement; the soul of his master appeared to him greater than that Rome from which Nero had banished him, and which he could so thoroughly despise.

But what had raised to the highest pitch the pupil's admiration was the fact that his master manifested a courage equal to his doctrine. Far above the heroic battles and combats in which he had afterwards taken part, there was one scene which took place at Tusculum that remained graven on his memory as the apogee of human pathos and sublimity.

One day some terrified peasants came running to the philosopher in his humble dwelling, exclaiming: "Flee for thy life! Cæsar's centurion, with two of his lictors, is hunting for thee!" This meant almost certain death, but

Afranius had replied with the utmost calm, "Lead me to him." Accompanied by his disciples, he went to meet the centurion at the door of his dwelling, and accosted him with the words: "What wilt thou with me?" "Cæsar has sent to ask of thee, who hast no fear of him, what is thy best defence?" "This," said Afranius, drawing from under his tunic a dagger which he always carried about with him. "Is it against him that thou wilt use it?" "No, against myself alone, were he to curtail my liberty or my speech." "Then give it to me!" the centurion had said furiously, snatching the dagger from the Stoic's hand. The disciples turned pale, thinking that Nero's envoy was about to slay their master. The latter said calmly, without moving a step: "Thou wilt thank Cæsar, for thus would he make me free!" Thereupon the centurion handed back the weapon to the philosopher, with an ambiguous smile. "Take it back," said he; "soon thou wilt have need of it. Cæsar merely wished to test thee; but if thou seest me again, thou mayst abandon hope."

When Nero's emissaries had disappeared, the disciples knelt before their master, kissing the edge of his threadbare mantle. He gently bade them rise to their feet, and forbade them to say another word on the matter. Then he sat down, and for a portion of the night, beneath the far-off

constellations, Afranius spoke to his disciples of
the Sovereign Good, the Providence and Soul
of the World into which the human soul is
gladly absorbed after death, when it has lived
according to divine law.

That night Ombricius had resolved to be
worthy of his master, though his determination
did not last long. Soon afterwards the young
man, happening to be in Rome, heard that his
master had been beheaded by hired assassins of
Nero, who had ordered the old man's head to
be brought to him. It had been the tyrant's
whim to have with the sage a dialogue in which
he had had the last word, thus assuring his
victory over his adversary. At the same time
all the philosophers in Rome were exiled.
Overwhelmed by this disaster, Ombricius asked
himself what was the use of such courage as his
master had shown. In his revolt against human
destiny he began to pity him and suspect the
teachings of his philosophy. Abstract thought
which is unable to reform the world seemed to
him a vain thing. He also made up his mind
to acquire sufficient power to be able to decree
life or death, and dispense justice as he pleased.
From that time he had flung himself with a
kind of savage fury into the career of a
soldier.

He enlisted in the army of Vespasian, and
afterwards in that of his son, Titus, then ruling

in the East. He grew to know military life,
its joys and sorrows, the hard drills and camp
watches, endless fatigue and the distaste of
obeying implacable chiefs; but along with all
this was the pleasure of self-controlled might,
the excitement of danger, and the intoxication
of victory. Especially did he learn the joy of
command when at the head of his cohort in
battle. As the instinct of domination formed
the foundation of his nature, an all-devouring
ambition awoke in him.

Much power, he thought, would be needed
before he could acquire greater influence than
Afranius, and avenge him by crushing his own
enemies. He quickly obtained the post of tribune
in a legion of Titus, at the siege of Jerusalem.
The highest honours seemed almost within his
grasp when an act of imprudence suddenly
destroyed his audacious hopes.

At a battle in Syria the general in command
of the legion was killed. Ombricius leapt on
his horse, took command of the legion, and won
the victory. The soldiers immediately acclaimed
him as their general. Each legion claimed to
have its own Cæsar, and a legionary exclaimed,
"Long live the Emperor!" Instead of punish-
ing the soldier, Ombricius had rewarded him.
This was reported to Titus, who was jealously
defending the empire for Vespasian, his father.
Instead of appointing Ombricius general, Titus

dismissed him with a crown of honour and a
rich reward.

Just about this time Ombricius Rufus, now
an orphan, had come to take possession of his
uncle's inheritance at Pompeii. Bitterly disappointed in his ambitious plans, he was on the
point of seeking in philosophy the forgetfulness
of all his troubles, when the sight of Hedonia
Metella had given a new perspective to his
desires. Had not a single glance of the haughty
patrician, reclining in her litter, sufficed to bring
beneath his eyes the procession of all kinds
of inaccessible delights? And, as though this
image were not sufficient to disturb him, another
had followed, reaching down to unknown depths
of his being. The priestess of Isis, after the
patrician lady. . . . Alcyone, after Hedonia
Metella! . . . the glimpse of a shining heaven,
after the sombre light of an imperial hell! How
simple and wonderful that seer's soul had appeared to him! It had glided over his own
burning soul like a breath of Elysian peace.
Suddenly it had transported him far from that
bloody arena, that infamous orgy called the
world. What name could he give to the women
he had hitherto known? Mean instruments of
pleasure, or dangerous animals. And the men?
Wild beasts in helmets and breastplates, intel-
ligent and treacherous, or unfortunate hunted
animals, victims of their tormentors. Could

even Afranius himself, the noble Stoic, his master, show anything else than a powerless reason? But Alcyone was a soul! a celestial, quivering soul in the pearly whiteness of a beautiful virgin's body. He had seen and heard that human lyre whose subtle chords were touched by some invisible genius, and whose vibrations were the breaths, impalpable though sweet, of a world beyond—breaths that awakened swarms of confused thoughts and distant memories. And behind Alcyone, the simple seeress so unconscious of herself, was the whole of that invisible world of which poets speak, and which no one has seen, perhaps the only true world. . . . Ah! if only this world existed, what a conquest to achieve, how much greater that joy and that sovereignty than those of empire! A new desire caused Ombricius to thrill from head to foot. Did he already love this virgin who had answered his imperious glance with a look so soft and sorrowful? And did Alcyone love him?

In fevered excitement he stirred the embers with a branch of dry vine. The fire had gone out. The oil in the terra-cotta lamp was now spent, and the flame gave merely a ruddy gleam to the surrounding gloom. Ombricius rose to his feet with a deep sigh, which ended in a kind of groan; then he left the room. Behind the Apennines the light of dawn was just appearing,

though the gulf lay there in gloomy, dark still-
ness. Pompeii looked like a black mass, dominated by the turrets and towers of the city, the
Temple of Jupiter and the Triumphal Arch.
As he gazed, the image of Hedonia Metella,
reclining in her litter, passed before the mind
of Ombricius.

It was followed by that of Alcyone in a state
of trance. Immediately afterwards the tribune
saw in his mind's eye his master Afranius, looking sternly at him, and seeming to say in solemn
accents, "Go to the Temple of Isis to receive
initiation."

Then, beneath the glowing stars, before the
slumbering town and vapour-topped Vesuvius,
Ombricius said aloud in the silence of the
night, "So be it, I will go."

Soothed by this determination, the tired
tribune sank to sleep in the bed of the veteran.

CHAPTER IV

MEMNONES

THAT night the sleep of Memnones too was troubled, nor was his insomnia any less feverish than that of the tribune. Returning hastily with his adopted daughter, he had found the old Nubian nurse at the door of the temple. Alcyone was plunged in a kind of dull stupor, the inevitable consequence of her trance. Memnones entrusted her to the faithful servant, who carried her away to an inner room, inaccessible to all except the hierophant. Meanwhile the priest mounted to a terrace on the roof of the temple, his wonted retreat for nocturnal meditation.

Here he breathed in the fresh night air and looked up at the starry sky. Instead, however, of calming him as usual, the constellations filled his heart with increasing uneasiness. He reflected upon the strange ecstasy of Alycone, her sinister prophecies and the violent tumult that had come over her whole being on meeting the audacious stranger. These unexpected events, like successive thunder-claps, appeared to him as supernatural signs and terrible warnings.

Not only did they illumine the whole of his past by stirring up the depths of his soul, they also threw dazzling flashes over the future.

He looked about him and sighed deeply. He seemed to need more air, more space and sky. Then he remembered that the decurion Helconius had, a few weeks before, shown him a rusty bronze gate opening into the thick wall of the adjacent building. It led to a corridor through which the theatre might be entered. With the key hanging from his girdle he opened the door. Fearlessly crossing the gloomy corridors, he rapidly reached the amphitheatre and ascended to the covered colonnade crowning the building.

In the moonless night the open theatre resembled the crater of a volcano. Beyond, lay the gulf; beneath, a veil of light mist, and the dim light of the stars. Memnones sat down beneath the covered colonnade. The abyss of his soul appeared to him no less murky than that vast amphitheatre. Beneath the intensity of his gaze the whole of his life seemed to pass before him; the main scenes at first isolated, then in groups, and finally bound in a living chain.

.   .   .   .   .   .

The studious son of a Greek in Asia Minor, he saw himself in the schools of the philosophers of Alexandria. The passionate love of transcendental truth had dominated his youth, as it was now ruling over his ripened years.

At the outset he was dazzled by the eloquence
of his masters, the brilliant scaffolding of the
systems they erected, demolished and built
again; but after a time he had come to regard
the discussions of Stoics and Epicureans, disciples of Plato and Aristotle, as being the
empty sport of sophists and rhetoricians. He
was given words and abstractions, whilst all the
time his mind thirsted after the living Word
which makes the universe transparent and fills
the soul with immortality. One day, as he was
walking with an old Egyptian, the latter assured
him that the doctrine of Hermes, as formerly
taught in the temples, and of which the popular
Egyptian religion was but a rude travesty, could
alone satisfy a mind like his. " Not only did
this teaching," he said, " enlighten the mind by
its solidity and grandeur, it also added practice
to theory and experience to thought, by enabling
the pupil gradually to penetrate into the source
of things, to that invisible world where the key
to all questions is to be found."

Where could this doctrine, this teaching be
met with ?

" Alas ! " the Egyptian had replied, " the doctrine still exists in the books of Hermes, preserved in certain temples of Thebes, Memphis,
and Lower Egypt. But it is a dead letter, for
the priests who were able to give it life have
disappeared. For centuries past the science of

the mysteries has been lost to a degenerate priesthood. The infamous Cambyses put to death the mighty prophets of that religion, and burned their books. Their survivors were tolerated by the Ptolemies, but the Roman Cæsars, divining that they would be secret enemies of their own power, exterminated them. Accordingly, the heads of the temples vainly call themselves by the mighty name of 'prophet'; they are only greedy holders of immense wealth, ignorant guardians of a science they do not understand, rigid observers of ancient rites and base tools of the Cæsars and their proconsuls."

" But is there not a single one acquainted with the tradition, and who knows within himself?" asked Memnones.

" Yes, there is old Sabaccas, dismissed by Tiberius; he lives in an old tomb by the Lybian range, on the confines of the desert, not far from one of the pyramids, in the sea of sand behind Memphis."

" Can I get to know him ? "

" Say you come from me, and he will advise you."

In the wild-looking rocks of the Lybian range Memnones found Sabaccas, who looked at his visitor with piercing eye, as he said :

"Thou seekest truth, young man. Knowest thou what the love of truth costs at this day ? Look at me; I was once rich, powerful, and

happy. I had a temple of mine own, fields and
cattle, a whole town at my feet. And this is
what I have become, through loving truth for
itself and above all else. Does my path please
thee, and my aim in life appear to thee a de-
serving one ? "

" Most worthy," exclaimed Memnones, with
the enthusiasm of youth, "I call God to witness
that I will accept my fate, if only I may obtain
light ! "

" Good," said Sabaccas, looking at him long.
" Thou shalt go to the temple of Sebennytic Isis
with this tablet, on which I will make a few signs.
Smerdes the pontiff will receive thee as a scribe.
He will give thee the books of Hermes, for he
alone possesses the genuine ones ; then he will
teach thee the sacred language. This is all he
can do. If thou wilt go farther, thou must seek
alone, for, rest assured, no one can be an initiate
except through his own efforts. Truth has
only one temple, though a thousand paths lead
thereto, and each one must find his own."

Memnones took the tablet covered with hieroglyphs, whereupon the old hermit seized him
forcibly by the arm, and, looking fixedly into his
eyes, said :

"I see that thy soul is pure and thy senses
chaste ; thou hast overcome voluptuousness.
This is much though not all, for thy soul is
passionate and thy heart too tender. I fear

weakness may vanquish thee. . . . He who would conquer truth must love it with firm heart and implacable will!"

Memnones felt the old man's hand tighten about his arm like a band of iron, whilst his flaming eye pierced his own like a sword.

"One thing more," added the old man. "When thou reachest the threshold of the third sphere, come to me again, for thou wilt not pass beyond."

"What is the third sphere?" inquired Memnones.

"That thou wilt learn when thou hast passed the first two."

Thus speaking, Sabaccas rose to his feet. He placed his fleshless hand on the head of Memnones, and the young man felt a sensation of warmth come over his brain and descend into his body. A wave of dumb pity showed itself in the powerful eye of the old man. Then, as though afraid of breaking down, he shook his rags, and exclaimed in commanding accents:

"Now, go!"

Memnones descended the rocky pathway of the mountain without a single backward look. He crossed the white smooth sand and soon perceived a body of women and children who greeted with noisy acclamations and shouts of joy the stranger who had been received by the solitary prophet, the healing saint of the country.

He himself was overcome with mingled joy and
terror, for he had freely chosen his destiny, the
faintest glimpse of which filled him with mighty
exultation. At the same time, he felt that this
destiny of his would bring about something
against which it would be vain for him to strive.
With iron band and the hand of a master it
had chained down his arm.

The temple of Sebennytic Isis was situated on
the vast plain of the delta, on the right bank of
the Nile, at a distance of twenty leagues from its
mouth. This majestic river, the father of all
Egypt, as it approached the ocean spread out
like a very sea itself, in which were reflected the
heavens with all their varying colours by day
and night.

Here were passed the happiest days in Memnones' life. Smerdes the pontiff, a timid though
prudent man, had given him a favourable reception on the recommendation of Sabaccas. The
Greek of Alexandria succeeded in winning his
confidence; in a short time he learnt the language of hieroglyphics and became the first scribe
of the temple. Smerdes allowed him to study
the books of Hermes, written on papyrus rolls
and preserved in a secret chamber of the temple.
By translating them into Greek he fathomed
their inmost meaning. The knowledge of this
doctrine was a kind of revelation to the neophyte,
who felt himself witnessing the birth of the

universe along the immensity of the ages.   The different periods of the world opened out slowly before him like white, blue, and pink lotus blooms whose closed chalices emerge every morn from the surface of the Nile, unfolding one after another beneath the beams of the sun.   So also his soul was expanding over the great river of life.   For years this passionate study sufficed to satisfy his intelligence.   Then followed a period of lassitude.   Was this vision of possible truth the full possession of the great secret, or only the sport of a dazzled reason?   No, knowledge was not there; this was only a more splendid, a more beautiful dream.   Not thus could he raise the thick veil hiding the life beyond and enter into the great laboratory of souls, of real beings and of life!

He had not yet quenched his thirst at the source of things; he still remained unsatisfied.

CHAPTER V

SOME time afterwards a great event took place in the life of Memnones, the source of nameless happiness and endless anguish.

One night, as he was walking along the banks of the Nile, he saw a large barque at anchor in a small bay. By its form he recognised it as being one of those Phœnician galleys which bring into Egypt silk from Persia and purple and perfumes from Syria. Its two slender yards, bent backwards like the wings of a bird, gave it the appearance of a hawk which has just dashed down among the reeds. Attracted by invincible curiosity, Memnones drew near. There was a narrow foot-bridge between the bank and the galley, by which the priest of Isis mounted on to the deck. He was alone there, for the boatmen were feasting in the neighbouring village and the tipsy pilot lay asleep on an empty leather bottle. Then, by the light of the moon shining full on the barque, Memnones perceived a child asleep on a bed of dry sea-weeds, near the poop. Clad in a torn robe, with a rag twisted round

49

her frail form, the little girl, scarcely twelve years of age, her golden hair mingled with the sea-weed, resembled a bird with a broken wing. She uttered a long dull moan as she slept.   So painful and plaintive did it sound that Memnones said aloud :

"What is the matter, child?"

After a long silence the child awoke.   With both hands she thrust aside the locks of hair from her eyes, which were now wide open, walked up to the priest and touched his arm, as though to make sure that he was a living being.   Then, falling on her knees, she stretched out to him her hands in supplication and cried aloud :

"Save me, save me from these men!   They intend to sell me!"

Memnones, deeply moved, raised the child to her feet, and, pressing her to his breast, said :

"Have no fear; come with me!"

Stealthily the priest of Isis and the little Greek girl, clinging to his arm, made their way in the direction of the temple.   Often did she turn round to see if the evil-disposed sailors were not running after her to snatch her away from her rescuer.   Only when they had passed the great gateway did she feel reassured and tell her story to the old man.   She was born in Samothrace.   When on a voyage, her parents had been shipwrecked on a reef in the Ægean Sea.   Pirates had killed them and left the child with some

merchants in Tyre to be sold as a slave in Upper
Egypt. The rough sailors were in the habit of
beating and ill-treating the little girl. One night,
terrified by their threats, she was on the point of
flinging herself into the sea, when a stranger
appeared before her on the prow of the barque,
waved her back, and disappeared like a ghost.
A week afterwards, on seeing the priest of Isis
rise before her, she had recognised in every
feature of Memnones the apparition of the
barque.

"Then I understood," she said, "that thou
wert my rescuer, a new father sent me by the
gods."

Memnones, on his side, was convinced that this
child, endowed with second sight, was the re-
compense of all his efforts, a daughter given
to his love-weaned heart, a living torch offered
by the Powers to lead him . . . perhaps into the
mysterious regions of the life beyond; a feeble,
flickering light, though capable of growing and
shining more brightly in his hands. He, too,
when he saw the child asleep in the barque,
when he saw her rise and walk up to him as in
a dream, had been conscious of a strange thrill
in his heart, and believed that he recognised her.
Ah! in what former existence had he been
brought into contact with that soul? An eternal
mystery, though the affinity was profound and in-
stantaneous. This supraterrestrial bond existed,

more powerful than all others, for no other
emotion could compare with that he had experienced in holding this child in his arms.   Had
not Plato said : " To learn is to remember " ; and
had not an unknown sage added: " Nothing is
more sacred than the mystery of remembrance,
for the love of two souls is the recollection of
their life in God " ?   In thinking over his past
life, another thrill of surprise and joy came over
Memnones.   He remembered that he had long
ago consulted the Pythoness of Delphi, and had
asked her whether he should in his lifetime ever
solve the mystery of the other world.   The oracle
had replied : " In the land of Isis a kingfisher
(alcyon) from over the seas will bring thee the
key of souls."   Had he not found this maid of
Samothrace in the barque of her ravishers, like
a halcyon in its floating nest ?   This was why he
called her ALCYONE.

.   .   .   .   .   .

At first Memnones gave himself up unreservedly to the happiness of possessing an
adopted daughter. A considerable sum of money
satisfied the merchants of Tyre, who had loudly
demanded the girl's return. Finally the priest,
without difficulty, obtained for her admission
among the *pallacides*, a name given to the wives
and daughters of the Egyptian priests, who were
attached to the service of the temple. They took
part in the ritual and the sacred music, and, when

they possessed the rare gift of clairvoyance, they were employed down in the crypts for the purposes of secret science. Alcyone was entrusted to the care of an old Nubian woman, named Nourhal, who was to teach her to play the lute, whilst he himself taught her poetry, sacred hymns, and the history of the gods. Though generally timid and of an untamed disposition, she had moments of passionate recklessness or mad gaiety. Then her eyes would change from blue to violet and glow in extraordinary fashion. Of a sudden, she would pass from one thought to another; two different personages early manifested themselves in her. When walking through the fields with her Nubian nurse, she would sport among the springing corn, or play with the kids like a young Bacchante. In the temple, with Memnones, however, her countenance assumed a stern, serious expression. From the first, she had entered the sanctuary as though it were her own home, looking fearlessly at the statues of the gods, the painted figures and hieroglyphs. Long would she gaze upon the ceiling, covered with the symbolic figures of the Zodiac. In silent, though not astonished delight, Alcyone seemed to recognise everything. Though incapable of following out an idea for any length of time, or setting in their places all the parts of a vast whole, she would at a glance see its meaning. One day, when standing before a statue of Osiris, she said:

" He never laughs, because he comes from the land of the dead."

Another time she said in presence of an Isis :

"She is always smiling, because she comes from heaven."

Memnones spent many wonderful hours with her in the sombre temple, for she listened attentively to him, sometimes lying at his feet with her head against his knees, or again standing upright before him, or even walking about with long strides, as though she needed to express by gestures the emotions aroused within her by the words of the priest. The legend of Isis and Osiris would plunge her into a kind of dream. Sometimes she would lean against one of the giant columns, her hands clasped over her head and lost in thought, as though recalling the memory of another world.

Occasionally Memnones would allow Alcyone to sail in the barque on the waters of the Nile, under the care of the old Nubian. Two rowers and a trusty pilot were in charge of the skiff. All the boatmen of the Nile knew the barque attached to the service of the temple, and revered it as though it bore the goddess herself. They would have regarded it as a sacrilege to touch it or even to approach too near it. Often would they land on the opposite bank, where they saw camels and captive ostriches pass in long files.

One of the small islands at the mouth of the

river was preferred by Alcyone to all the others. The Isle of Reeds was the largest of them all. It was surrounded by a dense girdle of papyrus. In the interior was a forest of palm-trees and far-stretching meadows, where the Bedouin children led the goats to pasture. In this abode of verdure, open to the winds of heaven, though protected from the sun, Alcyone loved to rest. From the outset, water-fowl, like the white ibis and the rose-coloured flamingo, would form a circle on the sand, looking inquisitively at the virgin as though she were a bird of a different species, *though still a bird.* She would fling them crumbs from the temple bread, or grains of maize. Then the winged tribe would come in flocks—storks and cranes, pigeons, and even the sea-gulls swarming about the delta. As though these aerial beings were more familiar to her than men, she would talk to them, summon them to her call, or dismiss them—and they seemed to understand, for they obeyed her. Seated on the banks of the bay, with a single motion of her scarf she would attract streams of swallows, which wheeled for a moment above her head and then fled swiftly into the dazzling azure sky.

Puzzled by these swarms of birds always descending at the same spot, the little Bedouin shepherd boys stole quietly through the reed, right to the bay, scarcely daring to raise their sunburnt heads above the thicket of papyrus.

With a kind of religious fear they looked at the " daughter of Isis " as they called her, feeding the birds of the air.   But since she smiled at their timid gestures and barbarous language, they gradually grew bolder and brought her honeycombs and figs wrapped in long leaves.   Respectfully they drew near, and, kneeling on the turf, laid down these offerings.   In return she brought them amulets from the temple or tiny images of Osiris made of black basalt.   Thereupon they would fling themselves in strange postures on to the ground and utter shrieks of joy.

Often during these scenes had Alcyone heard rustlings as of human steps in the copse of reeds. One day the Samothracian girl saw a youth of marvellous beauty.   Above his tunic he wore a lamb-skin, flung over his shoulder ; in his hand he carried a dog-wood staff, like the one used by shepherds.   His curly locks and countenance of the purest Greek type, however, showed no trace of Bedouin blood, whilst his great, limpid, pensive eyes shone like stars.   With his serious-looking mouth and manly form, he might have been taken for a grown-up Eros, disguised as a shepherd.   No sooner did Alcyone perceive him than he disappeared among the reeds.

She saw him again in the following fashion. Amongst the Bedouin boys was a mischievous little urchin, with the head of a satyr.   He alone secretly ridiculed and made sport of the "daughter of Isis." One day he caught by the wing a dove which Alcyone was very fond of, as it would eat from her hand. She uttered a cry of terror, but the little fellow disappeared among the reeds, carrying off his prey with a shout of triumph.

Alcyone, in great distress, burst into sobs, when, to her surprise, she saw the stranger issue from the reeds, holding the little thief by the ear. With many threats, he forced him to kneel before the bird charmer and deliver up the dove. In a rapture of joy she clasped the affrighted bird to her bosom, whilst the stranger asked anxiously and in pure Ionic Greek:

"Is Alcyone happy now?"

"Yes, wonderful shepherd, but who art thou, who knowest me so well?"

"I am an exile."

"From what country?"

"From thine own."

"Wherefore hast thou turned shepherd?"

"Shepherds live in solitude; no one troubles about them."

"Then thou wishest to be always alone?"

"I do."

"For what reason?"

"I cannot tell thee."

"Wilt thou return here?"

"Yes, if any one threatens thee with injury."

"What is thy name?"

"In this land I am called the Horus of the Bedouins. I am a stranger and have lost family, fortune, and name."

"Wilt thou not quit this island?"

"I know not, but if I disappear . . . remember that Horus always keeps watch over Alcyone!"

Saying which, the stranger smiled sorrowfully. Then his dark, dreamy eyes flamed up rapidly, like a dying torch rekindled by a gust of wind. Alcyone made a piteous gesture which seemed to say: "Do not leave me!"

The stranger, however, stretched out his hand to indicate that they were separated by an insuperable barrier. Then he suddenly disappeared among the reeds.

A few days afterwards Alcyone asked for permission to go for another sail on the Nile. This the priest granted, though he suspected something from the strange light he saw in the eyes of his adopted daughter. From the bank he saw the barque land at the "Isle of Reeds." Immediately summoning the ferryman, he followed her by a different route. He glided through the reeds right into the bay. Everything was silent; the Nubian woman sleeping in the barque, and the pilot and oarsmen fishing in the distance. Alcyone was asleep beneath a sycamore. Memnones remained long motionless, and, ashamed of his spying, was on the point of going away, when he heard a rustling in the reeds. The papyrus tops parted asunder and the stranger issued from the thicket. He looked around to make certain that there was no one near, and knelt down by the side of Alcyone. Was it pretence or was she really asleep? Gently the shepherd raised the light veil covering the maiden's face, and bent over her in a long enraptured gaze. Slowly his mouth drew near the face of Alcyone. Memnones, in panting anxiety, was on the point of rushing forward to prevent the fatal kiss, when an occult power chained him to the spot. The stranger's lips, however, did not touch the virgin's brow; he raised his head, took a few flowers from a basket he had brought, and dropped them on the breast of the sleeping girl, then he carefully replaced the veil. Slowly moving away, and looking back several times, he disappeared. Alcyone was still asleep. Shortly afterwards she awoke with a deep sigh, calling out: "Nourhal! Nourhal! whence come these roses?" "They are a gift of Isis, and have fallen from heaven," muttered the old Nubian woman, running up. "No! they come from Him!" murmured Alcyone, looking in the direction of the reeds. Memnones fled; he had learned enough.

On the evening of the same day the priest of Isis led his adopted daughter into the temple and asked her whom she had seen in the "Isle of Reeds." First she mentioned the little Bedouins; then, Memnones pressing her, she related without a blush the episode of the dove, the appearance of Horus, and her conversation with him.

"And thou hast not seen him again?"

"No."

"And thou hast no desire to see him!"

Alcyone replied simply, after a moment's silence:

"Oh yes, I do! . . . . I love exiles."

At the same time a tear shone in her azure-blue eye, as she looked up at the painted roofs of the temple, where appeared the dreadful sombre figure of Nephtys, the goddess of Night, in the centre of the Zodiac, enveloping the firmament with her dark outstretched arms. The tear, held back by the golden eyelids of the beautiful girl, did not roll down on to her pale cheek, but the pupils became violet as a pool ruffled by a breath of wind. Memnones was as terrified at the sight as the mariner who sees rising to the immaculate vaults of heaven a tiny cloud, precursor of the storm!

.   .   .   .   .   .

It was as though an arrow had pierced the heart of the priest. Alcyone was no longer his alone! An unknown power had taken possession of her. Who was this wretched intruder who dared dispute his treasure with him ? He uttered not a word of reproach against his adopted daughter, but a veil of silence fell between them.

Memnones made inquiries from the Bedouins on the other side of the river, and discovered that the stranger had come from Alexandria, offering to work among the Bedouins as a shepherd. The chief of the tribe had received him courteously by reason of his distinguished bearing and his gifts as a healer. He had given himself the name of Horus, and was generally called the Horus of the Bedouins. Some said that he had committed a great crime, and for that reason was hiding away in that quiet spot. His sole occupation in the dark camel-skin tent of the Bedouins consisted in reading rolls of papyrus, and, leaning against some palm-tree at sunset, listening to the shrill pipes of the little Bedouins in the cornfields. The crime committed by the youth, thought Memnones, must have been a very serious one, to have made him consent to become a servant to the Bedouins.

A week passed by. One morning before sunrise Memnones was walking about in the alley leading from the temple to the gateway, when the guardian came to tell him that a stranger wished to speak to him. Great was the priest's surprise at seeing the mysterious guest of the Bedouins. His face was thin and his general appearance grave and serious, though he wore his shepherd's garments with dignity and pride. Memnones felt his heart stand still as he said within himself: "This is the Enemy, come to steal away thy treasure. Be on thy guard!" Leaning on his crook, the stranger looked at the priest with dark, scrutinising glance. The following dialogue took place between them:

"What brings thee here?"

"I am a stranger, poor and persecuted; it may be that these three reasons give me the right to receive advice from a priest of Isis."

"Speak, what desirest thou?"

"I wish to be received as servant in the temple, and, later on, if thou deemest me worthy, to be instructed in the sacred science."

"Before I can answer thee, I must know thy name."

"They call me the Horus of the Bedouins; this is the only name I have. I am an exile seeking a port."

"What is thy origin and history? Wherefore art thou an exile?"

"I can tell no more."

"In the district thou art accused of serious charges. They say thou art a criminal, hiding away under an assumed name."

"If thou believest that of me, I will say nothing further."

"The temple cannot harbour a nameless

stranger, without family or surety of any kind."

The stranger's eyes shot forth a tragic fire.

"Who then art thou," said he, "if thou canst not read the heart and soul of a man? Thou art no initiate!"

With commanding gesture, Horus raised his finger and pointed it at the priest's head. Speechless with wrath, the latter made the same gesture, signifying: "Leave this place!" Already the two mistrusted each other. Memnones, however, quickly calmed himself and added:

"Know, thou foolish and audacious youth, that I am a priest whose life is devoted to the search after truth."

"What callest thou truth?" said the stranger, folding his arms with a smile of bitter disdain. "Does this truth of thine teach thee to refuse me shelter? If so, then thy science is base and false. Well, be it so—farewell! Live for thy truth . . . as for me, I will die for mine!"

And, turning his back on the priest, he departed with rapid steps. Without reflecting on the meaning of these strange words, Memnones breathed freely as though delivered of a mighty burden. The better to enjoy his victory, he mounted the inner staircase, on to the lofty terrace of the pylon overlooking the far-stretching surface of the delta. The sun was rising

over the vast valley of the Nile whose silvery
channels were lit up with ruddy glow, for the
tide was advancing. The Horus of the Bedouins
was walking resolutely in the direction of the
river : Memnones saw him depart with profound
satisfaction. The only adversary of his wonderful good fortune was away, and the priest now
felt that he had absolute possession of Alcyone.
Henceforth no one would rob him of the pearl of
Samothrace. What a relief it was to have put
off the bold, cunning ravisher who had been
prowling around, to see him depart—for ever!
He saw him embark on the river in the boat of
the ferryman, and was not completely at ease
until the stranger had disappeared on the other
bank. Then only did Memnones remember the
singular beauty of the youth, his air of nobility
and distinction, and he began to wonder whether
after all he had not repulsed one of those gods,
disguised as shepherds, of whom Homer makes
mention. This remorse, however, was of short
duration, and completely disappeared when he
saw Alcyone receive him with a limpid, beaming smile—Alcyone, who, thank Heaven, knew
nothing of the incident.

CHAPTER VI

THE PROPHETESS

A FEW weeks afterwards Memnones learned that the stranger who had been passing under the name of Horus had left the country. The Bedouins did not know what had become of him. Alcyone never spoke to Memnones of him; she appeared even to have forgotten her walks along the banks of the Nile, the friendly birds and her dreams beneath the sycamore. All danger seemed to have disappeared; she was beginning a new phase of her mysterious inner life. She neglected her lute, and paid little heed to the lessons of her adopted father. Utterly absorbed in herself, she fled from every one, and wandered about the quietest parts of the temple, as though she felt the need of gathering renewed strength from the darkness, away from all visible things.

One day she disappeared. Tired of searching for her, Memnones went down into the crypt, the door of which happened to be open. In former times the priests of Isis had brought there the neophytes to whom they entrusted their secret instructions. Ever since the art of initiation had been lost, this had been an abandoned spot. To his great astonishment Memnones found his adopted daughter, sunk in a deep sleep, at the foot of the central pillar of the crypt. This pillar consisted of a colossal statue of Osiris, cut out of a single block of grey granite. Lying on the pedestal, Alcyone was sleeping in a kind of lethargy; pale, with half-opened lips, and scarcely breathing. Her features seemed transformed by an inner flame, and her countenance had become transparent. A shudder passed over Memnones. Had the oracle said true? Was Alcyone at last about to reveal to him her power of prophecy?

At that moment he heard the solemn sounds of a lute, beneath the peristyle of the temple. It was the hymn to the solar god, Amen-Rā. Alcyone slowly rose to her feet, without leaving her magic slumber, and stood before Memnones in solemn attitude. Her eyes, wide open, saw nothing of the real world. Memnones felt himself in the presence of another being, purer and greater than himself. It was the Soul itself, the shining Virgin free from all earthly taint— the divine Psyche—appearing before him in all her beauty; like the lotus lifting its head above the waters of the Nile to greet the sun's first beams. Finally he said:

" Art thou Alcyone, my daughter? "

Thereupon Alcyone began to speak in gentle accents, though with graver voice than usual. She murmured:

"Yes, I am thy daughter, the prophetess. . . . At thy petition the gods have sent me to thee to conduct thee to the land of souls . . . in the sacred night of Osiris. . . . Thou shalt see by means of me. . . . The eyes of my soul shall be thine eyes. . . . Thine it is to lead and protect me."

"In what way?"

"Thy will shall be the Barque of Isis. Be thou its faithful pilot. Bear my soul on thy hands . . . and we will go into the country of the dead . . . to the land of resurrection!"

"I am ready. Here is the key and the cross."

"Ah! take care! We are menaced with terrible dangers. . . . A circle of defence must be traced round me . . . to protect me against demons . . . in the ocean of shades we shall have to cross."

"Seest thou where we shall go?"

"We shall cross the circle of the shades."

"And afterwards?"

"We shall ascend to the circle of light."

"And shall we go beyond to the solar circle, the circle of the heroes and demi-gods, dispensers of power and might?"

"Yes . . . if my Genius permits."

"Who is thy Genius?"

"I know not his name, nor do I see his face, for it is veiled. But there is a star on his brow, and in his hand he carries a Mercury's wand."

"Ask him his name."

"He is so high . . . so distant! I see nothing but his star and sceptre. . . . Now he calls us. . . . Hold me, I faint!"

The harmonious strains of the lute had ceased. Supported by Memnones, Alcyone fell back on to her stone couch in an ice-cold lethargy. Gently he warmed her hands, and laid his own on her brow, which was as cold as marble. At the end of an hour she awoke, feeling rather tired, but appearing in no way astonished at seeing Memnones by her side.

"Dost thou remember having dreamed?" he asked her.

"I remember nothing," she replied, "except that I was far, far away."

"Dost thou like to sleep in the crypt?"

"Yes, if thou watchest over me. Never leave me when I am here."

. . . . . .

From that hour an era of light began in the life of Memnones every day at sunset. Alcyone followed her master into the gloomy crypt, where a naphtha lamp, hanging from the vault, was burning. A few notes on the lute sufficed to lull the prophetess to sleep. Very soon she fell into deep sleep whilst replying to

her guide, whom she told everything she saw.
During Alcyone's magic sleep, Memnones experienced a pure, subtle kind of voluptuousness,
the sentiment of a perfect blending of soul with
his adopted daughter. She became plastic to
him, his thoughts passed into her without word
or gesture, like a fluid. She, too, read his soul,
as though it were an open book. When her
trance became more profound a new faculty
developed : she saw a whole world of unknown
beings around her. Then she had to drive them
from her with both voice and gesture. These
beings, whether spirits or visions, souls or
phantoms, invisible to Memnones, threatened to
overwhelm her. On rising to a higher sphere,
and approaching the ecstatic condition, a change
took place in the relation between seer and
guide. A more lucid and powerful mind suddenly
appeared in face and gesture ; loftier thoughts
and imperious commands fell from her lips.
Now the inspired prophetess dominated the
hierophant her master.

At these rare moments, he felt himself in the
presence of the most astonishing of revelations.
Was he to admit that the visions of Alcyone
were nothing more than the dreams of an over-
heated brain ? Whence came these marvels ?
what explanation could be offered for their
logical sequence and increasing splendour ? His
reason told him that the visions of Alcyone were

something other than the work of the simple-minded virgin. Their ordered sequences corresponded to a series of striking and sublime ideas. In it could be seen a kind of ascending panorama of universal life; the lower part quite dark, the middle shaded with light, and the upper filled with dazzling brightness. As the panorama unrolled, the very earth itself took on a new meaning. The visible world, judging by our physical senses, was nothing but a link in the chain of worlds, a mode of matter and life. Another world, invisible to our eyes of matter though visible to those of the spirit, was spread round this earth in ever-increasing circles. Ought it not to reach right to the central sun of the pure Spirit, the source of all things?

If only he could attain to that height, drinking in torrents of knowledge and power! Before such a perspective the priest of Isis was filled with boundless joy and pride; he forgot all else —even the soul of his dear Alcyone! This was nothing more than the marvellous skiff in which to cross the surging unknown main. These first experiments were painful and anxious. Alcyone could not escape from a dark chaos, in which moved strange, uncertain forms which she described to Memnones in incoherent though incisive words. It was useless for the priest of Isis to trace round her a circle with the cross, in the air of the crypt, pronouncing the formula for exorcising evil spirits contained in the *Book of the Dead;* the sleeping girl felt herself assailed by crowds of spectres and shades, some of which were called accursed souls, and vomited out on her their feelings of hatred or distress. Alcyone, with cold beads of perspiration on her brow, shrieked and twisted about. Memnones, with loud voice and imperious gesture, drove away the swarm of shades. The impression came to him that this obscure limbo, surrounding the earth, was a vast laboratory, containing both the spoils of his immemorial past and the floating germs of his future, a swarming reservoir of life, of which seers and prophets perceive only fragments, whilst a god alone can embrace the whole. This was the murky region called *Erebos* by the Greeks and *Amenti* by the Egyptians. Alcyone called it *the black zone.*

After a month's hazardous wanderings in the land of shades the black veil was removed, and the travellers entered a light, peaceful region. This the prophetess called *the rose-coloured zone.* In it Memnones recognised the circle of blessed and happy spirits, the abode of harmony and light. There the radiant purified souls create dwellings and scenes after their own desires. Away from the cold darkness, Alcyone felt herself plunged in a warm atmosphere of sweet perfumes; thrilling with perfect happiness, she would have liked to stay there for ever. Memnones, however, could no longer be restrained. His thirst for knowledge increased with his science, his ambition with his powers. The higher his seer bore him aloft, the higher he wished to mount. Had he not seized hold of the magic chain of spirits which ascends from earth to heaven and is lost in the infinitudes of space? By mounting this ladder of souls, step after step, might he not attain to that sublime elevation where the spirit of man is identified with the Soul of the world, drinking in from that spring things which the sacred books call *the sun of Osiris?* To do this, he must first enter the sphere of heroes and gods, doubtless the one which old Sabaccas had warned him against approaching. Already Alcyone had caught faint broken glimpses of this region, which she called *the zone of gold.*

Here Memnones met with an insuperable obstacle. No sooner did he order the prophetess to enter this sphere than she began to tremble, saying in tones of lament: "The light is too strong, it hurts me. Besides, I feel something holding me back." Memnones, in his obstinacy, would not be discouraged. He had sworn to himself that he would break the obstacle and vanquish his mysterious adversary, and, by the might of will alone, enter the circle of heroes and gods. Every evening he renewed the rash attempt.

Once when the priest of Isis had been more pressing than usual, Alcyone openly rebelled and suddenly broke out:

"I can go no further."

"Why?"

"An awful light dazzles me. He who has conducted us here, the veiled Genius, stands at the golden door through which lightning flashes are streaming. Beware of rousing his anger. . . . There he stands, armed with a fiery sword . . . he forbids thee to enter!"

"Ah! I will know who this strange Genius is; I must see this masked god with my own eyes!"

"Stop! . . . I beg of thee!"

"None can stop me on my path to a divine conquest. . . . If thy Genius bars the road against us, we will go on in spite of him. Onward! break through the door!"

As he spoke the priest touched the brow of the prophetess. She uttered a terrible, convulsive shriek. With a few passes of his hand, Memnones appeased her. Suddenly she rose, majestic and grave, as on the very first day he had seen her. But she had become another person, as it were, and now stood before him in an attitude of defiance. Memnones stepped back in fright, for the girl's features had changed, and had now assumed the proud, disdainful expression of a heroic youth. No longer

was Alcyone before his eyes; it was the shepherd of the Isle of Reeds, the mysterious lover
of the prophetess, who had come to brave him
at the very door of the temple. As before, he
now folded his arms and glanced with flashing
eyes at the priest, whose frame thrilled with
affright as he heard the voice of Horus himself
come from the mouth of the girl, saying to
him :

" Memnones, thou art not what thou believest
thyself to be!   Thou hast the breastplate of
might and the helmet of faith, but thou lackest
one thing—the sword of light, steeped in the
blood of thy heart—before thou canst enter
the circle of the heroes, who behold the sun of
Osiris ! "

The blood of Memnones seemed frozen in his
veins, but he found strength to stammer forth :

"In whose name speakest thou?   I am the
master of the soul of Alcyone."

"Thou art not master of her soul."

"Then whose is it?"

"It belongs to me by divine Love and the
might of the great Sacrifice.   Without me thou
canst do nothing; thou wilt fall back into darkness.   In thine heart there still burns the dull
flame of ambition and desire.   Cease to torment
thy daughter, for thou shalt go no further. . . .
Renounce—and obey!"

" Who art thou ? "

"The Genius of Alcyone."

"And what is thy name?"

"They call me Anteros!"

The prophetess uttered this name in solemn accents, and stood there for a few moments, motionless, her arm raised and countenance shining, in the attitude of a herald of the gods. Then, suddenly, the features of her swollen countenance relaxed. Her rigid body, transfigured by a superhuman presence, gave way and fell like a lifeless mass at the granite feet of the colossal statue of Osiris. Memnones, terrified, bent tenderly over the body of his daughter, whose heart had ceased to beat, though she still breathed. Only slowly did she come out of her deep lethargy. When completely awake, she was depressed and silent, unwilling to answer a single question.

CHAPTER VII

MEANWHILE Memnones was called away to Pompeii. Marcus Helvidius, in the name of the decurions of the town, requested that a priest of Egypt should be sent to reform the cult of Isis. Smerdes, the hierarchical chief of Memnones, proposed that the latter should go there as hierophant. Under other circumstances the chief scribe of the temple of Isis would not have consented to leave Egypt. Two things absorbed his entire existence—occult science and his daughter Alcyone. These two passions had become infused into one ever since the prophetess, through her marvellous faculties, had become the instrument of his discoveries. The last night spent in the crypt, however, had quite changed his plans. What was the meaning of this surprising, inexplicable manifestation of the Horus of the Bedouins, under another name, and through the medium of the prophetess? Whence came this superior and redoubtable power, suddenly stopping him in his progress and forbidding him all approach to the greatest of truths? Before his unknown guest he was perplexed and humiliated. A dull feeling of remorse had come over him, so that he hesitated when Smerdes spoke to him of Pompeii and asked for three days' reflection. Then, in a flash of light, he remembered Sabaccas. Had not the ascetic of the pyramid said to him: "Thou shalt not enter the third sphere. When thou hast reached it, come to see me." Thereupon Memnones set off for Memphis and the desert.

Sabaccas was not to be found at the entrance to his cavern, but a child from the neighbouring village told Memnones that the hermit was a short distance away, near the tombs of the prophets. After an hour's walk, beneath the burning sun, over rocks of red porphyry, the priest of Isis perceived the solitary old man in rags on the threshold of a dismal vault, closed by a bronze door.

"Ah! at last thou hast come," said Sabaccas, with a sharp, mistrustful glance. "I was expecting thee. Hast thou crossed the door of the third circle?"

"No."

"Did I not tell thee so? Then what wilt thou with me?"

"I have been summoned to Pompeii as hierophant of the temple of Isis. Ought I to accept?"

"Ah! so thou wilt be a hierophant?" said the hermit, with his fleshless face and eagle eyes.

Placing his hand like an iron vise on the priest's shoulder, he added:

"First come this way."

With his bony, though still vigorous hand, the old man opened the bronze door of the vault. They found themselves in a square room, supported by four Doric columns, cut out of the rough stone. Several tombs could be seen fitted into the sides of this funeral chamber, which had been dug in the very flanks of the mountain. At the end was a sepulchre, shaped like a mutilated pyramid. The only religious emblem on the monument was a gigantic eye, painted on the top of the *stela*. Below were Greek letters engraved in the stone. Sabaccas, pointing them out to his companion, said, "Read!"

Memnones, drawing near the tomb, read, not without difficulty in the gloomy vault, the following inscription:—

HORUS-ANTEROS
*gave his life
for Justice and Truth.
His body was cast into the sea.
His head lies here,
In the darkness of the mountain.
Clad in the splendour of the Gods,
His soul shines as the sun.*

The name of Horus joined to that of Anteros had produced in the heart and mind of Memnones the effect of a lightning-flash followed by a clap of thunder.

"Who lies here?" he asked, in trembling accents.

"A proud young man thou knowest well," said Sabaccas, in a tone of reproach, as he rested his hand like the claw of a hawk on the granite of the *stela*. "Destined for a great and noble life, he came to thee for initiation. Wherefore didst thou refuse it him?"

"Because he would not trust me with the secret of his destiny."

"He would not betray his friends. Hadst thou been a true priest, with the light of Isis shining in thee, thou wouldst have read that soul or divined it in his voice. The shelter of the temple and the knowledge thou thyself hast received were nothing but his due."

"He wished to steal away my prophetess, my daughter Alcyone," protested Memnones. "I know that he loved her and prowled about, spying on her when she was asleep. Had not I the right to defend her against him?"

"Thou hadst no right to banish into darkness the one who came to thee for light. Besides . . . who knows if he were not more worthy of Alcyone than thou art?"

"More worthy of her than I am?"

"Living, he was thy equal; dead, he surpasses thee," said the former prophet of Osiris, pressing his emaciated hand on the granite. "By his sacrifice he has now risen to the rank of a hero. No longer is he Horus—but Anteros —for ever!"

"How did he die?"

"With friends of his he conspired against Cæsar, but he alone was discovered. To save his life, he became a shepherd among the Bedouins. It was then he asked thee to receive him into the temple. Dejected and homeless, he returned to Alexandria and gave himself up to the prætor, sacrificing his life for his cause. He was beheaded and flung into the Nile. A fisherman found his head, which was brought here by a worshipper of Isis. The true initiates erected a monument to the man who lived his own Truth!"

Memnones bowed his head. Divine Truth, concealed behind the veil of nature, was beginning to shine before his eyes, though its light fell upon the barren abyss of his heart. Overwhelmed in the presence of the haughty old man, he murmured:

"And now . . . what am I to do?"

"Atone for thy sin. . . . Go with thy prophetess to Pompeii, there to toil and suffer and struggle. Search the initiates' secret, to catch a glimpse of which one must have lived it.

Only in supreme grief wilt thou find supreme
Truth!"

.   .   .   .   .   .

Thus in the silent amphitheatre of Pompeii,
beneath the canopy of the star-lit heavens,
Memnones had retraced the course of his life.
How impossible not to recognise the ways of a
mysterious Providence! His attention had been
aroused by secret warnings; striking signs had
guided his progress and marked the divers stages
of his path to the desired goal. To the cries
of his soul and the ardent appeals of his will
the Powers had replied, for his first interview
with Sabaccas, his admission to the temple, the
coming of Alcyone into his life, and the revelations of the prophetess, the whole chain of connected effects, was all their work. Finally, was
not the manifestation of Anteros, through the
face and voice of Alcyone, an undeniable proof
of the reality of the other world? Tragic was
his destiny, however, for the Powers, though
demonstrating the certain existence of that
Beyond, had said to him: "Thou shalt go no
further!" Alcyone, the only torch he had to
light his way through those dark regions, was
now no longer in his power. Her soul belonged
to him she called her Genius, who disputed its
possession with him in the other world. And
now another adversary, even more dangerous,
threatened to steal her from him in this world.

Between these two enemies, what would become of him?

Memnones had left the amphitheatre and reached the terrace of the temple. The priest held out his arms towards the curia where the prophetess was sleeping under the protection of the old Nubian nurse.

"A father's heart," he said, "is stronger than both the dead and the living!"

As the priest of Isis, however, went down into the darkness, along the winding staircase, to his bed in the narrow cell, he imagined he saw a thick veil fall heavily back on the divine dream of his life. The thought that he had caused the death of Horus tortured him like an unpardoning grief. Of all his troubled past, only two images rose to the surface of his mind—the young man's head carried away by the Nile to the sea, and the eye of Anteros, fixed on him from the depths of the tomb.

BOOK II

THE RAY

"Love is the interpreter and mediator between gods and men."—PLATO.

CHAPTER VIII

THE GUARDIAN OF THE THRESHOLD

THE curia of Isis was situated in the centre of Pompeii, in one of the most populous quarters of the town, at no great distance from the two theatres, the gladiators' school, and the gate of Strabies. It was a rectangular courtyard, with porticoes and small side rooms. At times voices might be heard from without, though the place was no less inaccessible than an Indian cloister in the Himalayas or a Persian seraglio in a king's fortress. Its only exit was a passage leading to the temple of Isis. In former times it was inhabited by priests, but now its only occupants were two women—the adopted daughter of Memnones and her old slave nurse.

The sunlight of a bright summer morn was flooding this peaceful retreat. Two colonnades of the portico were shining in all their dazzling whiteness, the other two stood in a grey-blue shade. From a fountain there shot a crystal jet into a round basin, through the mouth of a small sphinx, of grey marble. Between two pillars was suspended a hammock, almost touching the

ground. In it lay a graceful maiden dressed
in a white gown, caught like a bird in this
azure net. She was not sleeping, but rather
sunk in reverie, with eyes wide open and head
leaning on her hand. It was the prophetess
Alcyone.

Close by her side, kneeling on the flags, was
an old Nubian woman with crisp woolly hair
and face shining like a mirror of dark copper.
Nourhal had been bought, when quite young,
by some priests of Memphis, who wished to
make of her a servant of the temple. She had
been taught to play the lute in the sacred ceremonies, since her sole talent was for singing,
music, and dancing. Being appointed to serve
Alcyone, she worshipped her with all the passion
of an old woman, keeping guard over her like
a faithful dog. Seeing her mistress absent-
minded, and knowing that she had not slept
for three days, she tried to distract her. She
placed on the Persian carpet three caskets, one
of ebony, another of silver, and the third of
sandal-wood. Looking in turn at these caskets
and the motionless dreamer, she laughed and
chattered in a strange tongue, a mixture of
Greek and Ethiopian, which resembled the
warbling of a tropical bird. Doubtless in her
parrot talk she was affirming that these were
infallible remedies for dispelling the cares and
worries of her queen. First she opened the

ebony casket from which she drew Egyptian
amulets, pretty little figures of Osiris carved
in black basalt, or coquettish figures of Isis cut
out of Siena marble, all corroded by time. These
small idols she held out to Alcyone, who appeared not to notice them. Then, with a cunning smile, Nourhal took the silver casket,
containing Greek divinities carved in onyx,
porphyry, and ivory—Minervas, Dianas, and
Apollos, and cornelian cameos. These had
no more effect than the former. With a shake
of the head, Nourhal opened the sandal-wood
casket containing aromatic scent-bags and phials
of perfumes in glasses of an opaline shade. The
old nurse wished her patient to scent these, but
the latter pushed them aside. Finally Nourhal
had recourse to her greatest attraction. She
opened the painted box containing fans of pea-
cocks' and ostrich feathers, stuffed birds of para-
dise, metal talismans, pearl necklaces, and tiny
bells such as her country-women fasten to their
ankles when dancing. Then, in triumph, she
drew forth a roll of papyrus on which was
written Homer's Odyssey. She herself could
not read a word, but she remembered that in
Egypt Alcyone had spent whole nights bending
over the long unrolled strip, with a naphtha
lamp by her side, instead of sleeping. The
young girl took up the roll, looked at it tenderly,
then let it fall to the ground as though she

had not even the strength to hold it. Disappointed and irritated, the old woman picked up a copper mirror from the box and said: "Look at the dark circles round thine eyes." No sooner had Alcyone done so than she turned over and coiled up in her hammock, like a dove burying its head in its wings.

The poor old woman's eyes filled with tears. Why was her mistress so ill-tempered? A terrible fear came over her that she had offended the marvellous and incomprehensible being she worshipped as though she were a goddess. All her anxiety, however, was speedily quelled, for after a few minutes a shield was struck in the distance, and the sound, like the tinkling of a cymbal, reached the ears of Alcyone. Like a gazelle she leapt from her hammock, exclaiming:

"The guardian's signal! There is a stranger in the temple. . . . I must see who he is!"

"Stay here!" exclaimed the old woman. "Thou knowest that the master will not have thee leave the court without his permission."

Alcyone had already disappeared. She passed the portico and proceeded along the narrow passage winding round the temple, until she reached the bronze statue of Isis. Close by was a skylight, through which the priests could see the interior of the sanctuary without being seen themselves.

She saw Memnones seated with a roll of papyrus in his hand, which he was reading. Two men, who had just mounted the stairs, appeared at the entrance to the sanctuary. The first was Calvus the Stoic. Alcyone almost fainted on perceiving Ombricius Rufus following him.

The philosopher touched the priest on the shoulder, as he seemed absorbed in his reading.

"Hail to the hierophant," he said. "Here is a friend who wishes to speak to thee."

A quiver ran through the frame of Memnones as he saw the tribune.

"I recognise him," he said. "What can I do for him?"

"He was present at the marriage of Helvidius. Moved by thy words and the new rites, he asks to be instructed by thee."

"Is this true?" said Memnones, with the same piercing glance he had given the tribune in the porch of the house of Helvidius.

"Quite true," said Ombricius, as humbly as his natural pride would permit.

Memnones bowed his head, as though he had received a mortal wound; then, regaining his self-possession, he offered two seats to his visitors.

"Thy name?" asked the attentive priest, his eyes fixed on the soldier.

"Ombricius Rufus, son of a veteran, and a tribune in the army of Titus. I was a disciple of Afranius and practised the Stoic doctrines in my youth. Now I should like to learn the word of Hermes, which, I am told, gives full and complete enlightenment. I come prepared to receive it, if thou art willing to teach it to me."

"Good!" said Memnones; "we joyfully welcome true disciples. Knowest thou, however, the conditions under which thou mayest receive the instruction thou now demandest so eagerly?"

"I do not."

"The law of Hermes permits its initiates to bear arms only under certain circumstances. In order to obtain divine science, art thou ready, Ombricius Rufus, to renounce not merely the title of military tribune, but also martial glory and power?"

"Is the knowledge and power thou dost promise me equal to that thou orderest me to renounce?"

"The knowledge and power thou wilt acquire here will depend upon thy efforts and the purity of thy soul."

"How can I renounce what I know for what I know not? Give me first a proof of thy science, then I will choose between it and my past life."

"Thou refusest the first condition; that is a serious matter. Listen to the second. Art thou ready to receive, without discussion, the knowledge we impart to thee during the whole period of the test ? The reason of this thou wilt see later on ; meanwhile thou must submit to the will of a master."

"What ! Hand over to another my will, the thing that is dearest of all things on earth to me ? Is that possible ? Were I to do this, I should cease to be Ombricius Rufus, a free man and a citizen of Rome ! "

"Thou seest, young man, that thou art not ripe for initiation. Return to thy legions and come back here when experience has made thee more docile."

"Be it so," said Ombricius. "Thou refusest me thy science. Keep it for thyself, if I am not yet worthy of it. Still, as hierophant and priest of Isis, it is thy duty to give light and counsel to a citizen of this town, a crowned tribune."

"Speak ! "

"Thy science, of which thou art so proud and avaricious, does not come to thee solely from thy books and thy own resources ; it comes from the prophetess, thy adopted daughter ; of this I had proof three days ago. Was it not she who, in magic trance, pronounced the sacred union of Helvidius and Helvidia ? Did she not utter that marvellous prophecy for. them in a superhuman rapture of ecstasy ? Well ! I demand an oracle from Alcyone, as does the candidate of Delphi from the Pythoness ! "

Memnones rose to his feet. He held his folded roll in one hand, and leaned with the other against the Corinthian column of the small temple of Isis. He opened wide his eyes with astonishment. Then a disdainful smile came over his face and he said :

"Thy request is peculiar and audacious, Ombricius Rufus. So thou wouldst obtain in a single day, from a chance encounter and as the result of a young man's whim, what I have taken twenty years of my life to acquire by dint of study and austere practices? Know that even I could not obtain an oracle from Alcyone at any time, that her prophetic voice is the crown of an initiate's whole life given up to sacred study and submission to discipline?"

Ombricius had now risen in his turn, and, looking the priest full in the face, said boldly :

" The look she gave me promised me the oracle, when I gave her back the lotus flower!"

"Ah! Thou deemest it so?"

"I am sure of it!"

"And it was with a mental reservation of so insidious a nature that thou hast come to ask me for initiation and the wisdom of Hermes! Know then at once that the temple of Isis is closed against bribery and violence. Thou hast seen the prophetess for the last time!"

A pallor came over the face of Ombricius and his lips trembled.

"I came here in anguish of heart, and thirsting for truth. . . . Is this all that thou, in thy wisdom, canst answer me ? "

"Truth," said Memnones, " is for such as give themselves up to it without reserve, not for such as wish to use it to gratify their passions."

"Farewell," said the tribune, wrapping his toga around him and suddenly departing.

Before descending the stairs, however, he turned round to hurl at the priest his parting words :

"And this is the light of Isis ! "

. . . . . .

In a state of distraction Alcyone had followed this dialogue. The aspect and bearing of the proud tribune had inflamed her imagination. Her virgin's heart leapt passionately towards the young man who had appealed to her prophetic soul. The attitude and replies of Memnones, however, had shown her how profound was the abyss separating the two beings she loved most on earth. She saw herself torn in two for the rest of her days, and the pain of such a prospect caused her to utter a dull moan. This involuntary wail set vibrating the bronze statue behind which she was concealed. Terrified by this response from the hollow idol, which might have betrayed her, she fled rapidly along the passage.

"The statue sounds as though it were groaning," said Calvus, with an ironical smile, though all the same he was slightly startled.

Memnones, himself astonished, stood there for a moment perplexed; then gathering his wits together, he said aloud:

"What is Alcyone doing?"

With rapid steps he left the temple and entered the curia. He found his adopted daughter curled up again in her hammock, her face buried in her folded arm.

"She is sick . . . sick," groaned the old nurse. "She will not fall asleep. She has not stirred from here the whole morning."

Memnones looked at her attentively and finally said:

"Look up at me, Alcyone."

She lifted up a childlike face, her eyes red with tears.

"Hast thou been weeping?"

"Yes; I was thinking of Egypt."

"Dost thou still regret having left Egypt?"

"Always."

"Perhaps we shall return some day, who knows," replied Memnones.

Alcyone looked up at the priest in astonishment. He then saw that she was convulsively clasping in her left hand a wax tablet and a steel awl.

"What wilt thou do with that tablet?" he asked.

Alcyone blushed and bent her head, then, rising to her feet, appeared before him with beaming countenance. Profound is the dissimulation which love teaches so quickly to the purest of souls.

"Well, the tablet?" insisted Memnones.

"It is for translating into Greek the song Nourhal has just been singing," said Alcyone.

"Calm thyself, child, and sleep," said Memnones, reassured.

Thereupon he kissed her on the forehead, and was soon plunged in reflection. Nourhal resumed her song, as Alcyone, with fevered eyes, traced carefully in the soft wax with the pointed awl the first words: "To Ombricius Rufus, tribune."

Nourhal mumbled her lullaby, which, however, she did not finish, as she was speedily lulled to sleep by her own singing.

CHAPTER IX

THE GARDEN OF ISIS

OMBRICIUS was furiously pacing to and fro along the dilapidated portico of his deserted house on the banks of the Sarno. He had just said to his tenant, "To-morrow I leave for Rome," when he saw Calvus hurrying in his direction.

"What brings thee to my accursed dwelling, with this blazing sun striking on thee?" said the tribune peevishly, for the Stoic's impassive calm greatly irritated him.

"The decurion Helvidius and his noble spouse Helvidia have requested me to invite thee to the festival of Isis, which is being celebrated to-day outside the village, in a garden consecrated to the goddess."

"Memnones is to be there?"

"Certainly."

"Then I shall not go. Thou art well aware that this vain and jealous priest has refused me the initiation I asked of him, so I have no wish to meet him."

"All the same, read this message. I do not know its contents, but it is Helvidia who sends it thee."

"What can they want with me?" said the tribune, with a shrug of his shoulders. He had entertained feelings of hatred against the brotherhood ever since his interview with Memnones.

"I cannot say," said Calvus. "Doubtless the letter will enlighten thee."

Ombricius broke the seal, and read as follows:

To OMBRICIUS RUFUS, TRIBUNE, GREETING.

If thou wilt come to the festival of Isis, I will tell thee the message of the goddess at the lotus spring.

ALCYONE.

The eyes of the tribune flashed, and a wave of blood mounted to his bronzed countenance. So Alcyone was after all aware of the refusal of Memnones, and, in spite of the priest, now offered him the desired oracle. How had she guessed his inmost desire and won the decurion's wife over to his cause? Was it love or inspiration that had dictated this letter, instinct with a virgin's audacity? This time, the soul mystery, added to the power of love, attracted him to the prophetess. She was expecting him! He was overwhelmed with the joy and fear that had come over him.

"Wilt thou come?" said Calvus.

"I am ready!" murmured the tribune, completely absorbed in his own thoughts.

. . . . . .

On the undulating land stretching beyond

Pompeii, between the isolated peak of Vesuvius
and the chain of the Apennines, stood in those
days the ruins of a former temple of Ceres, surrounded by a wild and splendid garden. After
acquiring this domain, Helvidius had named
it the Garden of Isis, keeping it reserved for
the secret meetings of the community of Isis, to
which only friends who had been proved faithful
and true were invited. Away in the distance
above the vineyards could be seen a wooded
mound of cypress and sycamore trees, where stood
the chapel of Persephone. This chapel and the
portico of the temple of Ceres alone remained
standing of all the former buildings which had
been destroyed by an earthquake. It was surrounded by a wall of unequal height, bristling
with cactus and thorn bushes. An attendant
kept guard at the only door, through which
Ombricius and Calvus entered.

The tribune and the Stoic first crossed that
portion of the garden which the earthquake had
completely overturned. Nature, in her prodigality,
had already reclothed this volcanic soil with
an uneven, exuberant vegetation. The twisted
branches of olive-trees hung their pale foliage
over broken columns and the busts of goddesses
and heads of gods lying scattered about in every
direction. Tiny streams of water, flowing beneath
the mastic-trees and stones, kept alive the vegetation of this verdant wilderness. To the right, the

road ascended along a hill, covered with oak-trees, right to the temple of Persephone. This was the darkest, the sacred portion of the garden. From the depths of the grove rose a plaintive hymn.

"Whence comes this singing?" asked Ombricius.

"From the portico of Ceres. To-day they are playing a portion of the sacred drama: 'The death of Osiris.' We are now listening to a chorus of women."

"And who plays Isis?"

"Helvidia."

"Forward," said the tribune, "I will be with thee in a moment. Tell me where I shall find the lotus spring, for I have a rite which I must first perform."

Calvus pointed to a rocky path, bordered with roses and irises, leading into a grove of myrtle-trees, which he allowed his friend to enter alone. At the end of this labyrinth Ombricius found himself in front of a smooth-surfaced sheet of water, dotted with rose-coloured lotus-blooms. Drops of limpid water filtered through from a sombre grotto, which opened behind into a volcanic rock. A magnificent mimosa shaded the crystal sheet with its falling branches and flowers that resembled tresses of gold. In the distance rose the peak of Vesuvius.

In front of the grotto a maiden was kneeling,
bending over the spring. Her hand was delicately examining the water-plants, seeking something beneath the surface. Ombricius stood
still. This nymph wore the white robe of
a chorus woman. Her face was hidden by
her bowed head, but the tribune recognised the
priestess by the golden colour of her hair and
the wreath of narcissus she wore. At the sound
of approaching steps, Alcyone rose to her feet
and leaned instinctively against a marble *stela*
standing at the edge of the spring and crowned
by a miniature statue of Isis.

Ombricius looked at her for some time in
silence, then he said :

"Fear nothing from me, most noble prophetess; I have come at thy summons which
responds to my dearest hopes. Praised be the
god who has inspired thee with such marvellous courage, for it is from thee and none other
that I am determined to receive the oracle of
my destiny!"

Alcyone, still trembling, though without
daring to look at the tribune, replied in accents weak at first, though gradually becoming
louder:

"Thou must deem me mad, Ombricius, at this
strange boldness of mine. The other day, at
the marriage of Helvidia, I dropped the flower
of Isis I was carrying in my hand, and it was

thou who didst hand it back to me. Our eyes met in the torchlight, and in thine I beheld so strange a look of anguish that it pierced my heart like an arrow. But then, what could I do for thee? Three days afterwards, when thou wert in the temple, I chanced to be behind the bronze statue when thou wert speaking to Memnones, and I overheard everything."

Ombricius gave a start of joy.

"Ah!" he exclaimed, "and what then?"

"Seeing how thou wert athirst after truth, I determined that light should not be refused thee."

"Give it to me! Light can come to me from thee alone!"

"Alas!" she continued, bowing her head and looking at the crystal water of the spring, "it is not the prophetess who can speak to thee to-day as she would have wished; it is only the poor Alcyone, who was once rescued like a dying bird by Memnones, from a sailing vessel on the banks of the Nile. Perhaps, however, through her bruised heart, Isis also is speaking to thee now."

"What must I do?"

"Give thyself up unreservedly to Memnones, obey him in everything so as to obtain his promise that he will be thy master. If thou consentest, he cannot refuse to teach thee. Helvidius will protect thee. . . . I have his

wife's promise. Become the faithful disciple of
him who was more than father to me; he was
my deliverer. Then, some day . . . I am certain
of it . . . the prophetess will cause the ray of
Isis to shine on thee."

"Some day?" murmured Ombricius, bowing
his head and then suddenly standing erect,
as though he would break the obstacle that
was to be set up against him. Then he added
impetuously:

"And if I consent, wilt thou give me no
other promise? It is thy love I desire; without
that, what matters truth to me? Alcyone, dost
thou love me?"

For the first time Alcyone turned round and
looked him full in the face.

"I love thy soul, Ombricius!" she said, with
a smile whose frankness would have disarmed
a Nero, so sublimely fearless was it.

The dark pupils of her eyes quivered as
though she were in a trance. Suddenly she
sank down on her knees and plunged her hand
into the spring.

"Look," she continued, "the lotus stem I
wore at the marriage of Helvidia is hidden
beneath these waters. The new bud is not yet
open, but it will soon burst forth."

She showed him a large leaf, turning it over
in her fingers for some time. Then she fixed
on the tribune her tear-stained eyes, shining

with the pure flame of her love, and added in a
whisper:

"As I keep watch over these flowers, Ombricius, so will I keep watch over thy soul.
When it has attained its complete expansion, on
that day I will bring thee the lotus in all its
splendour!"

Ombricius felt himself gradually won over by
the tenderness and solemnity of this language,
which in the mouth of any other would have
seemed to him either ridiculous presumption or
childish caprice.   With quivering voice he immediately added in suppliant accents:

"And then Alcyone will be my wife?"

"Yes," said the prophetess, turning slightly
aside, "then . . . Isis will permit it."

And her long golden eyelids closed above
her blushing cheeks.

"Thou thyself art Isis!" exclaimed the
tribune, seizing the hand of the priestess with
all the impetuosity of a triumphant passion.

Before the violence of his embrace and the
breath of his lips grazing her locks and seeming
as though it would blight the narcissus in her
wreath, Alcyone, overcome with fear, again encircled the *stela* with her left arm, and leaned
her head against the statue of the goddess, as
though for refuge.   Her right hand remained
held fast in that of Ombricius, who covered it
with burning kisses.

At this moment a terrible voice was heard at the other end of the spring. Like a wail of despair or the outcry of an avenging deity came the name :

" Alcyone ! "

Memnones was standing close to the lovers, followed by Helvidius. The prophetess sank on her knees, hiding her head behind the *stela* which she clasped as though to defend herself against a deadly blow. Ombricius crossed his arms and looked at the priest with an ironical smile of triumph.

" Alcyone, why art thou here with this man, when thy place is at the head of the sacred chorus, chanting praises to the goddess ? "

The stern words of the hierophant met with no other response than the distant voices of women, singing: "The god Osiris is dead! Where lie his scattered limbs?   O goddess! With thee we seek, we lament Osiris! Osiris!" The broken fragments of the plaintive hymn were wafted over the lotus fountain, as though to give intensity to the question of the priest.   The only reply Alcyone gave was to bow her head lower and fold her arms more tightly round the *stela*.

Then Memnones turned to the tribune :

" Who gave thee permission to enter the sacred precincts?   By what right hast thou come into this place, which is reserved for initiates alone ? "

Ombricius was about to reply when Helvidius intervened.

"I invited him to our festival," he said. "This I did at the request of Alcyone and Helvidia."

"So I am no longer head of the temple! Is Alcyone a prophetess no more?"

"Listen, Memnones, and pardon me," continued the decurion. "If the tribune refuses to submit to our rules, I should be the very first to expel him from our body; on the other hand, if he accepts our laws, we cannot drive him away. Alcyone has promised that he will obey thee. Speak, Ombricius, dost thou accept Memnones as thy master?"

"I do," said the tribune, "if he will take me as his disciple."

"Thou seest he consents. Canst thou then forbid him the temple? One must refuse truth to the unworthy, but not to such as ask for it sincerely. Regarding the prophetess, he will obtain her only in case he prove worthy of her, after duly taking the oath of Isis. Meanwhile let him submit to the test; if he comes off victorious, he will be the staunchest defender of our phalanx. Our truth sets the hero's seal on the brow of the combatants . . . and since Alcyone loves Ombricius, it is possible that her love may be for him the ray of Isis."

"Unless," said Memnones, "the love of Ombricius be the end of the prophetess and

the death of Alcyone. Who will guarantee the
fidelity of this disciple ? "

Alcyone had risen to her feet, and in strong
prophetic tones exclaimed :

" I will . . . with my life ! "

" Dost thou then love him ? " said Memnones,
in accents of despair.

Alcyone had not heard; her thoughts had
mounted to a loftier sphere. With solemn
voice she continued as though she would have
liked to engrave her flaming words in the limpid
ether :

" That he may become a son of Isis and that
his might may radiate over Pompeii, I offer
myself as a burnt sacrifice."

Memnones continued :

" And if he comes victorious out of the test ? "

" I will be his wife."

" What wilt thou do if he proves false to thee?"

" I will watch the solitary flame of my glorious
desire burn away, and I will die like the Vestal
clinging to the altar on which burns the undying
flame."

Suiting the action to the word, she again sank
to her feet, her arms encircling the *stela*. The
three men stood looking at her, with an inward
thrill of awe, for there was something decisive
and sacred in the deed. Then Helvidius, taking
Ombricius by the arm, said :

" I too will vouch for the fidelity of this young

man, who is a Roman knight. And now, let us
return to the festival and leave the father alone
with his daughter."

.　　.　　.　　.　　.　　.

When Helvidius and the tribune had disappeared in the myrtle thicket, the priest and
the prophetess remained there motionless, he
standing with folded arms, she kneeling before
the *stela*. What had just happened to them
was so unexpected and wonderful that neither
understood it; it was as though the thunderbolt
that had flashed down had left them living,
though soulless. He felt that he had lost
his adopted daughter and his seer, the treasure of his heart and the eye of his spirit in
the invisible realms. He had been robbed of
his crown. She, too, discovered that by obeying
the irresistible impulse of her heart, she had lost
the confidence of her friend and deliverer. This
thought crushed her, and yet she had obeyed a
command of her soul that was superior to all
possible scruples. This was the reason these two
beings, united by the tenderest and most subtle
bonds, now faced each other like strangers astonished at finding themselves together. Finally,
Alcyone, still kneeling, raised her head, and,
holding out her hands in suppliant gesture to
Memnones, murmured:

"Pardon me, father, I could not do otherwise.
Some god impelled me."

"Which god?"

"I know not, but he spake here," said Alcyone, laying the palm of her hand on her left breast.

"Whoever he be, he is not mine."

"Pardon thy daughter, thy prophetess."

"Thou art my daughter and my prophetess no more," said Memnones sternly. "The alcyone of the seas, which I had gathered to my breast, has flown away. Thou art merely the child of Samothrace, stolen by pirates, an easy prey rushing headlong to thy destiny!"

The prophetess had now risen to her feet, her eyes swimming with tears.

"What, father, shall I never more be thy Alcyone?"

"I know not," said the priest. "Now go, return to the chorus and bewail thy lost god!"

Alcyone, by her attitude, implored a paternal kiss and embrace, but the outstretched arm of Memnones commanded her to advance. Slowly, with bowed head and face buried in her hands, she departed, followed by the priest. From the grove of Persephone, towards which they were advancing, plaintive voices were heard chanting melodiously: "Isis, Isis, what hast thou done with thy god?"

CHAPTER X

IN THE TEMPLE

MARCUS HELVIDIUS belonged to that rare category of men who join to the cult of the highest truths an energetic spur to action, and are happy on these higher planes only when they can group their fellow-beings together in one common effort to attain to their ideal. His birthplace and his natural bent of mind brought him into contact with the ancient school of Pythagoras, venerable mother of the noblest philosophies of Greece, but which, in a sense, was ostracised by the whole of antiquity, from feelings of mingled fear and disdain. A native of Croton, where the master had taught six centuries previous to that time, Helvidius was one of the few followers of Pythagoras who had preserved the master's teaching and tradition in its entirety. In politics he was in favour of an aristocratic government, which conferred power on a select few, who should consist of real initiates. He wished these chosen ones to be of the loftiest character and intelligence, quite capable, in consequence, of instructing and educating the people.

The hierarchy of souls, inherent in humanity and in the constitution of the universe, ought to be applied to the State, and men classified and employed according to their rank in evolution. All are destined to progress, though rarely to mount more than a very few rungs of the ladder in the course of a single lifetime. The institute of initiation should be the school of the governing body, and the political organisation of cities should be modelled after philosophical ideals and religious truth, which would be guarded, as in a sanctuary that must not be violated, by a chosen body of men, but translated to the masses only in proportion as they can be understood beneath the veils of art and symbolism.

This doctrine of a complete aristocracy, the enemy of tyranny and demagogy alike, has at all times excited equal hatred both in tyrants and envious demagogues. It was on this account that Pythagoras, who had instituted this kind of government in Croton, was exiled and perished at Metapontum in a conflagration in the midst of a popular insurrection instigated by Cylon, the demagogue, to whom he had refused initiation. For this cause also the Pythagorean exiles, who survived the disaster, were unfavourably received by the Greek democracies, and the few followers of the school who remained were suspected by the Roman Cæsars.

Helvidius was at this time a man of thirty;

open and generous, inclined to place too much
trust in mental influences, and willingly attri-
buting to others his own goodness of heart.
Deception was incapable of destroying his confidence in the final triumph of good. Devoid of
personal ambition, and finding his sole happiness
in the search after truth, he could afford to smile
at the treachery of rivals, and to disregard the
insults of the masses.

Julia Helconia, on becoming his wife, adopted
the name of Helvidia from her husband, who,
previous to his marriage, had travelled in Greece,
Egypt, and the East before settling in Pompeii.
This city of art and pleasure had a strange
attraction for poets, orators, and philosophers.
Helvidius hoped to make of it a centre for
Pythagorean ideas, and to introduce them by
degrees into the organisation of the city, to
spread them abroad in the towns on the Gulf
of Tarentum, which were still half Greek, and
afterwards into Greece and the East. In his
capacity as decurion he had sent for Memnones
from Egypt to restore the degenerate cult of Isis
to the importance it had formerly attained under
the direction of the true disciples of Hermes.
No sooner had he heard from his wife of the
passionate love of Alcyone for Ombricius Rufus,
than he immediately showed himself in favour of
a marriage between them, hoping to find in the
tribune an influential advocate of the doctrine

and its defender before Vespasian and Titus.
Accordingly, Helvidius used all his influence to
get Memnones to share his conviction.   Finally,
his arguments forced the latter to take Ombricius
as a disciple and subject him to the tests.   The
instruction was to be given by the priest in
the home of Helvidius and Helvidia.   To illustrate the heights and depths of the teaching,
which defies all analysis and can only be offered
through religious and poetic ecstasy, Alcyone
was finally to recite the best of the Orphic hymns
preserved in secret tradition, those dealing with
the celestial journeyings of Psyche.   Then they
would see whether or not there was in the heart
of the tribune that pure enthusiasm which is
almost always concealed like a drop of crystal
in the depths of the human soul.   Provisionally
they would demand of Ombricius only the oath
of silence on everything he saw and heard.
Should he come victorious from the test, he
would be solemnly received into the order on
taking the oath of Isis, swearing obedience to
the masters, and unquestioning devotion to
truth, after which they would take a voyage
to Greece and Egypt in a vessel owned by
Helvidius.   At that very moment the decurion
of Pompeii was having his splendid trireme
painted and decorated in the harbour of Stabiæ ;
and in it, Helvidius and Helvidia, Ombricius
and Alcyone, under the guidance of Memnones,

would go to Athens to be present at the festival of Eleusis. There the marriage of Ombricius and Alcyone would be celebrated, and they would return and continue all together the work begun in Italy.

With death in his soul, Memnones resigned himself to the decree of destiny. Both his science and his happiness were in mortal danger, he thought. He remembered, however, the words Sabaccas had said to him in the desert of the pyramids : " Only in the greatest grief wilt thou find the greatest truth." Accordingly he resolved to think no more of himself, but only of his duty—to make of Ombricius a perfect initiate, and of Alcyone a happy bride ; though, perhaps, not without a secret hope that he would not succeed. This cowardly thought he thrust back, however, determined for the future to be no more than the master—that is to say, one free from all earthly desires, more than a man, a living word of God.

.   .   .   .   .   .

The lessons began at the abode of Helvidius. The only ornaments of the domestic sanctuary consisted of a small altar, always decked with flowers and two marble Muses—Melpomene and Polyhymnia.

Helvidia, with a dozen women and maidens, stood in a crescent, whilst Memnones spoke from before the altar. In front of him, beneath the peristyle, sat Helvidius, Ombricius Rufus, and a few young men. All attended the daily lessons of the master with profound attention and assiduity.

At first Alcyone did not appear, and for two months Ombricius saw nothing of her. Though this trial seemed a hard one, he yet submitted to it without a murmur. He had confidence in the promise of the priestess, and now, thanks to the teaching of Memnones, his mind had regained some of its youthful enthusiasm. After roughly sketching, in its essential principles, the science of numbers, that key to the Hermetic doctrine, whose importance can be understood only by its many applications to all sciences and to the final synthesis of the universe, Memnones passed rapidly to the history of the human races in which is seen the perpetual descent and the visible incarnation of spirit in matter. He spoke of the buried continents whose very memory had been lost in popular tradition. He related the life of the first human races, more like animals than men—races whose deeds have been preserved by Egyptian priests in the hieroglyphs engraved on the walls of their crypts and temples. He depicted the Lemurians, cave-men who formerly lived in a hyperborean continent, to whom Aeschylus appears to allude when he makes Prometheus say: "They saw, but they saw ill; they heard, but they did not understand. Like phantoms of dreams they lived for centuries, inextricably confusing all things." He related the history of Atlantis, that mighty continent which once rose above the Great Ocean, far beyond the Straits of Gibraltar.

Plato, who had been initiated by Egyptian priests, mentions this continent in his *Critias* and his *Timæus*. After a series of cataclysms, the last island of the continent, which Plato called Poseidonis, sank beneath the waters nine thousand years before the foundation of Rome. This vast continent, which has now disappeared, was the theatre of a marvellous civilisation, which lasted thousands of years, as is testified by its immense temples and its cities with their gates of gold. A series of islands, swallowed up since then by successive deluges, connected Atlantis with Africa and Europe and facilitated emigration from one land to the other. Science and art, magic and sun-worship, were born among the inhabitants of Atlantis. From them issued the chosen races which came to people Europe, Africa, and Asia. The sacred science, however, was handed down in its purity by Hermes only and the initiates who reigned in his name. The science of numbers and the stars, of writing and divination; religion which transforms occult forces and cosmic powers into speaking symbols; and the art of governing men, which proceeds from the science of the soul, all reached their apogee in Egypt.

"Thus," concluded Memnones, "in all these mighty human annals, from century to century, through every race and innumerable cataclysms, the sacred tradition is the connecting link, the unbroken chain, the torch which is often veiled though never extinguished. It is only owing to the prophets and messengers of God, incarnating on this earth, that the blind masses of humanity progress at all, though so slowly. Around these collect the select few, leaders of the many. Thanks to the initiates who pass on to one another the torch of life, the sacred fire never dies, nothing essential is lost, and the storehouse of knowledge ever increases. Each prophet brings his message and each race its work."

"With the Doric race and Orpheus its prophet," continued the priest, "begins the era in which we are now living. Orpheus, who came from the sanctuaries of Greece, wished to transform for the Greeks the divine science into life and beauty, in city and temple, in marble and flesh. Before him the world knew only Priest and King. Into the dull wilderness of mankind Orpheus cast, like the living torches of Prometheus, the Hero and the Poet, the Lover and the Pythoness. We, the disciples of Hermes, Orpheus, and Pythagoras, wave these torches throughout the world; it is our keen desire to light brighter torches still.

. . . But one must believe divine science if one would engage in divine combats!"

Such bold words filled Ombricius with delight. They caused springs hitherto unknown to gush forth from the hard rock of his heart. Perhaps he would not have lent an ear to such strange chords had not their powerful harmony flattered his pride. Already he looked upon himself as an initiate, a prophet, a *magus*, more powerful than the emperor. He would awe the crowds with his prestige; his will would both make and unmake Cæsars.

The thoughts of Ombricius, however, took another direction; his attitude completely changed when Memnones commenced the second part of the secret teaching. Man and the human race have not only a terrestrial history, they have also a cosmic one, both before and after this life. How did the human soul descend from divinity? Through what series of falls and repeated ascents did it attain to its present state? What is its cosmic journey after each death? By what inevitable law is it forced to reincarnate itself after each sojourn with the creative gods? What are the conditions of its final deliverance, its return to full consciousness and power in its divine homeland? Of the terrible, the sublime wanderings of the human Psyche, painfully seeking after a divine Psyche, Memnones gave only a brief account,

opening out partial vistas, trying simply to unravel the thread that bound together these divers
existences and the general law governing them.
He also added that Ombricius would receive
more light on this matter in Eleusis, and that,
in order to form an approximate idea of the
wonderful mysteries both on this side and on
the other side of death, he must learn by degrees
to penetrate these mysteries himself. This was
reserved for the final stages of initiation.

As soon as the master began the celestial
history of Psyche, there came over Ombricius a
feeling of mingled giddiness and fear. Although
this doctrine of a multiple and graduated immortality sprang from the secret depths of consciousness and the divine centre of the universe,
it all the same inspired a secret aversion in the
mind of the tribune. As he listened to Memnones he felt like an inhabitant of earth, carried
off in spite of himself by reckless sailors over a
surging boundless sea. Was it that his inner
vision would not open up? or did an instinctive
dread hold him back in presence of the unknown? Very soon this feeling of uneasiness
changed into one of revolt. His narrow-minded-
ness and pusillanimity of soul set up a helmet
of pride as a mask and defence over against his
bedimmed consciousness. His reason refused
to admit these bold hypotheses offered to
him as transcendental truths, and of which

no tangible proof was afforded him. His
pride rebelled at the idea of having existed
under other forms, and at having to change body
and consciousness many more times still. What
was this doctrine which tears you away from
the *terra firma* of the senses only to fling
you into an abyss of uncertainty? By what
right did this presumptuous priest threaten to
draw the tribune's soul from his body and
hurl it into space? Was this fictitious heaven
worth the joys of earth that he could see and
feel? Better to live a single life, he said to
himself, with all the energy of the passions,
and find annihilation at the end of it, than
be hounded like a vain shadow by an unknown
power through countless existences!

The presence of Alcyone, when she finally
appeared, merely increased this feeling of irri-
tation. She did not leave the circle of women
and maidens who surrounded her as with a wall
of tender respect. Only furtive glances passed
between the tribune and the prophetess. The
mystery of that soul he could not penetrate
troubled him even more than the mystery of
the universe. Alcyone's attitude during the
final lessons of Memnones only deepened the
abyss separating them. Whilst Ombricius became more and more hostile to the ideas of the
hierophant, the prophetess rose with delight to
these inaccessible heights. Such transports and

joys which he could not share, filled him with
indignant wrath. To crown his humiliation,
Alcyone appeared to have forgotten him. Seated
on the pedestal of the Muse, round whose knees
her arms were folded, with face as pale as the
marble against which her head was leaning, she
seemed to be on the verge of ecstasy.

In such an attitude Alcyone listened to
the last lesson of the priest. Memnones depicted the happiness of the soul which has
reached the end of its wanderings and meta-
morphoses ; when, having arrived at its divine
abode, it sees the whole of its cosmic journey
in a single flash. On this occasion only three
persons were present in the semicircle—Memnones in the centre, Alcyone on the left, and
Helvidia on the right, with an ivory lyre on
her knees. The priest of Isis, finishing his
discourse, said : " No human words can describe
the visions unfolded before the transfigured soul
in the region of which I am now speaking,
though sacred art has at times attempted to
express them. To illustrate the WORD of Hermes
the prophetess will chant to you the Hymn
of the divine Psyche." Whereupon Memnones
left the semicircle and took his seat beneath
the peristyle, by the side of Helvidius.

Alcyone appeared to be coming out of the
dream which bound her to the statue of Polyhymnia. She walked slowly to the domestic

altar, and poured a little resin powder on to
the smouldering ashes. A bright flame shot
up. Then the prophetess raised her narcissus-
wreathed head to the vault and recited the
mysterious hymn to Helvidia's accompaniment
on the lyre.

When she had finished, a passionate outburst of applause arose: "All honour to Memnones! Glory and honour to Alcyone!"

Helvidius offered the priestess a garland of
flowers which she took with a smile. Then
she leaned over to Helvidia and kissed her,
as though ashamed of her boldness, and feeling
that she had once more become a feeble mortal
after playing the divine Psyche. The only
reply Helvidia gave was to press the maiden's
golden locks in her hands and bury the burning head in her bosom, after covering with
kisses her brow all moist with the sweat of
enthusiasm.

.   .   .   .   .   .

All rose in a tumult except Ombricius, who
remained in his seat, motionless and silent.
Though his brain was burning with excitement, his heart was cold as ice. His was the
disappointed look of a pointer which sees a
lark wing its flight from the ground, and
is unable to follow it through the realms of
space. Filled with a dull feeling of madness
against an enthusiasm he could not understand,

and which he regarded as absurd, he was bitterly angry with all—Memnones, his teaching, his disciples, and even the prophetess herself. And yet the superhuman beauty of Alcyone roused with an invincible charm and to the highest degree all the latent desires of his being. But then he considered that he alone had any rights over her, and that he was being robbed of a treasure laboriously fought for and won. Forgetfulness of self is the essence of a mighty love as it is of enthusiasm. These two sublime faculties, more powerful than all the rest, will ever be regarded as the height of madness by such as are incapable of sinking themselves in another soul, or losing themselves in God.

Alcyone had remained alone near the statue of Polyhymnia, toying with a wreath of laurel leaves. She seemed to be awaiting Ombricius, who approached her.

"For three months," he said, "I have not been able to speak to thee, Alcyone! Scarcely has a distant look of thine told me that thou hadst remembered me. . . . Thou hast wandered away into other worlds, to some far-distant, inaccessible heaven. . . . To-day those sublime strains of thine filled me with despair. . . . I lose my foothold in those boundless spaces, nor have I wings wherewith to follow the divine Psyche. That wreath of narcissus shining on thy head dazzles and blinds me.

. . . These flowers, Alcyone, are as intangible as the stars!"

Alcyone, whose eyes had remained downcast during this speech, now gave the tribune a look of astonishment, as though she did not recognise him.   Then a smile of infinite grace played on her expressive lips; she removed the narcissus wreath from her head, and, holding it out to the young man, said:

" In the early freshness of the morn I gathered these flowers.   In like fashion would I gather thy soul as an offering to Isis.   Breathe in their perfume; what does it tell thee?"

Ombricius took the wreath in his hands and began to inhale the delicate perfume, which was as strong as that of a jessamine.   He looked alternately at the narcissus and the smiling prophetess, then suddenly handed back the wreath.

"It tells me," he exclaimed, "that I love thee passionately, and that thou hast no love for me!"

She gave him a look of mingled sadness and pity.

" No love for thee?   Hast thou then forgotten my oath by the lotus spring?"

" If thou hadst," said Ombricius, "thy sympathy would bring thee down to me . . . otherwise, I cannot have thee by my side. . . . Never shall I mount so high as thou art! . . . Ah! if only thou didst love me . . . thou wouldst give me thy wreath . . . at once ! "

A quiver of terror ran through Alcyone, who clasped her hands over her breast as though to restrain the waves of emotion pulsating through her. Then, with a gesture of ineffable tenderness, she raised the narcissus wreath to her lips. From the contact she seemed to draw sudden inspiration, for she said in quieter tones :

" Yes, Ombricius, these flowers shall belong to thee, for I am wholly thine ! " . . . Then, with radiant countenance and proud mien, she placed the wreath on the marble head of Polyhymnia, with the words :

" We will rise together ! "

Just then a group of maidens came rushing down to greet Alcyone. They wound a garland of roses round her, exclaiming : " How beautiful she is ! Her countenance is transfigured ! She is now the divine Psyche herself ! "

"Thine be the lyre which binds souls together ! " said Helvidia, handing to the prophetess her ivory lyre. " And thine the immortal crown ! " said Helvidius, taking the wreath of narcissus from the head of Polyhymnia and placing it back again on that of Alcyone, whose cheeks flushed with pleasure.

Memnones, standing a few steps distant, was looking at his adopted daughter and contemplating his work with the eye of a conqueror.

The virgin received all these honours without pride or vanity. The dull, sombre look on the countenance of Ombricius gave her a feeling of uneasiness. She had glanced once more into his very soul and seen in it for the first time all the bitter desires and the inferno of egoism.

Ombricius, who had withdrawn beneath the peristyle, was watching the group from afar. He said to himself bitterly: "There she is amongst her equals, but I am not one of them. All these followers of Isis form one family; they possess her, but I do not." A secret envy and a dull feeling of anger was brooding in his heart. To calm this feeling, he added: "She loves me. . . . Well, I will have her by force!" And thereupon he took his departure without bidding farewell to any one.

CHAPTER XI

HEDONIA METELLA

THE following day Ombricius was walking with fevered steps under the large portico of the forum, where the wealthy Pompeians and their active, vivacious wives and daughters had come to breathe the fresh evening air, trailing toga and stole along the mosaic pavement. Suddenly Simmias touched him on the shoulder and took both his friend's hands in his own.

"Some propitious god has brought thee here," exclaimed the Greek. "I have just left the most extraordinary woman in Pompeii. Myrrhina, that fascinating coquette who is at times faithless to me, has promised that she will dance at this illustrious lady's mansion to-night, after supper. The queen of Pompeii spoke to me in some such terms as these: 'Since thou art bringing the most accomplished dancer of Pompeii, why not bring me also the haughtiest tribune in the army of Titus, who has become, they say, the most learned of philosophers? I should be glad to include this Roman knight among my guests. Three months ago thou

126

didst make me this promise regarding Ombricius
Rufus, and so far thou hast not kept thy word.'
I replied to this queen : ' If I find him, I swear
by all the gods that I will bring him to thee
this evening.' Was I wrong in making that
promise ? "

" What is this woman's name ? "

" Hedonia Metella."

Ombricius ransacked his memory in vain.

" Hast thou forgotten the patrician lady who
passed by in a litter on the day of the marriage
of Helvidius, and the Pæstum rose which fell, as
though by chance, into the lappet of thy toga ? "

" Now I remember," said Ombricius, who had
thought no more of the adventure, being meanwhile under the charm of Alcyone.

" I have no wish to take thee unawares, my
dear tribune," continued the Epicurean. " Thou
must know where I am about to bring thee.
The temple of Isis has its mysteries, which I
know nothing about; the house of Hedonia
Metella also has its customs, rites, and laws,
through the labyrinth of which I will act as thy
guide. It is a strange place, full of charms and
snares. Some meet with good fortune therein,
others are ruined. I must just warn thee of one
peculiarity regarding this dangerous woman.
Whosoever once sets foot in her abode becomes
of necessity either her friend or her enemy.
Take heed against becoming the latter ! Though

she is generous to such as pander to her whims, she is said to be terrible against all who resist her. Reflect, then, before accepting, and, if thou comest, be on thy guard!"

"Ah! Simmias," exclaimed Ombricius, who had suddenly regained his good spirits, "thou art a mighty orator, for thou hast discovered my weak spot. So there is danger, is there? Very good, I will go. Besides, I need a little distraction!"

"Then that is settled," said the Greek, clapping his hands. "Come and sup with Myrrhina and myself. Afterwards we will proceed to call upon the queen of Pompeii."

An hour later the two friends and Myrrhina, the actress, reclining negligently on sumptuous couches, were gaily partaking of a magnificent repast in the elegant *triclinium* of Simmias. On the walls, all painted with red, were figures of swimming Nereids, flying Cupids, and others of similar subjects. While the goblets of wine were being handed round, Simmias said to his friend, in grave accents:

"Thou must know that Hedonia Metella is the daughter of Metellus the patrician, and a Numidian princess. In her person she combines the superb pride of the Roman matron with the keen, subtle fire of an African race. She is a man-tamer, an indomitable one, and has, up to the present, succeeded in mastering herself. There is in her something of Agrippina and of a Bacchante, though both these phases of her nature are concealed beneath an expression of wonderful sprightliness. Her masculine will controls her feminine passions when working out some deep scheme or other, and holds them in check as though they were a pack of panthers. Were I a philosopher, I should describe her character as follows : profound voluptuousness in the service of unbridled ambition."

" What is the object of her ambition ? " asked Ombricius.

" No one knows ; her conduct is very strange."

" Don't talk of philosophy, please ! " exclaimed Myrrhina, throwing back her pretty head to swallow an oyster. " Tell us her history ! "

" I know very little of it," continued Simmias. " In her childhood they say she was a favourite of Poppæa. Nero's wife loved to take the little patrician girl on her knees. Hedonia was a precocious child, and seemed to absorb from the conversation of the fair-haired Jewess, the monster's mistress, the subtle essence of her treacherous grace and cunning plots. Did she learn that art of ruling Cæsar by smiles, tears, and threats, of exciting by refusals, controlling by caresses, and bewitching with languishing looks? I cannot say, though she succeeded, at the age of eighteen, in marrying the wealthiest proconsul of the Empire. The latter died after a few years, leaving her an immense fortune, a house in Rome, land in Epirus and Campania, a villa at Baiæ, museums and statues, innumerable treasures, and an army of slaves."

"How I should like to be that woman!" sighed Myrrhina, as she opened one of that species of shell-fish called sea-flowers, the white pulp of which stretched its still living flesh to meet the sensual lips of the mime.

At this point Simmias lowered his voice so as not to be heard by the slaves who were passing to and fro, carrying silver plates:

"Between ourselves, they do say that Helvidia poisoned her old husband with a phial she concealed in her hair."

"How did she do that?" asked Myrrhina, trembling with mingled curiosity and excitement.

"Oh! most beautifully," said the Epicurean, with a smile. "After a feast the old man was in the habit of untying the dark tresses of his young wife, and breathing in the perfumes with which they were scented. The small enamel phial was twisted into one of the curls, like a jewel. Whilst the proconsul's lips were touching the bare shoulder of Hedonia, she held her goblet in one hand, and with the other gently poured the contents of the phial into the wine. Then she offered the deadly beverage to her husband, intoxicated with passion. I know not if this be true, or simply the calumnious report of a slave. The story spread throughout Rome and the provinces as well. After all . . . I should have no objection to dying in the same way. What sayest thou, Myrrhina? . . . Wouldst thou consent?"

"Ah!" exclaimed the actress, her eyes flashing with savage indignation, "what a horrible woman! . . . But what a glorious scene for the stage!"

"And what then?" asked the tribune, who had ceased eating and drinking.

"Ever since that day Hedonia has lived a life of luxury and wealth without marrying again. When in Rome she had a series of lovers, for it may be said of her, as was said of Poppæa, that she could never distinguish a lover from a husband. The most famous of her adorers was Cecina, a general in the army of Vitellius, and a violent, ambitious man, though a brilliant soldier. They suddenly parted, without any one knowing the reason. Evidently she entertains bitter feelings against him, for she never mentions the matter. Cecina has since become a person of great importance at Rome. During the cruel war between the armies of Vitellius and Vespasian Hedonia Metella espoused the cause of Titus, our emperor's young son, over whom she has great influence through his wife. It is now a year ago since she came to settle in her house at Pompeii. What she is now meditating I have no idea, though meanwhile she appears to be enjoying herself."

" In what way ? "

" Oh, in a very refined fashion. She has founded the Hedonian brotherhood."

" What is that ? "

" A brotherhood consisting, naturally, of Hedonia's admirers. I do not belong to it, though I visit them occasionally as director of the musical and dancing *fêtes*. In this capacity I am made pretty well acquainted with everything that takes place. To belong to Hedonia's club one must take an oath of submission, binding one to obey her slightest whim. She rewards every one as her fancy dictates, each one according to merit, though not all in the same manner. I must do her the justice to say that hitherto she has maintained the most perfect order among them. Her favourite for the time being is to be regarded as the prince of the brotherhood, and is consecrated as such by a special ceremony. He receives the respect of all, whilst any who show jealousy or displeasure are expelled without pity. The rest obey and wait, hoping, often in vain, that their turn will come, though none the less pleased to belong to the brotherhood, and consequently privileged to assist at the *fêtes* of the queen of Pompeii. Many of her *protégés* have become prefects,

generals, or prætors. Never does she forget
them, but will take up their defence if necessary, if only they continue to obey her. This
is doubtless the reason why those belonging to
the brotherhood are so proud of it, and why
the rest envy and slander the Hedonians. In
a word, everybody blames the vices of the queen
of Pompeii, and yet every one pays court to her.
She is detested and worshipped, loved and dreaded,
because she is both charming and powerful.
I had almost forgotten to tell thee, my dear
Ombricius, that Hedonia Metella believes neither
in the wonder-working gods of the priests, nor
in the inert, abstract god of the philosophers.
Such notorious impiety might well do her harm
in high places, did she not publicly affect a
pompous worship of the divinity of Cæsar, and
this clears her of even the faintest suspicion of
sacrilege. It is also said that she secretly wor-
ships Hecate in a small temple built in her
garden at Baiæ. No one, however, has entered
this temple, and she forbids all mention of it.
This is all I know, my dear tribune."

"Quite enough to afford every promise of a
pleasant evening," said the tribune, rising to
his feet.

"I shall be afraid of dancing before this
sorceress," said Myrrhina. "She will cast an
evil spell over me."

"Nonsense!" said Simmias. "She will make

thee a splendid gift, which will bring good fortune for the rest of thy life."

The tribune put on his toga, whilst Simmias clasped over the shoulders of the mime a mantle which completely concealed her, and the three went out together.

.   .   .   .   .   .

The interior of Hedonia's abode shone brightly. Conducted by the nomenclator, Simmias, Myrrhina, and Ombricius crossed a number of dazzling halls, peristyles, galleries, and labyrinths, supported by columns of jasper and porphyry. Mythological scenes were depicted on the walls and Cupids of terra-cotta were sporting in the flower-beds. They found the mistress of the place surrounded by a dozen youths, all wearing the patrician *chlamys*. In front of a carved nymph, close by a shady fountain, three seats had been placed. On the centre one sat Hedonia Metella as on a throne, wearing a purple *peplum* fastened with a golden girdle, a diadem surrounding her hair, which was held in place by a net of precious stones. An Indian scarf, of rose-coloured silk embroidered with flowers, passed behind her neck and wound itself round her bare arms. A solitary lock of her shining, jet-black hair lay negligently on her neck, like a serpent that had been lulled to sleep by some strong perfume.

Only once before had Ombricius seen this

woman. Then, her haughty features had been engraved in his memory, but now he was struck by the morbid grace beneath her beauty. Her opulent bosom, imperious, broad forehead, and proud, oval countenance showed that she was a Roman patrician by birth, but her sinuous neck and quivering nostrils betrayed her African blood. Her large dark eyes, resembling those of a wild beast, were impassive mirrors, whose troublous depths reflect with equal calm the burning heavens and the whirling sand-spouts.

On Hedonia perceiving Ombricius, the fiery flash of her eyes grew softer, and she greeted her new guest with a graceful gesture.

" Welcome to my chosen company, my lord Ombricius. Thy illustrious name has long been known to me in connection with this city, and even more by reason of thy exploits in Palestine. I am aware that thou art the first soldier in the army of Titus."

" Long life and renown to Hedonia Metella," said Ombricius, bowing low. " With just cause art thou called the queen of Pompeii ; but thou hast forgotten that I am in disgrace."

"What an erroneous thought, my dear tribune! I well know that it is the contrary that is true, as I will prove to thee whenever thou wishest."

Ombricius drew nearer, and the two spoke in low tones for a few moments. Eyes full of mistrust and curiosity were directed towards the tribune, but the patrician immediately said:

"Thou wilt soon know the members of my brotherhood. I will introduce to thee only three who will make thee acquainted with the rest. . . . The first is the noble Lentulus, my oldest friend, a wise and eloquent senator of Pompeii."

Ombricius beheld an elderly grey-haired magistrate, who held out his hand, a stern expression on his face as he looked at the tribune from head to foot.

"The second," continued Hedonia, with a smile, "is the excellent Flavulus, a poet who has brought back the glorious days of my favourite Catullus."

Ombricius saw a bald-headed man, prematurely aged, whose loose swollen face had been furrowed with greenish-looking wrinkles by a life of youthful debauch. On his thick-lipped mouth played an impudent, vain smile.

"The third," she continued, "is the noble Crispus, a Roman knight, youthful in years, though with a life before him full of promise."

The tribune received the obsequious bow of a youth of slender form, elegant and charming to behold. Everything about him was delicate and refined—nose and chin, hand and mouth. There was a sparkling light in his eyes, whilst in his hand he held a goblet.

"This is the present favourite," whispered Simmias in the ear of Ombricius.

"Continue, my dear Lentulus," said Hedonia. "What is the news to-day?"

"During the past week," said the senator, "the only thing talked about has been the trireme belonging to Marcus Helvidius, the decurion. It appears that he has had it constructed in Liguria. It bears the name of Isis and is a wonderful vessel; not one of the ships belonging to the fleet of Misenum has such splendid sails or such a glorious prow. It has been painted and decorated in the harbour of Stabiæ, and no one is permitted to approach it."

"What will he do with such a marvel?" asked Hedonia.

"It is believed that he is meditating a trip to all the large ports in the south of Italy. They even say that he will travel as far as Greece and Egypt, where he will proclaim his ideas concerning the government of the aristocracy and establish a league of free cities against Cæsar and the Roman Empire. Beneath that modest, affable exterior of his Helvidius is a dangerous man. Never has he consented to worship Cæsar, and now he struts about as though he were a king or a demi-god. These new followers of Isis may be even worse than the obscure sect of the Christians, who are poor and ignorant, and convert none but slaves. The followers of Isis are wealthy and learned and appeal principally to the *élite*. They call themselves friends of the human race, though, like the Christians, they are the enemies of Cæsar and of the people of Rome. Some day we shall have to take measures against them also."

"What are you saying about Helvidius?" said Flavulus the poet. "At all events, he is a charming, handsome man; but what think you of this priest of Isis he has sent for from Egypt? Did you ever see a more hirsute or gloomy-looking individual? In silent, sullen pride he wanders up and down the streets, lost in thought. The panther's skin he wears on his emaciated body is an insult to Bacchus. I am surprised the populace has not risen as one man to drive him out of Pompeii!"

"You are speaking of the priest, my dear Flavulus, but you forget the priestess," said Crispus, with a cunning smile. "This man Memnones, it appears, picked her up somewhere from the pirates in the Cyclades. The Samothracian girl, however, is no ordinary person."

"Is she beautiful?" asked Hedonia, raising her head.

"No, she is not beautiful, but rather strange and wonderfully pretty. In the streets she is always veiled whenever she goes to see the wife of Helvidius, accompanied by her old Nubian nurse. I once saw her in the temple of Isis during the sacrifice of fire and perfume, the only sacrifice recognised by the followers of Isis. She has glorious golden hair and eyes blue as a hyacinth. It is affirmed that when she falls asleep in the priest's presence Isis appears to her, and that he then consults her, to discover how to treat his disciples. Isis appears bearing either a key, a mirror, or a whip."

"That is correct," said Hedonia Metella solemnly; "in the temples of the Nile the goddess may be seen represented with those three emblems. I noticed this fact on my trip to Egypt."

"What do these three objects signify?" was the general request of those standing round Crispus.

"Listen to me attentively. When Isis bears the key, the disciple is immediately accepted with much pomp and ceremony. When she bears the mirror, he is submitted to a lengthy test, which sometimes lasts for years. When she bears the whip, he is refused admittance."

The tribune stood apart, at a little distance from the semicircle. He would have liked to reply with cutting words, but he could not do this without betraying himself. He stood there in silence.

"Unless I am mistaken," said Hedonia Metella, raising her voice, " we have here a true initiate of Isis in our haughty tribune, Ombricius Rufus himself. Am I not right?"

"I am not an initiate, merely a disciple. My test is not yet completed," said Ombricius, slightly embarrassed, as he drew near the circle.

"What matters that?" murmured Hedonia, in gentle accents and with a bewitching smile. "In public I well understand thy discretion, but in private— Come and sit down by my side, generous tribune. . . . Thou shalt whisper somewhat of these mysteries into mine ear, if only concerning the lovely eyes and tresses of the priestess. . . . Hast thou too sworn never to speak of them?"

Ombricius, his head turned by a thousand opposing sensations, went up to the patrician and sat down by her side. For a few moments they spoke to one another in whispers. This was unexpected, and caused some stir in the group of young Hedonians. The senator became more imposing, the wrinkles on the face of Flavulus the poet turned a deeper green than before, and the handsome Crispus rose indignantly to his feet. He was quickly reassured, however, for Hedonia Metella, seeing his uneasiness, suddenly said :

"Sit down on my right hand, Crispus; we have had enough speaking, and will now finish the day with the spectacle of a dance. Terpsichore herself is in our midst. . . . Incomparable Muse, delight of the eyes, triumph of grace and poetry of pleasure . . . come hither, Myrrhina!"

" All hail to Terpsichore and her interpreter ! "
exclaimed all in chorus.

Myrrhina advanced. She had unrobed herself
in front of a large copper mirror, and was now
covered only with a filmy blue tunic, behind
which her graceful form swayed to and fro like
sea-weed beneath the rippling waves. A beryl,
in imitation of a winged insect, sparkled in her
jet-black locks, and her eyes shone with joy.
Clasping her hands, she made a profound rever-
ence before the queen of Pompeii. The flute and
tambourine players commenced their humming
and droning music, and Myrrhina began the
dance of the bee. At first she saw it afar off in
the air, following with her hand its capricious
flight. By degrees it drew nearer, its approach
being signified by suppliant gestures, movements
of head and body bent backwards and forwards.
The invisible bee, however, which seemed to be
on the point of descending, always flew away
again, to Myrrhina's great despair. Finally, with
a sudden sweep, it descended on the dancing
girl, settling in turn on her breast, her arm, and
her face. In vain did she attempt to catch it,
for it bounded away and came back more per-
severingly than ever. Suddenly she uttered a
cry, and leaped into the air, as though the cruel
insect had stung her. Then the panting mime,
ever pursuing and pursued, began to whirl madly
round with so rapid a motion that the two adver-

saries seemed to be fleeing and clinging to one another in turn.   Myrrhina had become a winged being, a human bee.   Suddenly she stopped, motionless and erect.   Standing there in serious attitude, like a *canephora*, she picked up from her hair the captive bee.   Humbly kneeling before the mistress of the house, she held out her open hand, and offered the beryl to Hedonia Metella.

A cry of delight and admiration rang out from a dozen throats, and the queen of Pompeii exclaimed:

"Most excellent of mimes, henceforth I will never call thee by any other name than Myrrhina the divine!"

Thereupon, unfastening a splendid cameo from the fine purple garment covering her breast, she offered it to the girl.   Then she drew her head towards her lips and imprinted a kiss on the mouth of the dancer, all radiant and half fainting with joy.

Whilst the dance was proceeding, Hedonia Metella had turned her eyes on her two neighbours with a passionate or languid expression, causing divers emotions in Crispus and the tribune. . . . The band of youths crowded round Myrrhina with words of praise and congratulation.   "Divine Myrrhina!" said one of them, "whose mouth has touched the lips of Hedonia Metella. . . . Henceforth she is en-

dowed with magic power. . . . Give me a kiss
. . . just one . . . it will bring me good luck
from our queen!" "Come to me," said another.
"No, to me!" "To us all!" they shouted in
chorus. Still trembling with the excitement of
the dance and with face and neck trickling with
perspiration, Myrrhina laughed and uttered faint
cries of joy, prancing about in the middle of the
group like a high-spirited horse steaming with
moisture after a race. She was on the point of
yielding to the entreaties of the youths, when
she was checked by a stern look from Simmias,
and, beaming with triumph and delight, she
crossed over to him.

The three most intimate companions of
Hedonia, Lentulus the senator, Flavulus the
poet, and Crispus, had taken up their posts in
front of their idol. Flavulus said :

"To conclude this glorious festival, we will
ask our sorceress to read the future for us."

"By the eyes or the hand?"

"By both."

"Be it so. I will begin with thee, Lentulus."

Taking the senator's hand, she fixed her large,
dark orbs on the sad eyes of the magistrate.

"Rejoice, Lentulus," she said, after a moment's
pause; "soon wilt thou become duumvir of
Pompeii."

These words had no other effect than to deepen
the expression of sadness on the old man's face.

His hand still clasping that of the patrician, he said :

"Rather than be duumvir of this town for the rest of my life, I would prefer to be the prince of the Hedonian brotherhood for a single day."

"Hast thou not held that office for three months!" she said playfully, "and well thou knowest that I never willingly grant this title twice to the same friend, whatever be his merit. No matter . . . hope on. . . . Hedonia, in a single day, promises nothing and gives everything . . . if the fleet-footed Hour permits."

Flavulus now stepped forward, with suppliant eye and derisive mouth, as though he were making for the hundredth time a prayer he had no hope of seeing granted. Hedonia carelessly took his hand, and cast a sidelong glance at the uneasy eyes of the bald-headed debauchee.

"What shall I prophesy of thee, unlucky poet? The muses are incensed because thou hast sacrificed too freely at the shrine of Venus. Well, I will reveal to thee what I read in thine eyes. For the fine verses thou hast composed in my honour thou shalt be crowned prince of poets by Titus, and thy bust shall be in his library."

Flavulus humbly kissed the hand of Metella as he murmured :

"Many thanks, O Cypris!"

Then he added in accents of self-pity and with a tragi-comical air:

"A bust! How gloomy and cold! A bust which some day will be flung into the Tiber and commented on when two thousand years have passed, by some learned scholar in Gaul or Germania, when I shall be nothing else than dust and clay! A bust which ridicules its model because it remains young whilst the former grows old! A bust which says, 'I am immortal and thou art not!' Ah! I would give all the busts in the world for the privilege of spending a single night at Baiæ in the temple of Hecate in the company of Hedonia Metella!"

Hedonia shuddered as she listened to these words, flames shot from her eyes, and she proudly raised her imperial head.

"Silence!" she said. "Thou knowest not what thou sayest!"

"But Hecate is thy goddess, is she not?"

"My worship of her, if such be the fact, concerns me alone. No one has ever accompanied me into her temple, nor has any one the right to speak of her! . . . Thou hast infringed the strictest law of my brotherhood. I condemn thee to a month's silence."

"That is a severe punishment for a poet," said the senator, with a half-smile at the defeat of his colleague.

Flavulus, crestfallen, hung down his head.

The rest looked at one another in trembling and fear before the mistress of the house and Hecate her familiar. Hedonia had turned pale, though two cold steel glances shot from her eyes. The burning atmosphere emanating from her whole person had suddenly become cold as ice. Embarrassed by this sudden chill, Ombricius rose to his feet and moved away a few yards, the better to observe another episode.

The handsome Crispus stepped forward and said assuringly:

"I will be more modest. I lay no claim to know the future, nor do I wish to know it, for I am too happy in the present. May it only endure! Since I am now prince of the Hedonian brotherhood, I only ask to renew, in your presence, my vow of obedience and submission to our queen by bestowing a kiss on her divine foot. Such is my privilege, and I am proud of it!"

"It is also thy right," murmured Hedonia, who had now regained her wonted cheerfulness.

"Look!" whispered Simmias to the tribune. "Thou wilt now witness the ceremony of consecration."

A slave brought an ivory stool, which he set before his mistress. On it she placed her bare foot, covered only with a small Tyrian sandal. In the light of the lamps this wonderful foot resembled pale amber, and appeared to be as transparent as alabaster. Crispus knelt and kissed it devotedly, then he bent his face over the cushion which covered the stool. Hedonia placed her foot on the neck of the youth, her toes leaving rosy marks on the pale skin. A look of joy on his face, he rose to his feet. His companions came up to congratulate him, whilst the two rejected candidates stood apart, in gloomy resignation.

"Well, friend Ombricius, what sayest thou to my ceremonial?" asked the patrician, beckoning to the tribune.

"I say that this foot of thine is the wonder of the world, and that there is not its match among all the queens of Asia. Assuredly the wife of Darius, whom Alexander refused to see for fear of yielding to her charms, was not possessed of one so beautiful. Had I been in Alexander's place, I would have taken the wife of Darius, though I would never have submitted to her foot. No woman shall ever subject me to this."

"Art thou quite sure?" murmured, with ironical gentleness, the daughter of Metellus, bending her head slightly forward.

"Absolutely certain."

"Then thou wilt not belong to our brotherhood?" she asked.

"Great is the honour thou offerest me," said the tribune, "but I fear I am unworthy of it.

I thank thee for thy favour and bid thee fare-well.   In thee I acknowledge the most beautiful and powerful of Roman women."

" Good-bye, Ombricius Rufus," said Hedonia, in loud accents.

To signify his departure, he stretched out both his hands and bowed his head, then he went away without noticing any of the rest. When he had advanced a dozen paces along the passage, he heard the shrill voice of Hedonia call after him: " Beware the scourge of Isis!" He neither turned round nor replied, but the whole company greeted the exclamation with a burst of Homeric laughter.   This shout of scorn gave his departure the appearance of a defeat, and delivered them all from the feeling of insolent pride which the tribune had imposed on them.

.   .   .   .   .   .

No sooner had the tribune, the Greek, and the actress issued from the gorgeous rooms, all ablaze with light, than they found themselves once more in the gloomy streets of the city. Ombricius took leave of Simmias to return to his home beyond the walls.

" How dost thou like the queen of Pompeii?" asked the Epicurean.

The tribune, who had become as sombre as the night, after a moment's silence replied in dry tones:

"She is a powerful woman, but I am stronger than she is."

"Who knows? All that is decreed up above," said the Greek, raising his hands to heaven.

A shooting star sped through the August sky like a golden, fiery-headed serpent. The three companions saw it shine brilliantly forth and then die away.

"Dost thou believe in the Gods? I have always heard thee swear that they have no existence," said Myrrhina.

"No, I believe in thy beauty alone!" replied Simmias, as he flung his mantle around the shivering body of his companion.

Then the loud laughter of the dancer suddenly rose like a fountain jet, falling in silver cascades through the silence of the night in the streets of Pompeii.

CHAPTER XII

MASTER AND DISCIPLE

OMBRICIUS passed a troubled night on the hard couch of his uncle, the deceased veteran. The cunning patrician had instilled into his veins a host of sensations which caused him keen suffering and which he could not disentangle from one another. Though he felt nothing but contempt for the servile group of Hedonians, the queen of Pompeii herself had inspired other sentiments. Her beauty, wealth, and power had called forth in him the desires of old. To her keen physical charm and wide intelligence she added a fascination that was unique, the mystery of evil, of which her superb body appeared to be the temple, just as her mind must have held the science of evil and her soul its religion. Cruelly had she tortured the tribune's senses, finally piercing him with the darts of bitter irony. It was with the utmost impatience that he had borne the mischievous and calculated jests of Crispus, but the patrician's final words, "Beware the scourge of Isis!" had stuck in his flesh like a poisoned Parthian dart.

"After all," he said to himself, "she may be right. Can this strange cult of Isis be anything else than a mighty plot hatched by the ambition of Helvidius and Memnones? They are looking for adepts to serve as docile tools. The prophetess is their bait, and doubt-less I am their dupe!" No, he could not admit that Alcyone was an accomplice. But wherefore did she submit to their every whim and ceremony? No sooner had these doubts entered his mind than they grew beyond all proportion, and were followed by a torrent of tempting thoughts. He was even now pos-sessed by this dangerous magician, who seemed to control with so light a touch those rampant steeds—ambition and desire. Did not Hedonia Metella reign over the mightiest empire of all, and he could enter it through her, would he but speak the word! Why should he renounce such a magnificent realm? Would the doubtful promises of the priest of Isis be any compen-sation to him? Alcyone alone might be; but then, was she sincere? Like all men of action, Ombricius detested uncertainty. As an escape from these poignant doubts, he determined to force the consent of Memnones to his immediate marriage with the priestess, instead of waiting for the voyage to Eleusis. First, however, he must obtain Alcyone's consent. After thinking over several pretexts to obtain a secret interview with

her, through the influence of Helvidia, he fixed
on the idea of offering her a betrothal present.

.   .   .   .   .   .

The moist autumn morning decked the fields
with dew. To make his purchase, Ombricius
entered the city by the Sarno gate, crossing
the business streets and alleys. Beneath the
rough canvas coverings swarmed motley groups
of slaves, whilst in front of the open shutters
of the shops crowded the shepherds of the
district with their goats and sheep, jostling
quarrelsome freedmen and gossiping servant-
maids. Everything testified to plenty and effeminacy. It would have been an easy matter to
stumble over heaps of gourds, oranges, and
melons. The odour of new wine, fermenting
in wide-mouthed terra-cotta jars, mingled with
the flavour of fried fish in rolling iron stoves.
Everywhere, even on penthouses, were branches
of laurel and garlands of flowers. Then the
tribune passed through the working-class quarter,
which was less populous though quite as noisy.
Here could be heard the rollers of the fullers
bleaching the togas, the creaking of the benches,
the grinding and groaning of the stone-cutters'
and sculptors' chisels. At the stands of the
money-changers the clinking of the coins mingled
with the frenzied hammering of the makers of
bronzes. Ombricius finally stopped in front of
a shop where a number of small ivory figures

were exposed for sale. A small boy was in attendance.

"Where is thy master?" asked the tribune.

The child opened the door and led his visitor to the back of the shop. Here a flat-nosed Greek was engaged in sawing in two an elephant's tusk.

"Show me the prettiest casket thou hast."

"For a wedding-present?" asked the carver, a look of cunning in his sparkling eyes.

"Exactly."

"I will show thee a marvel."

From a cupboard in the wall the artist took a beautiful ivory box. The four sides were ornamented with groups of tiny Cupids, in embossed work. On the lid reclined a Venus, gazing into a mirror. After a little bargaining, Ombricius paid for his purchase in golden sesterces, which he had brought with him in a leathern purse. Then he proceeded to a jeweller's, where he bought a necklace of pale rose coral, silver clasps, and a few onyx cameos, the whole of which he placed in the box. Then he went into the wealthy quarters of the city, where he saw none but elegant freedmen and others of every colour, with shining skins and supple limbs. There were shops here also, but of a better order, exhibits of new fabrics, transparent gauzes, weapons and tapestry, kept by men wearing togas and women dressed in *stolas* with long sweeping trains. At the street corners were small fountains from which the limpid water trickled away into the ruts and gutters between the red brick footpaths and the white pebbles with which the streets were paved. Through the bronze gratings could be caught glimpses of rich furniture and painted columns; white statues and shady gardens. Everywhere on the marble thresholds could be seen inlaid in mosaic the hospitable greeting, "*Salve !*" inviting the passer-by to enter.

Ombricius thought of calling upon Helvidia and confiding to her his plan, for she saw the priestess almost every day. As he went to the back of the house of Helvidius, he saw that the small entrance door was ajar. The tribune pushed it open and entered the private garden of the decurion, but he rapidly withdrew as he saw Alcyone standing beneath a vine-arbour in front of a weaving machine con-sisting of two columns of satin-wood. The movable panel fastened to the joist contained the threads stretched from top to bottom. The maiden held the ivory shuttle and was passing it into the woof, laying it on the horizontal board of the loom. The tribune could only see the back of Alcyone, though he recognised her by the slender form concealed beneath the folds of the upper garment, the pearly whiteness of the neck, and the dark golden hair, twisted on her head in Grecian fashion. Her wonderful locks seemed set aflame by a tiny sunbeam, piercing through the arbour. Advancing lightly over the fine sand, he made his way round the grove, and suddenly found himself face to face with Alcyone.

Dropping the shuttle, she stepped backwards and exclaimed:

"What has brought thee here?"

Ombricius held out his hands in an attitude of supplication.

"Pardon me! I was looking for Helvidia when I saw thee. Then I plucked up courage, for I must speak with thee. Besides . . . I have brought thee a betrothal gift."

"A betrothal gift!" said the prophetess, looking at the tribune with dreamy eyes, now beginning to express a gentle curiosity.

"Here it is," said Ombricius, laying the ivory casket on a small round table of green jasper, standing on three griffins' feet close by the marble seat.

The dainty box, with its frieze of tiny Cupids and the reclining Venus, resembled a living group of miniature gods. Alcyone had sat down in front of this masterpiece in mute contemplation and timid hesitation.

"Open it!" said Ombricius gently.

She opened the box, saw the cameos and clasps, and with her dainty fingers took up the coral necklace which fastened by means of a small rose-coloured dove with wings outspread.

"How beautiful!" she said, holding up the ornament to her neck for a moment. "But then, may I wear it? The betrothal day has not arrived; and thou hast not yet come out victorious from the test."

"What matter?" said the tribune, his eyes flashing and an expression of bitterness on his face. "If we should ever part, thou wilt keep this souvenir of me."

In panting accents, Alcyone exclaimed:

"Is it then thy wish to leave us?"

"No, but my mind is full of suspicions regarding Memnones. . . . He is my enemy, and I am afraid of becoming his victim. Perhaps, when I have submitted to every test for thy sake, he will refuse me my reward after all. All this delay and waiting is slowly killing me, Alcyone . . . I cannot live without thee any longer!"

Perplexed and uneasy, Alcyone had risen to her feet. She felt her heart beating violently and her head was all in a whirl.

"Art thou forgetting thy promise, and thy novitiate which was to last a whole year?"

"That is the very thing I object to; it is too much to ask of one. I can endure the torture of suspense no longer, for I feel there is within me

a devil which will master me . . . unless thou
art willing to chain it down with thine arms,
and, by appeasing it, convert it into a god, a
king of earth! The time has now come for the
sacrifice thou hast promised me. Dost thou
love me, Alcyone?"

In deep anguish Alcyone buried her face in
her hands.

"Then thou hast ceased to love me?" said
the tribune.

"Ceased to love thee!" . . . repeated the
prophetess, with choking voice, as her head fell
on the shoulder of the young man, whose arms
were now clasped round her form.

His passionate glance plunged deep into her
violet orbs, which shone, like a starry sky, with
the glowing radiance of a boundless love. Intoxicated with his triumph, the tribune took
her head between his hands and passionately
kissed her on the lips. So overpowering was
the sensation that Alcyone almost fainted. She
lay in the arms of Ombricius, her head thrown
back, white as marble, her lips apart and a pallid
expression in the shining glow of her startled
eyes. Falling back on to the marble seat, she
covered her face with her hands and murmured:

"Wretched Ombricius, what hast thou done?
Isis . . . Isis, can I still remain thy prophetess?"

"Yea, more than ever!" exclaimed Ombricius,
with a victor's assurance. "On the morrow I

will request Memnones to grant his consent to our immediate marriage."

With anguished look, Alcyone said to her betrothed:

"Thinkest thou he will give it?"

The tribune flung back his toga over his shoulder, then stretching out his arm, with a gesture of triumph, he added:

"I am certain he will! For the future I am the master . . . it is for him to follow me!"

A sound of steps was heard on the sand behind the grove. Alcyone gave a start. "Away, I beseech thee," she whispered, "it is Memnones!"

"Farewell until to-morrow!" murmured Ombricius, as he escaped by the door of the porch.

It was not Memnones, however, but Helvidia. She noticed how excited her friend was, and saw the ivory casket and the coral necklace on the jasper table.

"Who has given thee such wonderful trinkets?" asked the decurion's wife.

"Ombricius," sighed the maiden. "It is his marriage gift."

"Already?" said Helvidia, with a smile and a shake of the head.

Then Alcyone fell sobbing into the arms of her protectress, who, divining her anxious heart,

consoled her with gentle words and loving
embraces.

.   .   .   .   .   .

Rejoicing in his victory and impatient to shake
off his yoke, Ombricius, the following morning,
entered the temple of Isis.   There he found
Helvidius and Memnones engaged in conversation.   They both appeared to be expecting him,
for they seemed in no way astonished at his
coming.

" I should like to speak with thee alone,
Memnones," said the tribune.

" Helvidius and myself are only one," said
Memnones.   " We are united in the bonds of a
brotherhood in which secrets have no place and
confidence is unlimited.   I desire that he remain
with me."

"All the better," said Ombricius, with a feigned
assurance which ill concealed his embarrassment.
" I hope to find that the noble decurion will
second my demand."

" Speak freely," said Memnones.

" For three months," continued the tribune,
in fevered accents which betrayed a dull irrita-
tion, " I have faithfully attended thy lessons,
Memnones, admiring thy eloquence and wisdom.
I abandoned and forgot my past life to listen to
the Word of Hermes, so fruitful in surprises and
disquieting intelligence.   Now a troubled feeling
of doubt and uncertainty have taken hold of

me ; I wish to know whither I am being led, to
learn the object of all this hidden science and
the reward of all my efforts.   In a word, I love
Alcyone . . . and she loves me. . . . She told
me this three months ago in the garden of Isis,
and she loves me even more to-day than she did
then. This I know, for I have the proof. Neither
she nor I can wait longer.   Before continuing
my novitiate, I exact . . . yea, exact thy consent
to my immediate marriage with the prophetess."

"What thou now askest is impossible," calmly
replied Helvidius, bent on supporting by his influence the refusal of Memnones. "Reflect well
and ponder over thy solemn promise. Not without perjury couldst thou exact this sacred union
before returning from Eleusis, and issuing victorious from the tests. The effort thou hast
hitherto made is nothing compared with the one
incumbent upon thee if thou wouldst merit a
wife like Alcyone, a human lyre responding to
the divine breath. Be patient then, and per-
severe. Thy reward will surpass thy expectations
by the distance that separates thy present desire
from real love."

"What reward?" asked Ombricius, with a
thrill of emotion.

"Let me tell thee, tribune of Titus, what we
expect of thee and the object we have in view.
We wish to set up, in this corrupt and depraved
society, the noble hierarchy of heroic times, the

labour of such as are truly inspired and the
crown of the human family, through which alone
truth is made manifest to men. These initiates,
whose work we are continuing, and many of
whom lived among the people unknown to
them, are the mystic kings of mankind, powerful rulers, though ever prepared for sacrifice
and renunciation. In city and nation we intend
to establish the sacred hierarchy of Soul and
Spirit, forming in the invisible sky a living
empire whose image should be reflected by a
true people. We appoint each his rank, and
freedom must be won by rising stage after stage.
We honour the gods, cosmic forces and divine
souls ; we spell out their names and create their
symbols. Above all we worship the unfathom-
able, sovereign God, from whom emanate the
creative Spirits and the whole of Nature. Each
god corresponds to an infinite force, each soul to
a stage of consciousness. We fight armed when
necessary, but only to set free, never to crush
and destroy. In order to give our pupils liberty,
we exact submission and trial. We want disciples, to make masters of them."

" What do these disciples do ? How does this
doctrine act ? "

"The doctrine is only the quivering envelope
of truth, the million-rayed sun ; its home is in
its centre, a living fire—and that centre is Love.
To raise the nations that have fallen into crime

and effeminacy, there is no more powerful lever than an elect husband and wife. In their love they radiate truth, and in their children they spread abroad pure strong life. If thou wilt accept our rule, Ombricius, thou shalt have the greatest of privileges. The prophetess shall be thy shining torch. Sometimes, in the heroic days of the Doric race, a priestess of Apollo conceived a passion for a Doric hero, and renounced heavenly marriage, which confers divination, to become the hero's bride. Then both consecrated themselves to the heroic life. The same life and death devolved on them, whether in the war chariot or on the funeral pile. Together they and their children belonged to the Solar God in every action. Such a spouse hast thou found, Ombricius, and Memnones will abandon all claim to his beloved daughter, his prophetess, if thou art willing to join us!"

"Yes," said the hierophant, in a firm, grave tone of voice, "I will give up my Alcyone, on condition thou makest thyself worthy of her."

"To accomplish this end, what must I do?"

"Thou must begin by taking the oath of Isis."

"What oath?"

Memnones fixed his piercing eyes on his disciple's face, and then said, after a moment's silence:

"First, the renouncing of earthly glory; then, absolute devotion to Truth; and, lastly, submission to the Master right on to the final initiation."

The frank, earnest words of Helvidius had considerably shaken the tribune, but a shudder ran through his frame at the claims of the priest, and he said, with a shrug of the shoulders:

"Truth! How shall I recognise it? Where is it to be found?"

"Within thyself. Until thou hast greeted the glorious God manifested in the contemplative soul, thou wilt never know what Truth is, never be ready for the initiation which gives final liberty."

"To obey a master is not being free."

"Were thy master to order thee to do something against thy conscience, thou wouldst be right in disobeying him. But we never do this, for we ourselves have masters, invisible and more powerful than we are, and they watch over us, inspire by restraining us, and, if need be, inflict punishment on us. Never do we ask anything for ourselves from our disciples. Were we to do this even once, that very moment we should lose all our powers so dearly won. It is for the sake of liberation that we demand temporary obedience. Liberty is only attained through conquest of oneself and devotion to the sublime All, the Only One. Helvidius and myself are thy sureties and guides. Art thou ready to keep thy oath?"

"Art thou ready?" repeated Helvidius, taking hold of the tribune's arm.

It was a solemn moment, for an oath binds irrevocably. Ombricius, seduced by the lofty thoughts of Helvidius and almost won over by his magnanimity, seemed to feel the scourge of Isis lashing his back at the words of Memnones. The decurion's hand on his arm appeared to him the collar of an immense chain mounting into endless space, in which he would remain for ever captive. Filled with suspicions once more and humiliated at not having caused his will to prevail, he felt that he must avoid compulsion at all events. Turning aside his head, he murmured in low tones :

"Within a week I will give you my answer. I must have time to reflect."

Thereupon he suddenly held out his hand to the decurion and the priest and took his leave, without looking at them.

"I have good hopes of him," said Helvidius, when he had gone.

"I don't know," said Memnones; "his eyes had the look of a wild, untamed beast."

CHAPTER XIII

OMBRICIUS walked along in mad fury. So troubled was he by doubt and tortured by his thoughts, that he imagined himself once again at the siege of Jerusalem, with the arrows of the Jews pouring upon him, whilst rivers of molten gold streamed from the roof of the burning temple. On reaching home he found an old man, with a searching expression and wearing a brown mantle, awaiting him.

" Art thou not Ombricius Rufus, the tribune ? " said the stranger.

" That is my name."

In spite of the rustic surroundings and the quietness of the spot, the man looked furtively all around before he whispered :

" I am a freedman of the house of Hedonia Metella. My mistress invites thee to come to her villa at Baiæ to-morrow. She has something of importance to communicate to thee."

" How am I to know that thou art telling the truth, and that she has sent thee ? " said Ombricius, looking closely at the old man.

" Here is her sign," said the other, taking from beneath his mantle an onyx cameo, representing a front view of the head of Medusa which Ombricius had admired in Hedonia Metella's girdle.

It was the sign of her sovereignty over the Hedonian brotherhood.

"My mistress ordered me to give it to thee," said the servant, with an ambiguous smile, which showed his toothless mouth and lewd, though lack-lustre eyes.

The tribune took the jewel and examined it critically.

"I do not know Baiæ," he said. "How can I find the way to that distant villa?"

"A barque will be in readiness at the port of Stabiæ on the morrow, at the twelfth hour after sunrise."

"Where must we disembark?"

"At the temple of Hecate, where my mistress will be in waiting for thee."

"At the temple of Hecate?" exclaimed the tribune, with a start.

He was amazed. The haughty patrician permitted none of her friends, not even the prince of the Hedonian brotherhood, to approach this mysterious spot, or even to mention its name in her presence. Was this woman, whom he had seen only once at her home, about to receive him in her inmost sanctuary? Evidently she held the disgraced tribune higher than all the rest in her

esteem! What State secret, what gloomy magic
was she about to reveal to him? In what wonderful adventure or shady intrigue did she wish
to involve him? Such were the thoughts that
followed one another within a few seconds in the
mind of the tribune. Horrible doubts as to his
future seized hold of him. He would have liked
to solve them, but now he preferred to forget
them for a time. Pride, curiosity, and a kind of
insatiable eagerness proved stronger than doubt
and hesitation.

"Very good!" he exclaimed at last. "Tell
thy mistress that I will be there."

.   .   .   .   .   .

The sun was sinking into the sea, between
Capri and Cape Miseno, when the tribune's barque
entered the Bay of Naples. Towns, villas, coast,
and islands all shone and burned beneath a
light veil of transparent purple. The wonderful gulf of Parthenope, surrounded by mountains,
resembled the golden goblet of a Bacchante.
When the barque was close to Baiæ the sun
had sunk beneath the waves, and right beyond
the promontory of Sorrento could be seen the
island of Capri, like a sphinx of porphyry over
against the orange-red furnace of the horizon.
Twilight brought with it a dull, heavy feeling of
weariness both over the land and the motionless
surface of the gulf. Then Ombricius noticed
that the boat was making towards a woody pro-

montory, which sank perpendicularly into the
sea.   On the top of this steep, inaccessible rock
there shone a dim, uncertain light.

"That is the temple of Hecate," said the freedman to the tribune.

It was quite dark when they reached the shore
behind the rock, in a small creek, guarded by
Libyans.   There was a garden on the sulphurous,
volcanic ground round the Bay of Puteoli.   On
this spot the surface of the earth is continually
undergoing the influence of the subterranean fire.
Everywhere are to be seen ashes, and pumice-
stone, pebbles covered with crystallised metals,
yellow or bluish-looking sulphur.   Sometimes
small mountains, peaks of burning ashes, would
come up from the ground in a single day, laying
waste fields and woods.   An exuberant vegetation, however, covers this moving soil, where
smoke is seen issuing here and there from holes
and crevices, and boiling water heard splashing
beneath the rock.   Hedonia had had her country-
house built on a small bay, hidden from obser-
vation.   Ombricius passed onwards with his
guide.   By-and-by he saw slaves bearing torches.
The freedman led him to the entrance of the
wood of Hecate, behind the promontory, and
separated from the garden by a wall.   Here
they found a Libyan, armed like a centurion,
with buckler and sword.   He looked suspiciously
at the tribune, appeared to recognise him, opened

the door, and shut it after Ombricius had passed
through. He was rather puzzled at being left
alone and treated like a prisoner, but followed
the narrow way ascending between the cork oaks.
From time to time he noticed in niches of foliage
gigantic marble urns, statues of emperors, or of
grave, stately-looking matrons. Reaching a cross-
path, Ombricius perceived two women standing
motionless and wearing long grey veils. They
seemed to be awaiting him, and he brushed past
them inquisitively. The tall, thin one, showing
an old woman's face beneath her hood, pointed
to a steep path which buried itself in a thick-
spreading grove, then she raised her finger to
her lips. The other, evidently a younger woman,
touched the tribune's hand and whispered in his
ear : " Along that path ! " It was very dark, but
he finally came out on to a small terrace from
which a magnificent view could be obtained of the
gulf. In the Bay of Puteoli there shone lights
from innumerable pleasure-boats, one of which
was just passing by the foot of the promontory.
Lit with torches, it glided over the dark waters,
crowded with youths and maidens, two by two,
some seated or reclining, others standing by
prow or stern. A voluptuous song, chanted in
rhythm with the stroke of the oars, reached his
ears :

" Wandering Bacchus, thou gentle, untamed
god, hast thou come back to us ? Betrayed by

the virgins, hast thou remembered the smiling Bacchantes? Now they come to greet thee. Seek thy spouse, seek her everywhere. There are innumerable Bacchantes, but only one Ariadne! . . . We are languishing beneath sweet caresses and embraces, but Ariadne is pining away and dying. O Bacchus, Bacchus, take thy goddess to thyself once more!"

The barque disappeared and snatches of the song were wafted to him by the breeze. A feeling of giddiness came over Ombricius and he stepped back in terror. Turning round, he found himself in front of a portico supported by only four columns and looking on to a dark grotto, at the farther end of which a light could be seen. At the entrance stood a Libyan, more fierce-looking than the first, and impassive as a statue. Overwhelmed by opposing sensations, the tribune wondered if he were about to be assassinated by Cæsar's orders for conspiring with the followers of Isis. He grasped tightly the dagger concealed beneath his toga, ready to defend himself to the death. Then he advanced with resolute step. Great was his astonishment at entering a small grotto, carpeted with leaves and flowers, and brightly illuminated with enamel lamps, surmounted with winged Cupids. Hedonia was half reclining on a purple bed, covered with a panther's skin. As queen of the Bacchantes, she wore the costume of Ariadne, a light transparent silk gauze, like a rose-coloured tunic.

In silence she looked at him, holding his hand in hers, as though to take possession of him. In her sumptuous costume, as a half-naked goddess, with fixed, wide open eyes, she seemed another woman.   So powerful was the influence passing from her glance and her warm hand into the very being of the tribune, that he fell on his knees before her, as though stunned by too strong a draught.

"Long have I waited for thee . . . Ombricius Rufus . . . ever since the day of the rose. . . . Dost thou remember? Why hast thou come only now?"

"Perhaps I was afraid of thee . . . but now . . . mine eyes seem to behold thee for the first time!"

With both hands he had seized hold of the patrician's arms, and seemed bent on drawing down her lips to his own. With an imperious gesture, she checked him.

"What is this?   Not yet hast thou the right to approach the lips of Ariadne."   In grave tones she added: "Do not forget that thou art in the temple of Hecate. My goddess must grant her permission, as I must myself!"

Ombricius made an effort to rise to his feet, but, placing her hand on his shoulder, she forced him to remain on his knees.

"Inhale the odour of this rose; it will calm thee," she said. "Come, do as I tell thee, child!"

As she spoke, Hedonia held up to his face a full-blown rose, at whose delicate perfume and soft caressing touch, Ombricius closed his eyes, feeling as though he would swoon away. In melting accents she continued:

"They caused thee much suffering . . . in the temple of Isis . . . did they not?"

"It is true," said Ombricius briefly.

She immediately added in eager, wheedling accents:

"Tell me all about it!"

"I cannot now," he said. "To-day . . . I wish to forget!"

At the same time he turned away his eyes from the woman's keen, scrutinising glance. Once more he attempted to rise to his feet, but Hedonia, with a supple movement, took the tribune's head between her hands and looked at him searchingly.

"Art thou he whom I expect?" she exclaimed. "Art thou the object of my desire? . . . Speak!"

"Who is that?" said Ombricius, alarmed.

"Thou shalt soon know."

"But who art thou? I do not know thee."

"True. Then listen to me."

Ombricius sat down on a bronze seat, and Hedonia, resuming her proud, tranquil attitude on the couch of Ariadne, began as follows:

" Like Aphrodite, I came forth from an ocean all swarming with monsters, from whose jaws and tentacles I was preserved in a mother-of-pearl shell.   Festivals and pleasures of every kind, like the sea foam, have always been around me.   My childhood was spent under Nero, who witnessed the spectacle of lions devouring virgins, and set fire to Rome.   I saw this terrible madman in the midst of his minions, his courtesans and play-actors—himself a play-actor who regarded the earth as his toy—led like a dog in a leash by a smile on the lips of the fair-haired, lascivious Poppæa.   Then I saw the greedy, mean-souled Galba, who merited no loftier a position than the one of tax-gatherer, receive the death he well deserved at the hands of his own legions.   Afterwards I saw poor Otho kill himself after a lost battle, and Vitellius, stupid glutton, dragged away to the gibbet, his hands tied behind his back and the point of a sword beneath his chin.   I had married Carnutus, the proconsul.   When this worthy man died—I was very fond of him, by the way " (here so insinuating and treacherous a smile came over Hedonia's face that Ombricius wondered if this woman had not in very truth poisoned the wealthy old man, as was bruited abroad in Rome) —" I found myself alone in the world, still young and possessed of those feminine wiles which influence rich and poor alike.   In all that mob of slaves, of degenerate knights and senators, I sought for a man worthy of the name, and imagined I had found one in the person of Cecina. . . . He deceived me, the wretch! He is nothing more than a fool and a coward, and some day I will make him repent."

Here Hedonia lowered the corners of her feline lips, which assumed the contour of a bow stretched to let fly an arrow. They soon abandoned this bitter expression, however, and formed into a sinuous line, expressive of mingled desire and languor.

"I had allied myself to the fortunes of Titus and his wife. After Cecina's treason, I formed an idea of the man predestined for me. I wished him to be as beautiful as Adonis, passionate as Achilles, and strong as Brutus. . . . A virgin Cæsar! . . . whom I would help with all my might. With him, I said to myself, I should feel strong enough to overcome a world, to bring an empire into subjection. I should feel as invincible as the Amazon armed with her javelin. In vain did I seek him. . . . Finally, however, I saw him from my litter, at the forum of Pompeii, the day I met thee!"

"Me?" said Ombricius uneasily. "And now . . . what dost thou wish to make of me?"

"Something great, which I must not tell thee. . . . Thou shalt know later on. . . . For the present, trust in me."

As she uttered these words, Hedonia struck a bronze ball, fastened to a tripod. The two maid-servants whom Ombricius had seen in the grove entered by a door concealed in the rugged walls of the grotto, and flung a grey mantle over the shoulders of their mistress. Ariadne seemed to have changed into a stern-visaged vestal virgin.

"Follow me," she said.

Crossing the dark, gloomy portion of the grotto, they reached the small terrace from which could be seen Baiæ with its innumerable lights and the whole of the Gulf of Naples. Around the peak of Vesuvius spread a ruddy gleam, reflected in the sea like a fiery plume.

"Seest thou this gulf?" said Hedonia. "It is the reflection of my power. I feel myself its queen and drain from it my strength, but my real influence stretches far beyond. Wilt thou share it with me?"

"Share it . . . with the ephemeral princes of thy house . . . the sport of thy caprice . . . those feeble creatures I saw crawling at thy feet?"

"No, thou art the Only One, the Elect. To-morrow, if thou wilt, they shall be nothing, thou shalt be all!"

On hearing this rapturous promise, Ombricius gently wound his arm round this fascinating woman, who seemed to have become intangible beneath her priestly robes, and said :

"Then be my Ariadne!"

She made no attempt to free herself from the strong arm encircling her waist, but continued with the same insinuating gentleness:

"I will, on one condition—that thou art willing to take the oath of Hecate."

"I have been informed that Hedonia Metella does not believe in the gods."

"True, they are phantoms which lead men astray."

"And yet thou worshippest one divinity?"

"One only—without her I could not live, for from her I hold the secret of my power. To tell the truth, I know not if it is I who have created her, or she who has made me what I am. She exists in the shadow . . . all around me. . . . She haunts me, and in turn obeys and commands me. She and I are only one. . . . Stay, I will show thee her image."

Overcome, in spite of himself, with a dread he could not explain, Ombricius hesitated. Hedonia, however, took him by the hand and led him back to the large grotto, where there was now to be seen a lighted chandelier at the foot of a statue, set up in a niche. The grotto of stalactites resembled a room of a palace in the infernal regions, where flames rained down from the vault and flashed their fiery tongues along the walls. Ombricius saw nothing but the awful statue; he stood in silence before its terrible beauty.

Clad in a mantle of shining black marble, with
countenance white as wax, and ruddy-looking
eyes, the statue resembled Hedonia Metella; but
it was a more gaunt and stately Hedonia, of a
deathly pallor and most sinister and dreadful
expression.   In her right hand she held a blood-
stained sword, set vertically into the ground; in
the left was a small winged Victory.   Her very
aspect froze the veins of Ombricius.   His will
seemed to leave him; he knew not whether it
would remain powerless, or spring to sudden life
again.   Slowly and solemnly Hedonia unwound
the sombre veil which covered her from head to
foot, and with it enveloped the statue.   Then
she placed on the head of the goddess the
crescent-shaped diadem which adorned her own,
and knelt before her.

"Hecate," she said, in low accents, "thou one
and only goddess! these offerings I now dedicate to thee.   Powerful sovereign, my other self,
strong to succour and to avenge, I promise to
dedicate myself to this man if he will dedicate
himself to thee in our mutual labours . . . if he
will keep the oath!"

Dipping her hand into the warm water of the
spring which fell into a marble basin, she sprinkled
it over Ombricius, uttering the words: "May
he be consecrated to our work."   On rising, she
appeared extraordinarily beautiful in her transparent, rose-coloured tunic, her eyes all beaming

with triumph.   Then delicately drawing a dagger
from her breast, she pressed it to her lips, and
offered it to Ombricius.

   " Swear by Hecate," she said, in a deep, almost
masculine tone of voice—" swear that thou wilt
be mine, for life or death.   Swear by this consecrated weapon that thou wilt be in action as is
this cold blade in my burning hand—so will I
make thee strongest of the strong and greatest
of the great.   Swear to obey me—even as I
obey Hecate ! "

   " And thou wilt be mine ? "

   " Both now and for ever."

Ombricius drank in the penetrating power of
these words, along with the breath from that
fascinating mouth.   Beneath the rose-coloured
gauze he saw the amber neck and bosom of the
queen of the Bacchantes.   He felt the beams from
those fixed eyes enter his very brain, like the
sharp blade of the dagger which Hedonia offered
him in her open palm . . . and he trembled . . .
for he felt that he was about to take the oath
in spite of himself.   Perfectly self-possessed and
certain of victory, she kept her eyes fastened on
him, ever drawing nearer and nearer.   Suddenly
she placed her hand on the tribune's arm and
said to him, with a sarcastic curl of the lips :

   " Above all, swear that thou wilt never again
see the priest and priestess of Isis."

   " Alcyone ? " sighed Ombricius, turning aside

as though emerging from the depths of the ocean into the light of the stars.

"Yes," continued Hedonia, raising the steel blade to the lips of the tribune. "She is my enemy. Thou must choose between Alcyone and me!"

On hearing this gentle name uttered in accents of hatred, Ombricius beheld, as in a flash of light, the prophetess in a state of ecstasy and the luminous paths which the Word of Hermes opens out into the Infinite. Turning round to Hedonia, he saw that the face and expression of the patrician had become those of Hecate. Then he exclaimed forcibly :

"Never!"

"Farewell, then! Thou art a coward like the rest," she said, in a hissing tone of voice. In haughty accents, she added: "Woe to thee, Ombricius Rufus, thou votary of Isis and enemy of the Empire. Woe to thy master and thy priestess!"

On hearing this insulting threat, the tribune felt the blood mount from his heart to his brain in a wave of anger and wild raging desire.

"Why bring me here," he exclaimed, "if thou dost not want me? Thou hast provoked and incensed me, as the gladiators do the lions in the arena. Tremble in thy turn! Hedonia Metella, thou hast made sport of a Roman knight,

but I will get the better of thee.   Know that I
am not thy slave. . . . I am thy master ! "

As he spoke, Ombricius violently tore away
the rose-coloured gauze with which Ariadne was
enveloped.   Terrified for the first time, the
patrician fled to the end of the grotto.   Here
she turned round, and, in defending herself
against the tribune who tried to seize her, she
wounded him severely on the arm with the
weapon she still held in her hand.   Ombricius
tore it from her by twisting her wrist.   During
the struggle he had slightly wounded her on
the neck without any intention of doing so.
Hedonia raised a cry and sank down on to her
couch, her head thrown backwards.   The pupils
of her beautiful eyes had retreated beneath the
eyelids, and nothing was seen of those immense
orbs but their pearly whiteness.   Ombricius,
terrified at the thought that she might be dead,
bent over the beautiful body of his proud victim,
and involuntarily touched with his mouth that
amber neck on which lay a single drop of blood.
Eagerly his lips drank it in.   With a deep sigh
she slowly rose, and, seemingly moved to pity,
whispered mysteriously into his ears :

" Thou hast drunk my blood. . . . Henceforth
thou art mine . . . irrevocably ! "

The tribune stood there like one thunderstruck
on hearing these terrible words, with which the
cunning magician regained possession of her

rebellious prey.   His inmost being was conscious
of the echo of this cry, uttered by a wounded
woman . . . now wounding in her turn, and
that in deadlier fashion.   Well did his fierce
savage heart understand this triumph of the
conquered Hedonia, who seemed to have already
turned the tables on her victor.   In anxious
tones he stammered :

" What dost thou mean ? "

Rising to her feet, she continued :

" Haughty child, foolish athlete, art thou
without understanding ?   Dost thou not know
what has just taken place ?   Thou wert not
willing to take the oath : now I need not ask
thee to do so.   For thou hast fulfilled the rite
of Hecate by receiving on thy lips the blood
of the wound thou hast inflicted on me, far
more certainly and irrevocably than by any
verbal promise.   Vain now is thy will ; thou
lovest me . . . in spite of thyself."

She continued :

" I too love thee, for in the madness of thy
passion thou didst wish to kill me . . . thou art
the only one who has dared this." . . . Taking
him by the arm, she pressed it tightly, and
said : " Confess that thou art afraid of me . . .
and that thou lovest me ! "

In presence of this strange love, a mixture
of voluptuousness and hatred, promises and
threats, the tribune was torn between desire and

fear. A feeling of pride came over him, and gathering himself together, like a centurion in front of his cohort before attacking the enemy, he exclaimed in loud, ringing tones: "No, I am a free man!"

She released his arm, with a bitter, almost savage laugh.

"Free? Think thyself fortunate to be alive! Know that with a single word I could have had thee killed by those around me. So I could even now . . . but I take pity on thee. Free? Well, be free then! But do not forget that my image will never leave thine eyes or thy heart. Wert thou Cæsar himself, my phantom would come to whisper in thine ear. I am in the blood of thy veins; I am ever with thee! In vain wilt thou clasp thy priestess to thy breast. I shall drink in thy breath, for I live in thy thoughts and hold sovereign sway over thy soul. Thou wilt go to thy Memnones and thy Alcyone, wilt thou not? But thou wilt come back to me. . . . I read it in thine eyes! . . . Now, go! Leave me!"

Overcome with fear, Ombricius rapidly left the spot. He reached the terrace and descended the path in the darkness. Veiled servant-maidens opened the door leading to the grove. Crossing the deserted garden, he found in the creek a small barque moored there, the boat-man lying asleep. He aroused him, and the gondola was soon gliding silently over the surface of the water. The full moon was sinking beneath the sweeping clouds into the black sea. On reaching the middle of the gulf, Ombricius rose to his feet, with a desire to repeat aloud in the face of a threatening sky, overcast with clouds that resembled dishevelled demons and monstrous serpents, those last few words he had said to Hedonia: "I am a free man!" Why did the words stick in his throat? Overwhelmed with dismay, he sat down again. An oppressive light vapour, like some subtle poison, seemed to have entered his heart and brain and limbs. Was this the imperious, deadly breath of Hedonia?

Ah, feeble indeed was the freedom left to him! . . . He must now bind himself for ever in one direction or the other. The choice must be made between the oath of Isis and that of Hecate! Was he already in the toils of the goddess of Evil?

CHAPTER XIV

THE KISS OF ANTEROS

AFTER her meeting with Ombricius at the home of Helvidia, Alcyone shut herself up with her Nubian nurse in the *curia* of Isis. The audacious deed of the tribune had troubled her virgin senses, suddenly bringing her soul from the heights in which it was sojourning down to a mirky, troubled region. She sank into a grim, sullen silence. In the daytime she meditated on her future, so dreaded and unknown, and which she could no longer separate from Ombricius. At night frightful dreams disturbed her slumbers. Sometimes she saw groups of Fauns and Bacchantes scornfully laughing at her; then, again, a superb-looking woman, wearing the diadem of an empress, whose eyes were fixed on her, like those of a bird of prey. When this woman stretched out her arms they became filmy wings, like those of an immense bat, threatening to strangle her victim. Every night Alcyone dreamed of Ombricius, wearing the arms of a military tribune, and carried off by the harpy in a blood-red cloud. Be-

neath them galloped wildly a band of cen-
taurs. After these nightmares she awoke in a
pale sweat, half dead with fear. Foreseeing
disaster, Memnones endeavoured to quiet her,
but she did not answer his questions. Dragging
her to the temple, he sent her into a profound
sleep, but as she was passing into the second
stage, she exclaimed: "I will see nothing! I
will know nothing! I am surrounded by storms
and monsters. . . . Awake me!" "Mount higher!
Mount to the door of light!" commanded
Memnones. "I cannot," she answered, sinking
into a lethargic state. Seeing that he had no
control over her, the hierophant determined to
leave the priestess to herself and keep watch
over her. When she awoke, she gently, though
firmly, requested permission to spend a week
with Helvidia in the garden of Isis, where there
was a rustic dwelling near the temple of Persephone. Memnones granted the request all the
more willingly as he reflected that a rest in the
country might cure his adopted daughter, and
that this departure might prevent the possibility
of a meeting between herself and the tribune
until the time when the latter should take the
oath of Isis.

.   .   .   .   .   .

When the day came, Memnones and Helvidius
were awaiting Ombricius in the temple, but all
in vain. In the afternoon, however, the priest,

now left alone, saw the tribune approach. His eyes were haggard and the features of his livid countenance contracted, whilst his every movement was abrupt and feverish. His whole attitude gave token of the most violent inner struggle. In halting tones he said :

" I cannot take the oath of Isis without seeing the prophetess once more. I wish to hear her repeat with her own lips that she still loves me . . . that she will love me in spite of everything."

The hierophant fixed his eyes for several moments on his disciple, and a feeling of profound pity came over him. Taking in the situation at a glance, he said after a short silence :

" I see that thou art suffering, my poor friend, and I can guess everything. Thou hast reached the time when a choice must be made between the path of darkness and that of light. The darkness fascinates and seizes upon thee, almost winning the victory. . . . There is still time to tear thyself away ; to-morrow will be too late. I will show thee the light . . . and thou shalt choose. Come ! we will go and see Alcyone."

A flash of fevered joy shone in Ombricius' anxious eyes. Without another word, priest and tribune crossed the city of Pompeii, in the direction of the garden of Isis. A freedman of Helvidius opened the door, and they advanced a few steps into the uncultivated garden, where trees and shrubs grew rank and wild round the ruins of the temple of Ceres. Ombricius saw from the distance the lotus spring where the priestess had proclaimed her love for him and braved the anger of Memnones. The spring appeared to be abandoned and overgrown with verdure. They came to an alley of cypress-trees, mounting in the direction of the chapel of Persephone. The front consisted of four caryatides, which supported its cornice. The abandoned temple was sheltered by spreading sycamores, whose leaves, tossed about by the wind, rustled on the dark pediment.

"Here she spends her days with the wife of Helvidius," said Memnones. "For a whole week she has been unwell; perhaps she is asleep this very moment. We must enter cautiously, and not speak to her if she is in prophetic ecstasy."

Through the open door they made their way into the chapel. The interior was so dark that at first the tribune could perceive nothing whatever. By degrees the architecture appeared. There were no columns, nothing but bare walls, with empty niches and unlit chandeliers at intervals. On a square pedestal stood a double-coloured statue of Persephone. The head and arms, of white marble, emerged from a black marble upper garment. On the head was a wreath of poppies. The goddess held her sceptre as queen of the dead in her right hand, whilst in her left was a burning lamp, whose gentle beams played over her grave features and lit up the darkness like a star, with its glorious misty light. "What a contrast," thought the tribune, "between the nobility of this statue and the sinister beauty of Hecate, in the sanctuary of Hedonia Metella!" Suddenly Ombricius was conscious, in the depths of his being, of a trouble for which he could find no words. It was a kind of explosion of desire, grief and fear. On the pedestal of the statue of Persephone he saw Alcyone lying asleep, in the most graceful posture imaginable. To the left of the priestess embers were smouldering in a brazier on a bronze tripod. Chaste aromatic fumes were escaping, of so keen and penetrating a nature that they seemed as though they would separate soul from body. To the right of the prophetess, Helvidia was seated on a bronze chair. Alcyone was pale and transparent as alabaster in the light of the lamp. Her face bore the expression of sweet, perfect happiness. The tribune had the presentiment that this happiness was not for him; besides, the magic sleep set a wide gulf between himself and the prophetess. This gulf he determined to cross.

"May I speak to her?" said Ombricius to Memnones.

"Try," said the priest, at a venture.

The tribune drew near the sleeping girl. No sooner had he touched Alcyone's warm hand than she sprang with a cry into the arms of Helvidia, who leaped to her aid.

"Oh!" she exclaimed, "not that man now! . . . He is hurting me . . . he is murdering me! . . . Let me go to sleep."

Her eyes had remained closed all the time, but she was twisting about in Helvidia's arms, with a look of anguish on her face.

"Now thou seest how impossible it is to force her will," said Memnones to the tribune. "Let us leave her in the lofty regions where she is now hovering, and from which she may perchance deliver to thee her message. We will perform such rites as will aid her to mount to the heights of ecstasy."

Memnones plunged her once more into profound slumber by touching the brow of the prophetess with his finger. She fell back on to the cushions in the same attitude as before. Then he threw some styrax on the brazier. Volumes of smoke leapt up, filling the chapel. Thereupon the hierophant uttered aloud the following prayer and invocation :

"Sovereign spirit, thou who reignest over the worlds by the Soul of Nature, making one with her, Osiris-Isis, we now invoke thee, praying that the pure Genius who looks down upon this virgin may manifest himself in her and speak by her mouth, as he has spoken to me in the past, telling the truth to this man and showing him a beam of thy light, the ray of purity and salvation!"

Whilst Memnones was speaking Helvidia had taken up her stand by the side of the lute, whose chords she now began to strike. The powerful sonorous tones seemed to have some kind of plastic action over the clouds of incense, which came winding round the prophetess. They were pierced from time to time by vivid flashes of light, whilst right above, close under the vaulted roof, a shining star appeared for an instant and then vanished. Just at this moment Alcyone rose to a sitting posture and murmured, with extended arms and head erect:

"The betrothal day has come. . . . Approach. . . . Oh! Come to me, my Anteros!"

"What is the meaning of this?" asked Ombricius, filled with anguish.

"Fear nothing," said Memnones. "At this moment she is living her other life. The gods alone have power over her. We must wait."

The hierophant himself, however, soon began to feel uneasy, for the approach of the mysterious Genius had never hitherto assumed this form. Alcyone was enveloped in a dense cloud of incense, as a gust of wind, coming through the open door of the chapel, extinguished the lamp, and passed like a rapid, mysterious breath over the lute. Hedonia cried aloud and the two men stood nailed to the spot. Alcyone had

again sunk on to her couch, with closed eyes
and lips apart.   A luminous form was bending
over her in a kneeling posture.   He might have
passed for a tall young shepherd, but he was
beautiful as Apollo and shining as Eros.   His
locks glittered like living gold, and the lamb-
skin, passed cross-wise over his breast, flashed
like silver armour.   Memnones recognised him
as being Horus, though his eyes could not be
seen, for he remained bending over the prophetess.   His face lit up her own with dazzling
whiteness.   His lips drew near those of Alcyone,
imprinting thereon a nuptial kiss, during which
the two figures appeared resplendent as though
inundated with the same stream of incandescent
light.   Then suddenly everything grew pale.
Priest and tribune were for a moment plunged
back again into dense darkness.   Immediately
afterwards they imagined they perceived through
the smoke a human bust half way up the vault.
It was that of Horus-Anteros.   His great eyes
could distinctly be perceived, the shining passionate eyes of Eros.   From the clouds of incense
he appeared to be gathering white roses which
fell on to his sleeping fiancée.

Ombricius had followed the apparition with a
feeling of astonishment which had taken away
all power of reflection, such as happens in a state
of dream.   He now regained his full, waking
consciousness, and without reflecting on what he

had seen, or even attempting to explain it, a feeling of concentrated rage and base treachery came over him.   Scarce knowing what he said, he exclaimed :

"I do not believe in your spirits nor care I aught for them, but I will know whether Alcyone still loves me or not.   In spite of you all, I will know this!"

As he spoke, he made as if he would fling himself upon her.   Memnones tried to hold him back, for the shock might be fatal to his daughter.

The tribune tore himself from his grasp with the violence of a wild beast about to spring upon its prey.   Then he suddenly stopped, with a feeling of intolerable pain in his eyes and throughout his whole body.   Behind the sleeping girl and in front of the smoking tripod, he had seen the same figure which had just been bending over the prophetess.   This time, however, he was standing, his eyes flashing with a terrible light and a flaming torch in his hand.   The dazzling ray had entered the eyes of Ombricius, whilst at the same time he felt as though a knife had pierced his brain.   The phenomenon, coming like a lightning-flash, had lasted no longer than a few seconds, but the tribune seemed paralysed in every limb.   He trembled all over, and his mouth foamed with fury.   All the same, nothing unusual appeared to be taking place in the chapel

of Persephone.   Alcyone was still asleep, and
Helvidia, kneeling by her side, was warming the
virgin's ice-cold hands in her own.   Through the
open door of the sanctuary the sun could be seen
setting behind a clump of cypresses.   The lightning vision had been too immediate a response
to the sacrilegious gesture of Ombricius to be
anything else than the result of the invisible
power against which he had flung himself.   In
that secret part of the soul which is the seat of
convictions impossible to coerce, the tribune felt
that, after the kiss of Anteros, he himself had no
further influence over Alcyone.   His powerless
condition only increased his anger.   The invisible
and intangible enemy who had torn from him
his prey exasperated him far more than a living
opponent would have done, a lover of like flesh
and blood with himself, whom he could have
struck with his fist or pierced with his sword.   His
pride, however, stronger in him than any other
sentiment, would not allow him to recognise the
reality of this formidable power which humiliated
and checkmated him.   Consequently—with a
sudden revulsion of his whole being—down in
the depths of his consciousness he refused to believe in the reality of what he had seen, attri-
buting everything to a priestly artifice, or the
power of delusion by an exercise of will.   All
the influence Memnones had obtained over him
was immediately annihilated, and the teachings

he had provisionally accepted were swept away in a moment, nothing being left in the heart of the disciple except the bitterness of a resentment which showed itself in an outburst of mingled irony and blasphemy.

"Evil magician and impostor," he exclaimed, "thou hast deceived me! This virgin was destined for me. She was my betrothed wife! Thou hast bewitched her with the poison of thy foul arts, thinking to captivate and enslave me also by alluring me with thy phantoms. Now I utterly despise thy teachings and thy visions, thy counsel and thy prophetess!"

Memnones listened with folded arms as though in a deep reverie. He replied sadly:

"It was thyself who didst seek the path of light and hast this day chosen that of darkness. Maddened with pride and ambition, the fault would be insignificant indeed, hadst thou done nothing more than forsaken a love-stricken virgin, or denied thy master. That is nothing; thy real fault and unpardonable crime is that thou hast poisoned thine own soul at its very source. Thy greatest punishment will not be one that men can see; it will be the loss of the very meaning of truth. Thou hast blinded the eyes of thy spirit by expelling every trace of tenderness and love from thy heart. Thy savage appetites have made of thee a hypocrite, and thou hast desired my instruction for no other purpose than to dominate others and myself.   Thy punishment will consist of the darkness which will shortly wrap thee about in the midst of luxury and grandeur. Thy hardened heart can now lead thee in no other direction than that of evil.   Now I leave thee to thy fate, henceforth inevitable.   Go thy way ; when thy final hour comes, perhaps thou wilt remember what I now say to thee.   As regards the prophetess, thou hast no longer any power over her."

"Perhaps not," said Ombricius, in cold, bitter accents.   "But when once Cæsar is made acquainted with your intrigues, then tremble !   For myself, I no longer believe in anything but the will ruling in my brain, the blood beating in my veins, and the sword I hold in my hand.   By their help, and their help alone, I will win truth and power!   Farewell."

He drew his short sword, which he had never ceased wearing at the girdle of his tunic ever since the night he had spent at Baiæ—his tribune's sword—and brandishing it aloft as though in defiance of a host of invisible enemies, he departed.

.   .   .   .   .   .

With pained expression, Memnones watched him disappear, fleeing for ever from the master's friendly care to pursue his fatal destiny.   What dreadful events had taken place during that tragic hour !   A ray of light had pierced the veil ;

the Invisible had appeared visible, fulfilling the
desire of the initiate and setting the crown on
his science.   An immortal spirit had intervened
in human destinies to help them forward, but
though the dazzling flash had preserved the prophetess and driven away the profane Ombricius,
the hierophant himself remained cast down like
a tree struck with lightning.   He was losing his
disciple and his daughter at one and the same
time.   Alcyone loved Ombricius in this world,
and Anteros in the other !   The best of her soul
belonged to her Genius, who possessed her in
Eternity !   Though the tribune was rushing
inevitably to some disaster or other, he still had
the intoxication of passion to silence his grief.
Whilst as for himself, Memnones, the suffering
seer, he was alone, with all the torture of the
Infinite in his heart !

The prophetess awoke.   She sat up, very
pale and grave-looking, absorbed in her own
thoughts, apparently receiving illumination from
within.

" Art thou not in pain ? " asked Memnones.

" No," she said, touching her breast with her
outspread fingers.   " My heart is gratified and
a diamond cuirass has been given to me."

" Dost thou know that Ombricius has left us ? "

" Yes," she said.   " A whirlwind of passion has
carried him off."

" We must forget him."

"No," said Alcyone, with a gentle calm which brooked no opposition, "we must save him!"

Memnones saw how lasting were the two loves of Alcyone, the earthly and the divine, both ineradicable, and each representing a stage of the soul in a separate living sphere. And yet a link had been established between the two regions, a progress effected in her power of vision. On previous occasions she had retained no memory of the events of her sleep on returning to waking consciousness. Now, she appeared to remember, though she refused to speak of them.

Alcyone, Helvidia, and Memnones left the chapel of Persephone, halting for a moment beneath the peristyle. It was twilight and the distant mountains reared themselves aloft like flaming altars round the pallid waters of the gulf. A few stars were shining, like flowers of light in the vault of heaven. The prophetess watched them, and suddenly, letting go the hands of her friends, raised her own in greeting to the flaming lights.

"What do they say to thee?" asked Memnones.

"I feel that they are all within me," said Alcyone, placing both hands on her heart. "Between me and the universe there are no longer any barriers. I am free . . . free!"

Then Helvidia took a laurel wreath, hanging from one of the caryatides of the peristyle, and placed it on the head of the prophetess. They descended the steps of the temple and crossed the garden without a word. A solitary tear trickled silently down the cheeks of Memnones. Gentle and resolute, the crowned priestess resembled a victim proceeding to the sacrifice.

BOOK III

DARKNESS

"The whole of magic consists of the two words : Love and Hatred."—Plotinus.

CHAPTER XV

IN THE TEPIDARIUM

THE warm light of a beautiful autumn morning
fell on the lava-flagged squares, the mosaic courts
and the innumerable colonnades of Pompeii. It
illuminated as with silver streaks the small
streams flowing into the ruts of the streets, which
were paved with white and grey shingle. In
the entrance-halls, indolent women were dressing
themselves, with the help of eager, active slave-
girls; children were playing with dogs, whilst
shopkeepers were bargaining with their cus-
tomers. The freedmen were walking to and fro,
making their purchases or engaged in business.
In the temples the priests were praying or preparing sacrifices. The whole city was awakening
to its everyday life of indolence and pleasure.
To the eagle of the Apennines flying over
Pompeii from the height of Vesuvius, the ex-
quisitely dainty city, lying on the edge of the
gulf, must have looked like a shell, or a piece of
coral on a wreath of oak-leaves. The passer-by in
the street, however, looking at this eagle soaring
aloft in the azure sky, could see it only through

the light, rose-coloured mist, spread out in the intervening space.

The door of Hedonia Metella's house was wide open ; the porter, a swarthy giant, wearing a blue turban, standing there, looking disdainfully at all who passed. Perhaps he was thinking of the free life of the desert, the galloping of horses over the sand whenever an oasis appeared on the horizon. Suddenly a young man appeared, with eager feverish eyes and contracted features.

"Is the illustrious patrician Hedonia Metella at home ? I must speak to her immediately."

"She is in, but cannot be seen."

"When she hears my name she will receive me."

" Wert thou Cæsar himself, thou couldst not enter. My mistress will admit no one in the mornings."

Notwithstanding this refusal, the obstinate young man was determined to enter, but the African took hold of his arm, which he almost broke with his powerful grasp. A scuffle was about to break out when a slave, a cunning-featured, soft-footed man, came from the vestibule.

"I know this man," he said ; " he is a Roman knight."

"What matters that to me ?" said the porter ; " I have my orders to obey."

" At all events, I will give his name to our mistress."

The slave held out an ivory tablet and a piece of red lead to the visitor, who wrote down a few words. A few moments elapsed, when the slave returned and said :

"I have orders to lead the tribune to the tepidarium."

"Then let him enter," muttered the surly Numidian.

Preceded by his guide, the young man passed through a number of peristyles and passages. The guide opened a door, and when Ombricius had gone through, closed it behind him and returned. Crossing a dark corridor, the visitor entered a vaulted hall, filled with a warm, soothing vapour. The walls were bare, but all along the frieze were Cupids in coloured terra-cotta, sporting with a group of children. On the roof a few thick glass windows toned down the light of the azure sky. In the centre of the room a brazier was burning in a brass basin. At the far end sat Hedonia, wearing a violet cloak deeply fringed with gold. She had just left the bath, and a slave-girl was engaged in plaiting her luxuriant tresses and arranging her complicated head-dress. The tribune, intimidated and abashed, remained standing, some distance away.

"Ah! Ombricius Rufus?" she said, with an almost imperceptibly ironical accent, which was more a caress than anything else. (As she spoke, she quietly fastened to her shoulder a soft silky dressing-gown, only half veiling the magnificence of her superb arms and neck.) "Thou dost indeed astonish me, illustrious philosopher. I thought thou wert imprisoned in the temple of Isis, for ever lost to simple mortals like ourselves. And here thou art, back again! Can I believe mine eyes?"

"I am unworthy of thee," said the tribune, with bent head. "Noble Hedonia Metella, a great misfortune has befallen me. I have come to beseech thy pardon . . . and help."

"First tell me what has brought thee here?"

"I can only speak to thee alone."

"Leave the room, Galla!" said Hedonia; "I will call thee shortly."

The girl dropped the heavy tresses in disorder on to her mistress's neck and disappeared.

"All my hopes have been broken," continued the tribune. "Thou wert quite right, illustrious daughter of Metellus, glory of Rome and Pompeii, for they have deceived and scouted me. With the utmost sincerity I sought after truth from the lips of that rascally priest and his false priestess. Isis made jest of me! I looked upon Memnones as a master and upon Alcyone as inspired. . . . Well, he is a vile impostor, whilst she——"

"What of her?"

"This virgin prophetess . . . has a lover!"

"Really?" said Hedonia, amazed, as she dropped to the ground an opaque glass bottle of perfume.

The phial broke to pieces on the mosaic, and in the large dark eyes of the patrician there appeared a savage curiosity, almost akin to admiration. After a moment's silence, she added:

" Hast thou seen him ? "

" Yes, in the garden of Isis, at the chapel of Persephone. He is a glorious youth, beautiful as a god. I saw him through a cloud of incense, kneeling by the side of Alcyone, who was asleep. He was leaning over her, touching her lips with his own . . . drinking in her breath ! "

" Meanwhile what wert thou doing ? "

" I tried to strike him . . . to seize hold of him. Impossible to do so ! He paralysed me with what appeared to be a lightning-flash . . . then everything vanished. It was not a sense illusion, though it might have been an empty form, a phantom created by the magic of Memnones. . . . Perhaps it was really a spirit ! "

Whereupon Hedonia filled the tepidarium with a mocking laugh, which echoed back from the vault on to the flags like a shower of pearls. Then she suddenly became pensive.

" And yet," she said, " all this is very strange."

Her eyes assumed an expression of anxiety, as though they were attracted by some unknown power.

Then she continued, in serious tones:

" Dost thou still love this Alcyone of thine ? "

Ombricius answered with sombre energy:

"Ah! thou knowest not how much I hate her now, and all connected with her!"

"Then what wilt thou do?"

"Leave this cursed city and return to the army. I will do my utmost to forget these cunning wretches . . . till the day of vengeance!"

"All this redounds to thy credit, proud tribune. Hast thou obtained the pardon of Titus?"

"No: without it I can do nothing. Shall I ever obtain it?"

"Wait a moment. All the time thou hast been infatuated by thy priestess, I have been working for thee, my dear Ombricius."

She clapped her hands. The slave-girl immediately returned.

"Galla," she said, "bring me the gold casket in the ebony cupboard of my bedroom."

The girl returned with the casket. Hedonia took from it a papyrus roll, encircled with a thread of gold to which hung a red wax seal bearing the image of Cæsar. Opening it, she held it out to the tribune, who read:

"*Titus Cæsar, son of Cæsar Augustus Vespasian, to Hedonia Metella, greeting!* Since thou dost vouch for the fidelity of Ombricius Rufus with thy head and blood, I pardon him. As soon as he sets foot in Rome I promise him the command of a legion."

Utterly astonished at what he read, Ombricius dropped the sheet of papyrus to the ground.

" Thou hast done this for me ? " he stammered.

" Why not, since I love thee ? " said Hedonia, carelessly tying behind her head her glorious tresses.

" My goddess ! " exclaimed Ombricius, in a whirl of emotion, " thou hast pledged thy life for one who has wounded thee.   Would I were thy slave ! "

Flinging himself at her feet, he kissed her knees.

" Beware, proud tribune ! " said Hedonia Metella, in ironical accents.   " Thou art no longer the free man thou didst say thou wert a week ago. . . . I too am anxious for thy liberty ! "

" My liberty ! " exclaimed the tribune.   " Thou hast restored it to me by delivering me from my enemies and avenging me on them.   Now let them tremble !   Free ?   I can no longer be so except by thee and with thee !   It shall be my ambition to obey thee.   Command me, torture me if thou wilt, and I will accept all with the utmost delight.   I am now prepared to take the oath of Hecate."

She bent over him, looking into his eyes with that domineering kind of voluptuousness, which was the only form of tenderness she ever manifested.

" There is no longer any need.   Do I not know that thou hast belonged to me ever since thou didst drink a drop of my blood ? "

" Then permit me at least to kiss thy foot."

"Is such indeed thy desire?" said Hedonia, with a smile which seemed to fill her dark eyes with a golden light.

"It is . . . I beseech thee to grant it!"

The daughter of Metellus slightly raised the edge of her cloak, exposing to view her alabaster foot, to which the violet dressing-gown and the blue light in the tepidarium gave an ivory tint. Ombricius, in an outburst of passion, pressed his lips on to the foot, which she then gently placed on the head of the young man kneeling before her. In a rapture of delight he felt the claw of the human panther pressed on the nape of his neck. This frenzied servility appeared to him the most striking revenge he could take on what he called Alcyone's treason and betrayal. In the sudden and complete revulsion of his soul he imagined he had regained his lost power.

"Speak, and I will obey thee," he said, rising to his feet. "Must I leave at once for Rome?"

She seized the young man by both shoulders.

"Leave for Rome? Now? Thou shalt not leave this dwelling until a month has passed. . . . Meantime, thou shalt be its king!"

The tribune almost swooned with delight. His trembling hands wandered over the cloak and the bare arms of the patrician. He closed his eyes beneath the warm, intoxicating perfumes emanating from that queenly form; then a sudden desire came over him to clasp her to his breast as he uttered the stifled cry:

"Come to me!"

She checked him with an imposing wave of the hand, flashing on him a domineering, proud glance.

"Be prudent," she said; "our slaves might take us by surprise, and we must see to it that we remain the masters here. Take up thy toga and follow me."

Ombricius quietly obeyed, flinging his toga over his shoulder. Hedonia. with a majestic smile, had also risen to her feet.

"Come!" she said.

They crossed several porticoes. in which were fountains playing on every side, and flowery lawns. Freedmen and mute slaves bowed as they passed, making their way to a quiet dark retreat, overhung with gorgeous tapestry.

CHAPTER XVI

SORCERY

A YEAR had passed. Ombricius Rufus, appointed by Titus propraetor of a legion in Britain, had won three victories and repulsed the enemy right to the fastnesses of the mountains. On returning to Rome, he lived in the house of Hedonia Metella. The Senate had decreed in his honour a statue and a crown of gold, in short, all that could possibly take the place of a triumph. Titus, too great to be jealous of a subordinate, had consented to all this. These lofty distinctions, however, had not satisfied the protectress of the tribune who had become head of a legion. Hedonia wished him to solicit the vacant consulate. Titus had frowned and made no reply to this proposal of the daughter of Metellus. Ombricius wished to desist, thinking that he would prejudice his future by showing too great boldness; but on seeing him hesitate, the proud patrician had disdainfully shrugged her shoulders, an evil expression coming into her face. " What appears impossible," she said, " is never so when one knows how to set to work." Still she maintained an ambiguous silence as to the methods to employ. All the same, Ombricius felt that she remained firm in her plan, in accordance with her indomitable and mysterious will.

The Roman house of Hedonia Metella stood like a watch-tower on the side of Mount Cœlius, perched like an eagle's nest between the temple of Claudius and the marble fountain of Nero. It was approached by a narrow path winding upwards between lofty walls. From the top of the terrace the centre of Rome could be seen, as from an observatory. In the large valley between the Aventine and the Palatine Hills were the groves and ponds of the gardens of Nero. Behind stretched the Great Circus, like an immense race-course, with its sandy arena and ruddy benches, staked out with poles adorned with multi-coloured streamers. The numerous entrances, which pierced its lower circumference as with holes, made it resemble some huge mouse-trap prepared for gladiators and wild beasts.

On the roof of the Hedonian house, Ombricius was seated on the terrace, his arm leaning over the balustrade. On his breast he wore large brass medals, embossed with eagles' and lions' heads, tokens of his victories. There were yellow fringes to his red tunic, reminding one of the metallic thongs of a sword-belt. On his

closely-cut hair was a golden crown. In this
costume the chiefs of a victorious army were
accustomed to appear in public, at feasts or the
Circus, or in the theatre. The propraetor was to
be present that evening at the banquet of Titus ;
for the moment he was looking on Rome, lying
at his feet, thinking of her past and present,
and the destiny in store for her.

After a month's complete seclusion, spent at
Baiæ in the company of Hedonia, the tribune
had resumed his military life, at the head of a
legion in a cold climate and in the midst of
barbarian tribes. The ambitious patrician had by
this time completely mastered him ; he belonged
to her, body, soul, and spirit. Her voluptuous
image, which had become almost living, beset
him in his hours of repose, promising the most
entrancing delights on his return. Her imperious glance impelled him to issue implacable
decrees against the vanquished, with the object
of hastening on his conquest. True, there were
times in the still night, as he lay on a bear-skin
in his tent with no other sound about him than
the challenge of the sentinels, when the image
of Alcyone came back to him. He saw again
the prophetess, the melodious messenger of
the divine Psyche, and the solemn, stern-faced
Memnones, whose words seemed to tear away
the veil of nature and lay open limitless hori-
zons before his eyes. Then a painful thought

entered his mind : was it not here that he would find the source of all light and happiness ? The approach to this source he had shut off for ever ! No sooner, however, did he think of Anteros than his fury and rage drove away all regret. Besides, the memory of Hedonia intoxicated him. The priestess of Hecate had appointed him to the fulfilment of some distant goal or other. What was this goal ?

Now that he was a glorious conqueror, his trouble and distress redoubled. After the first ecstasies of his return, Hedonia had become feverish and sombre-minded. During the day-time she received foreign emissaries with whom she held secret conference. At night she abandoned herself to lengthy meditations before a small statue of Hecate, a copy of the large one at Baiæ. For some days past she had shown herself cold and harsh towards Ombricius. What was the danger threatening her ? What terrible plot was she meditating ?

Ombricius looked at the Palatine Hill, the Circus and gardens. In spite of the honours he had won, Imperial Rome shut him in like a prison, weighing him down like heavy armour.

Suddenly he saw Hedonia standing before him. He had not heard her as she passed through the proprætor's room overlooking the terrace. Robed in a large matron's *stola*, she held in her hand a roll of papyrus.

"Read!" she said sternly.

Greatly astonished, Ombricius read an inflammatory proclamation to the legions of Italy, an incitement to revolt against Vespasian and Titus, and finally an appeal to choose a new Cæsar.

"What is the meaning of this?" asked Ombricius.

"It is written in Cecina's hand. He is conspiring against Titus and Vespasian. The revolt has been fixed for the festival of Augustus three days hence. Titus is to be assassinated in the Capitol."

"Who gave thee this papyrus?"

"A freedman of Cecina, whom I bribed."

"What wilt thou do with it?"

"Show it to Titus. Before that, however, Cecina must be put to death; only in that event will the news be acceptable to Cæsar. He could refuse nothing to the bearer of such news. Besides, I know that Titus hates Cecina, whom he looks upon as his deadliest enemy, though he has invited him to this evening's banquet, at which we also are expected to be present."

"And who would be so bold as to do this?"

"Thyself!" said Hedonia, handing him the dagger dedicated to Hecate.

Ombricius leapt to his feet.

"I? Commit such a murder?"

"If thou dost not slay Cecina, thou wilt not be consul."

"I prefer not to be, rather than to become
one in this way. I will not sully my victories
with the blood of a Roman general."

"Then thou wilt remain a slave . . . and I
must have a master for my husband. The Capitol
can only be mounted along a pathway of blood.
Once the summit is reached, the lustral water of
a triumph carries off the blood that has been
shed."

"Such assassin's work is none of mine."

"Knowest thou not," said Hedonia, in hissing
accents, "that this man deserves death a thousand times over? He is my worst enemy. In
bygone days he betrayed, insulted, and disgraced
me. By killing him thou wilt have avenged
me!"

"Thy revenge is less important than my
glory."

"Thy glory?" said Hedonia, in tones of
scorn. "That is my work! . . . So thou wilt
not avenge me?"

"I would rather fight with wild beasts in the
arena in the presence of all Rome."

As he spoke, Ombricius pointed to the hel-
meted gladiators, armed with masks and nets,
practising in the Circus at their feet.

"'Tis well," said Hedonia Metella; "I will
seek for a true Roman, one with more courage
than thou hast. Now for the banquet of Titus."

An hour afterwards the proprætor Ombricius

Rufus and the patrician Hedonia Metella were
borne along in a litter to the Palatine Hill.
Not a word was exchanged between them during
the journey.

.   .   .   .   .   .

The table for the imperial feast had been set
in an immense hall surrounded with porphyry
columns.   The flames of chandeliers, the jasper
and marble of vases, and the precious stones on
bare necks and arms sparkled and glistened with
a thousand different lights.   Thirty guests reclined on sumptuous couches, whilst fifty slaves,
bearing gold and silver plate, craters of wine and
boxes of perfume, wheeled round these favourites
of the Emperor like a swarm of bees.   Titus,
majestic and grave in his purple tunic, of few
words but all observant, was the personification
of self-possessed power, more terrible in calm
than in anger.   His wife was on his right hand,
Hedonia on his left.   By the side of the latter,
Cecina, a broad-shouldered giant, keen-eyed and
rough-featured, was leaning on his elbow.   Ombricius was in front of them, on the other side of
the table.   Amid the hubbub and noise of the
feast Ombricius could catch no more than a
few chance words of the conversation of those
opposite him, but the engaging attitude of the
patrician, in the presence of her former lover,
filled him with dismay.   This man, whom her
implacable hatred had just condemned to death,

she was now clearly endeavouring to win back, speaking lightly of their past life in common. At the outset Cecina remained unmoved, but as he saw Hedonia's eyes continually fixed on him, and her beautiful arm stretched out to fill his goblet, the dull, heavy colossus gradually became animated and finally turned his uneasy, fascinated eyes on to his beautiful neighbour. Often did they bend over and whisper to each other. When Titus rose to go into another room, where an Atellan farce was being performed before his guests, Hedonia took leave of the imperial couple and left the building without making the slightest sign to Ombricius, who seemed no longer to exist for her. Cecina followed immediately after, and Ombricius, grinding his teeth, descended the stairs at some distance behind. Numerous litters were stationed there, the entrance to the forum being kept by the prætorian guard with their shining helmets and drawn swords. Ombricius saw the patrician turn round and meet his gaze, so she was aware that he was following her. Concealing himself behind some *fasces*, he saw Hedonia stop in front of her palanquin, and heard the following sentences exchanged between herself and Cecina :

" I have news for thee. Mount the litter and come with me to my house."

" I do not trust thee."

"Thou art wrong not to do so. Thy life is at stake. I know thy secret; if thou dost not come now, thou art lost."

Aided by her slaves, she mounted the litter; Cecina took his seat by her side. Drawing the curtains, the slaves raised the palanquin and departed with their burden under the raised portcullis of the Palatine. Following behind, the propraetor saw the litter make its way in the direction of the Velabrum, a marshy piece of ground on the left. A cold sweat came over Ombricius. He wondered if Hedonia, in a sudden revulsion of feeling of which she was quite capable, had changed sides and joined the conspiracy of Cecina, whilst he, Ombricius, would be swept on one side and murdered along with Vespasian and his son. He had no idea what he was about to do; he simply walked on like a hunter on the track of a wild beast. The lanterns of the Libyans waved to and fro before his eyes. On the right there appeared through the dark azure of the night the temples, porticoes, and triumphal arches of the forum in black uneven piles. With what supreme irony these monuments now dominated this man, a son of Rome, maddened with ambition and torn with jealousy! They seemed to him to be oozing blood, and to be cemented together with his own flesh. He almost cried aloud as he noticed the bronze She-Wolf, with her twin

nurslings, defying him from the top of a
column, and seemingly ready to devour him.
The litter had now passed the Great Circus, and
the slaves were climbing the slope of Mount
Cœlius, along a steep pathway in the direction
of the abode of Hedonia Metella.

There was only one thought in the mind of
Ombricius : he would slay the two monsters who
had united against him ! He hid himself close
to the door. Cecina sprang from the litter, with
the single word :

" To-morrow ! "

With a bound the proprætor sprang upon him,
plunging his dagger into Cecina's neck. The
latter, a powerful man, seized his opponent and
attempted to fling him to the ground. Ombricius, however, who appeared to be endowed
with superhuman strength, clutched him by the
throat, and, stiffening his sinewy arms, nailed
the other to the wall. Neither of the combatants
released his hold in this terrible struggle ; not a
word or cry betrayed the mute, but fearful determination, each to overpower the other. Finally,
Cecina, strangled by the steel-like grip of Ombricius, and choking with his own blood, rolled
over, a lifeless mass, on the steps of the staircase.

Hedonia had watched the struggle, without
leaving her litter, by the dull light of the lanterns.
She was as calm and self-possessed as a lioness, for

which two lions are fighting, whilst she quietly
awaits the victor.

The death of his rival, however, had not cooled
the blood of Ombricius. With haggard eyes and
raised weapon, he turned on the patrician. The
Libyans sprang to the rescue, but Hedonia
said "Stay!" and placing her hand gently
on the shoulder of her exasperated lover, she
exclaimed :

"At last thou art thyself again!"

Unmoved, she fixed her eyes on him, ready
to receive the death stroke. After a moment's
silence, Ombricius dropped his weapon to the
ground.

Without a second's delay Hedonia said to her
slaves, "Return to the Palatine," and, pointing
to the house as the servants were opening the
door, she said to Ombricius :

"Wait for me in thy room."

Half-an-hour afterwards Hedonia appeared
before Cæsar at the Palatine. Seated on a
raised platform, and surrounded by his guests,
Titus, looking pensive and bored, was watching
the actors.

"I would speak alone with the Emperor of
Rome," said Hedonia Metella, aloud.

Approaching him, she added, in a whisper :

"It concerns the life of Vespasian and thine
own, as well as the safety of the Empire."

"Let all present depart," commanded Titus.

When they were alone, Hedonia drew from beneath her *stola* the roll of paper on which was written the speech of Cecina, inciting the legions to revolt. Glancing over it, Titus could not restrain an exclamation of surprise. Hedonia continued :

"What hath he deserved ?"

"The chastisement of all criminals. I will take that upon myself."

"His punishment has come," said the patrician.

"Who has struck him down ?"

"Ombricius Rufus."

"He is very ready to avenge insults offered to Cæsar!" said Titus, with a piercing glance.

"We have ensured the sovereignty of the Flavii," said Hedonia, humbly bowing her head. "Cecina was their last, their most dangerous enemy. Henceforth, noble Titus may act according to his natural disposition, and be clement."

"'Tis well," said the son of Vespasian sternly, though with secret satisfaction. "'Tis well, Hedonia Metella. Ombricius Rufus shall be consul within a month."

"Thanks, mighty Cæsar. Long live Vespasian Augustus. Victory and immortal glory to Titus Cæsar."

As she spoke Hedonia bent to kiss the imperial ring on the hand of the prince, and left the room.

"Let the play continue," said Titus to his courtiers, when the whole assembly had returned.

.   .   .   .   .   .

Near his couch, covered with precious silks and draperies, and seated between a chandelier filled with sweet-smelling perfume and a naphtha lamp, was Ombricius, his elbow leaning on a seat of bronze. He had plunged into the inmost depths of his conscience, in which a man no longer understands his own being, shrinking with horror from his own actions. What had he done? Was it a courageous deed or a shameful murder? Who was he? Had he acted of his own initiative, or in obedience to the will of this terrible woman? Ah, how skilfully she had made use of his passion for her! He had been nothing more than the toy of her will, a dagger in her cunning hand. What was he now? A mere necklace for her, or an axe, fit to fling into the Tiber? What would she bring him back from the Palatine? Glory or the gibbet?

After this enormous expenditure of fury and determination, he sat there, passive and crushed. Alas! he now knew that his will, his desire, everything was engulfed in this terrible woman, as in the depths of an abyss. And yet he was longing for her with all the passion of his nature.

From her alone, her eyes and lips, would he receive the reply of destiny—life or death.

The sleeping chamber looked on to the terrace. Through the open door could be seen a corner of the Palatine and an expanse of azure sky. Suddenly Hedonia appeared, dressed in her Syrian tunic of soft, transparent purple.

"Thou art consul!" she exclaimed. "Hail, my Bacchus and my king!"

The haughty patrician, transformed into a fiery, impetuous Bacchante, flung her arms round Ombricius, as a lioness would have seized her prey.

"What did Titus say?" asked the young man, trembling with mingled fear and delight.

"I care little for Titus, or Vespasian, or for all the Cæsars in the world," laughed Hedonia, toying with the gems of her necklace. "I know only one thing, that now thou art mine as thou hast never been before!"

Seated on his knee, she covered with kisses the head, neck, and arms of Ombricius. They rained on him like June roses, burning right through his tunic. The long pent-up passion of Hedonia Metella seemed now to be pouring forth like a torrent of lava. Overwhelmed by this fiery stream which overcame all his fears, the tribune whispered:

"Tell me everything."

"To-morrow, my Bacchus, to-morrow!"

Taking his head between her hands, she looked long into his eyes until Ombricius could no longer resist the intoxication of his delight, and their lips met in a burning kiss.

.   .   .   .   .   .

Peaceful and serene was the night when Hedonia came out on to the terrace, holding the future consul by the hand. The heavens were ablaze with stars, whilst Rome, dark and silent, lay asleep at their feet. A sombre look of sadness and strange anguish was apparent in the eyes of Ombricius.

"Art thou not happy?" she asked.

"Yes," he replied, as in a dream.

Pointing to the Eternal City, she said:

"Look at that empty Circus in the blackness of the night; it is the arena of every ambition. See the Aventine Hill, that mount of the people, a mob often victorious in its revolts, but ever dominated by a monster, born of its rage and fury. And there stands the Palatine—the throne of the Cæsars. Wert thou only willing, all this would be ours!"

Ombricius stepped back with a shudder of horror. The patrician laid her hand on the shoulder of the astonished Roman, and continued in a scarcely audible voice, as though afraid lest the night wind should waft her words to the echoes of the black Palatine, apparently asleep, though guarded by sentinels.

"Military tribune. . . . Head of a legion. . . .

Consul! . . . Wherefore shouldst not thou be
Cæsar thyself some day?"

She looked grave and majestic in her robe of
rose-coloured muslin, resembling the splendid
mantle of a marble Venus whose voluptuous
form is chastely moulded in its clinging drapery.
In presence of the city by night, of its monuments, huge and relentless like the offspring
of the She-Wolf, she seemed to be the Genius
of Imperial Rome.

"Wilt thou?" whispered Hedonia.

A sudden gust of wind, coming from the distant sea, passed over the Seven Hills, howling
beneath the sombre portico of the temple of
Claudius, and moaning through the gardens of
Nero. The giant cypresses bent and groaned
like phantoms of the night. For a moment the
stars grew pale, then they flamed forth, nearer
and more brilliant than before. Fascinated and
awe-struck, Ombricius looked at Hedonia, and
answered :

"Yes. . . . Cæsar, if thou wilt. . . . Augusta!"

These words, scarcely uttered aloud in the
silence of the night, partook of the solemnity of
an oath, sworn before the invisible gods. At
the same time, by a strange ebb and flow ever
present in the human soul, the tear-stained face
of Alcyone came into the mind of Ombricius, but
the vague, uncertain image was rapidly dispelled
beneath the caress of Hedonia Metella, whose

arms enfolded him like an unbreakable chain.
The blush of dawn was now spreading over the
Palatine Hill, and in the vaults of the Great
Circus the famished lions were beginning to
roar.

CHAPTER XVII

BLACK AND WHITE MAGIC

DURING the four years following the departure of Ombricius, Pompeii was a prey to violent public dissensions and feuds. Lentulus the senator had been appointed duumvir, along with Marcus Helvidius. These two magistrates, declared enemies of one another, governed the city. The whole of Pompeii was split into two camps— the Hedonians and the followers of Isis. The prophetess, who lived in an inner world of her own, either knew nothing of all this, or paid no attention to it.

Ever since the thrilling scene of the kiss of Anteros, a great transformation had taken place in the mind and life of Alcyone. A kind of heavenly peace had come down upon her, filling her with a divine sadness. By her mysterious suffering and silent martyrdom she had indeed become the prophetess, one, however, now free from her master. Memnones watched over and religiously listened to her, though he had ceased to control her. All the same he noticed that an indescribable longing now attracted the prophetess to that powerful consoler, that invisible

friend who had visited her one tragic hour ; and
also that, by abandoning herself to this desire
of her soul, she ran the risk of snapping every
bodily tie, and drifting into the other world
through the gate of death.   Terror took possession of him, and he made a vigorous attempt to
bring her back to life, in which he was doubtless seconded by Anteros himself, who said to
the virgin, when sunk in profound sleep : " Go
back to earth ; thou must still suffer in order to
heal and save.   Then thou shalt see me again,
as thou hast never yet seen me." From that
moment Alcyone had regained her love of life. At
times she would speak of Ombricius to Memnones
or Helvidia as of a far distant friend, who would
some day return and enter the light of Isis.
The priest and the duumvir's wife made no
attempt to check her, nor did they inform her
of the military triumphs of the former tribune
and his brilliant destiny, which was reported to
be irrevocably linked with that of Hedonia
Metella.   Following the advice of Memnones,
she acquired the habit of receiving in the temple,
in the presence of the priest himself, all kinds of
candidates for help—the sick or the suffering, or
those labouring beneath a painful destiny.   A
single look or touch sufficed to indicate their physical pain.   She read their secret thoughts and
past lives, and was ever ready with counsel and
advice.   At times, though seldom, she foresaw

the future, either dimly or distinctly. Hence
the increasing popularity of the prophetess, who
had become transfigured by misfortune, and
seemed to have discovered new powers and
faculties in her resignation.

This calm existence was disturbed by an un-
foreseen event, destined to cause a violent upheaval in the soul of the priestess, as well as
throughout the whole city of Pompeii.

One morning Alcyone was sleeping in her
hammock in the curia of Isis.   Nourhal, her old
nurse, was lying at her feet, playing with ostrich
feathers and glass trinkets.   Suddenly a shout
was heard in the street : " Long live the consul,
Ombricius Rufus ! "   Alcyone awoke and leapt
to her feet.

" Ombricius ! " she exclaimed.   " Nourhal, go
and see what all this means ! "

The old Nubian woman went tottering away,
and soon returned with news.   She had discovered that the consul, Ombricius Rufus, was
celebrating his triumph in Rome, and in a few
months would make his solemn entry into
Pompeii.   Troops of Hedonians were filling the
air with acclamation, in anticipation of the
joyous event.   At the name of Ombricius,
shouted by the crowd, the slumbering past had
awakened once more in the heart of Alcyone.

" Bring me the ivory casket," she said to the
Nubian woman.

Seated on a stone bench, in the court of the curia, Alcyone placed the box on her knees. Long she gazed on the tiny Cupids that formed the frieze, and the carved Venus on the cover. Was not this betrothal gift a pledge of the love of Ombricius? Slowly she opened the casket, her delicate fingers stroking the heavy bracelets. Then, with a sudden movement, she picked up the coral necklace and lifted it to her lips. At the same time a shrill cry escaped her, for she imagined she felt once more on her mouth that terrible kiss by which the audacious tribune had once taken possession of the senses and the heart of the prophetess.

"I cannot stay here," said Alcyone. "Take me back to Helvidia!"

The two women dressed themselves in long *stolas*, wrapped veils round their heads and went out through the crowded streets.

Alcyone found Helvidia near the colonnade of the entrance-hall, close by the smiling statues and the babbling fountain. Before her stood a weaving loom, and on the jasper table by her side lay spools of wool of all colours. She had left her work for a moment to look at her second child, a two-year-old boy, sleeping in a wicker-work cradle which resembled a small skiff. Hearing Alcyone's step behind her, she raised her head and said :

"Just see how beautiful he is! When asleep he is very like Helvidius."

The prophetess looked at the child, without uttering a word. The mother rose to her feet and the two women took each other by the hand. They formed a striking contrast. Helvidia, a majestic brunette, manifested in her calm eyes and open expression a peaceful though strong element that indicated the height of bliss. On the other hand, a stormy wind seemed to have twisted Alcyone's golden locks all about her head. She looked terror-stricken, and a passionate expression was apparent in her eyes.

"What is the matter this morning?" asked the duumvir's wife.

"Nothing. I only wish to hear thee sing the hymn Helvidius is so fond of—*The Chant of the Doric Woman.*"

"I would rather not sing a hymn which always gives thee pain," said Helvidia.

"It will do me good to-day. Sing it, I beg of thee, if thou hast any affection for me!"

As she spoke Alcyone took up an ebony lyre, inlaid with ivory, hanging from a gilt hook on the column. This she placed in her friend's hands, forcing her, with a kiss, to sit down by the side of the cradle. Persuaded by the caress, Helvidia yielded, and began, in deep melodious tones, the following passionate chant, the im-

perious glance of the virgin fixed on her all the
time she sang :—

> Deep in the wild and pathless woods,
>   I slept on a couch of stone.
> The tempest howled around ; behind the leafy trees
>   Apollo came, the Solar God.
> His glance pierced my heart with a dart of light.
>   Love-stricken, I languish
>   Sad and wan
> In this lone cavern the bleak night long.
>   In my despair,
>   I curse the light of day,
> Tearing my locks, vile slave, till morn appears.
> Alone I see thee stand, haughty and free,
> My glorious hero, in thy car of war ;
> Methinks I see once more my lord and god,
>   The solar king !
> Henceforth close watch I'll keep over the flames
> High leaping on thine altar.   Spear in hand,
> Erect in thy bright car, I'll take my stand,
>   Thou lion-hearted man !
> The arrow from mine heart I've torn away,
> For now thou art my hero and my lord,
> Thy burning glance has pierced me through and through,
>   Apollo's son !

Alcyone, her arms entwined round a column
against which she was leaning her head, had
listened motionless right to the end. When
Helvidia, carried away by the poetic rhythm,
finished her song in a burst of enthusiastic joy,
Alcyone sprang to her feet, and, tearing away
the lyre from her friend's hands, exclaimed :

"Stop! Thou hast a husband, a hero, a son of Apollo—whilst I—I have no one!"

"I knew it," said Helvidia, clasping the priestess within her arms, in a burst of mingled tenderness and anger. "Why didst thou force me to sing?"

"I wished to know whether I too had strength to draw my hero to myself. I believe I have!"

"Of whom dost thou speak?"

"Of Ombricius Rufus, the consul, who will shortly come to Pompeii."

"Poor creature! Art thou not aware that he is in the power of a terrible, an evil-minded woman, a black magician, an infernal sorceress?"

"My dreams have told me this long ago."

"Dost think thou canst tear away the wretched man from her arms? Thou wouldst be going to thine own ruin."

"What matters that? I must try to save him. Come with me to the garden of Isis where I have not been since the kiss of Anteros. I wish to see once more the lotus fountain where I swore to love Ombricius until death."

Alcyone buried her weeping face in the bosom of her friend; then suddenly regaining her self-possession, she said:

"Come!"

Proceeding along the sun-scorched fields, beneath the blossoming vine-branches, hanging in festoons from the trunks of the elms, the two

women made their way to the garden of Isis.
Ruin and neglect were visible on every hand,
the lentisk and the euphorbia growing everywhere.   Weeds covered the footpaths.   At the
lotus fountain, reeds and common water-plants
covered the basin, the moisture from them
choking the sacred flower of Egypt.   Alcyone's
eyes turned to the spot where Ombricius had
breathed out his words of love, and she had
bound herself to him by a solemn oath.   Instinctively they sought the small statue of Isis, but
in its place she perceived a funeral urn to which
hung a piece of black crape, already torn to a
rag by the wind and the rain.   Three young
cypresses were growing close to the small monument.

"What is this?" asked the daughter of Memnones.

"Dost thou not know the custom in the school
of Pythagoras?" said Helvidia.   "When a disciple has become faithless to the teaching of the
masters and has turned against them, he is looked
upon as dead.   This is the tomb of the Ombricius
of former days, of one who is now no more."

"Is it possible?" asked Alcyone, trembling
from head to foot.

"Look and read!" said Helvidia.

Bending forward, Alcyone read the following
words carved on the stone:

"*Here lies OMBRICIUS RUFUS.   He is*

*more dead than the dead, for he has returned
to a life of evil. His body moves among the
living, but his soul has departed. Mourn for
it, O disciples!"*

Sadly Alcyone sank to the ground at the foot
of the *stela*, which she encircled with her arms.
After long weeping she rose to her feet and
exclaimed with sombre energy :

" I will bring this soul to life again ! "

" Do not attempt what is impossible," replied
Helvidia, in suppliant tones.

Nothing, however, could break the will of the
prophetess. A few days later she replaced the
funeral urn with a small statue of a winged
Cupid, with torch thrown back, symbolising the
Genius of Resurrection keeping watch over the
dead. Every day she returned to the garden of
Isis to meditate and pray near the *stela*. Her
thoughts were often concentrated on her enemy
Hedonia Metella, whom she had never met,
though she saw her often in dreams at night.
The patrician would at times appear before her,
nude, of marvellous beauty, an intense fixed
look in her flashing eyes. Her arms were extended, whilst a diadem crowned her proud,
imperial head. Then a horrible thing happened;
her body suddenly increased in size by the addi-
tion of a large filmy tissue, grey, almost black
in colour. This film, joining together legs
and arms like two fans, had at each extremity

enormous claws, causing this superb-looking woman to resemble a gigantic bat, or rather a harpy ready to pounce upon Alcyone to tear and rend her to pieces. The latter, however, projected on to the vision her powerful will, and the ghastly form became paler and paler until it faded completely away. Alcyone saw Ombricius looking gloomy and excited; her love brooded over him like the white wings of a dove. She could never keep her attention fixed on him, however; he always escaped her. By such intense, concentrated meditation the prophetess gained the conviction that she was working upon her distant enemy, succeeding in keeping her in check.

.   .   .   .   .

About this time Hedonia Metella had returned to Pompeii, where she was engaged in gathering together her partisans, skilfully preparing the city for a worthy reception of Ombricius Rufus as consul, and for her marriage to him. For several days she had been in her retreat at Baiæ. Guarded by her Libyan slaves, she spent her entire nights alone in the small temple of Hecate. Here she was accustomed, in times of crisis, to commune with herself and renew her might.

The daughter of Metellus was nearing the goal of her desire. What else was the triumphal entry of Ombricius into Pompeii with full consular honours, followed by her marriage, but the

crown and completion of a life of luxury and
ambition ?   Long had she sought for a man who
would be her equal, and whom at the same time
she could control and dominate.   At last she
had found him in this doughty, fierce tribune,
whom she had slowly but surely fashioned to
become the instrument of her will.   And now
she loved him alone, with jealous passion, for
was he not her tool, her creation ?   Woe be to
the woman who should dispute with her this
husband !   Who was able, who would ever dare
to do this ?   For all that, vague feelings of uneasiness would suddenly assail her.   It is just
when one is attaining to the supreme goal of
life, grasping the prize so long and ardently
desired, that the anguish of losing it reaches its
height.   Hedonia passed bad nights, dreaming
of kingfishers and lotus-flowers which terrified
her without her knowing the reason.   The woman
who dreaded no human being became suddenly
afraid of the silence of the night.

One morning, in the pale dawn of day, a furious
storm burst over the Bay of Naples.   No sooner
had the first few gusts begun to howl along the
coast than Hedonia sprang from her couch and
made her way to the parapet of the promontory,
where she could enjoy the sight.   Shaking off
her terror, she could now breathe at her ease, for
she was in her element.   Thick heavy clouds
filled the eastern sky and the tempest moaned

and hissed on every hand.   The blue sea changed
to an inky black, then a white foam covered the
surface of the waves.   More feeble and fragile than
flies driven about by the wind, all the barques
made for shelter in the creeks.   Speedily the vast
bay resembled a foaming cauldron.   An army of
deafening waves assailed the coast, dancing round
reefs and islets like the nymphs of Amphitrite.

Bending   eagerly   forward   over   the   abyss   of
waters, Hedonia drank in with delight wind and
foam, space and ocean.   Ah! this sea . . . in
which she had bathed the previous night, becoming impregnated with its might, was it anything
other than herself?   When plunging therein her
beautiful   body,   seeming   to   dissolve   entirely
away, had she not absorbed it and become, in
her turn, wave and sea-weed and siren?   What
she loved in the sea was its devouring fury
and cruel, insatiable rage; its wealth of wrecks
and indomitable calm.   This sea was like her
own immense desire, with all her latent strength
and energy.   And the hurricane, which now
lashed her cheeks and beat upon her breast, was
it not the will of Hedonia herself, controlling
this strength and moulding this desire to her
pleasure?   The better to enjoy the wild rush of
the elements, she flung aside her veil, untied
her hair, and bared her arms and bosom to
the raging storm.   The spray of the waves
mounted to the temple of Hecate, lashing the

face of her priestess.   Woman and tempest met
in passionate embrace.

She shouted aloud : " Hither, demons of air
and ocean !   Enter the heart of Hecate, that she
may tame and dominate the heart of Pompeii ! "

And now it appeared to Hedonia that this
furious wind lashing the sea was Ombricius
trying to tame and dominate herself.   In this he
could not succeed.   The sea always fell back on
to its own mass of waters, howling and raging
on the surface, but tranquil in its depths.   In the
long run it wore out its master, absorbing him,
mistress both of itself and of the wind.   Then
they became a single force capable of overpowering every obstacle.

Pleased at having regained her calm and self-
confidence, Hedonia returned to the villa behind
the promontory.   Here she wrote letters all day
long, received emissaries and gave orders.   When
night came she returned to the grotto, behind
the temple of Hecate, where she was accustomed
to sleep.   The storm was now over, but the waves
were still splashing at the foot of the cliffs.
Black, jagged clouds rode through the sky, the
moon seeming to make her way through them on
foam of opals and silver.   Hedonia flung herself
on to the couch, close to where she had received
her first kiss from Ombricius—that kiss of blood
whose awful charm was working in them both, no
one being able to foresee its final issue.   There

was something disquieting and sinister in the blackness of the night. Outside, the wind moaned in the trees; she had boldly faced it when howling around her in mighty gusts, but now it seemed a traitor, come to spy into her very thoughts. A bat had penetrated into the grotto and was now fluttering against the walls dimly lit by the ruddy light from the chandelier. In the twilight Hedonia imagined she saw myriads of eyes of larvæ fixed on her, their soft wings and hairy feet brushing against her quivering skin. What were these fluid, fleeting phantoms, that came from the deep abysses of the air? Hedonia, who loved the tempest, who neither feared men nor believed in the gods, was afraid of this twilight, this gentle wind which made its way everywhere. A dog "bayed the moon with hideous howl." She imagined she heard a murdered man's death rattle and then an assassin's step. Snatching up the dagger which never left her side, she leapt to her feet and went out on to the terrace. The noises which had disturbed her proved to be nothing more than the moaning and creaking of an oak, through whose branches the wind swept in fitful gusts. Returning to the grotto, which served as her bedroom during her magical operations, the patrician drank a goblet of Sicilian wine, spiced with laurel and cloves. This drink sent her into a heavy sleep,

which, however, was disturbed throughout with
nightmares. She seemed to see Ombricius enveloped in the blood of Cecina as in a purple
mantle. He looked at her with reproachful
eyes. A virgin, clad in white, approached
him with suppliant mien. Ombricius immediately flung himself on Hedonia, in an attempt
to tear from her the dagger that Hecate had
consecrated. She struck him with it, but at
the same moment the magician felt her throat
clutched by iron claws, like those of Nemesis,
the goddess of vengeance and reprisals, with
feet and hands of brass.

Hedonia awoke, with a cry resembling the howl
of a wild beast. Was she to be overcome by a
paltry virgin? She had recognised her, and was
well aware that her great enemy, her only one,
was . . . Alcyone. She felt that the priestess
of Isis, from afar, was attacking her with the invisible sword of her virgin will, and that she was
exercising an occult influence over Ombricius,
threatening to unravel the cunning plot woven
by the patrician. Hedonia raised her hand to
her temples, wet with a cold sweat. Lighting
a torch of resin, she entered the large grotto
of stalactites, where stood the one goddess she
worshipped, Hecate, an enlarged image of herself,
in which, though created by herself, she imagined
she believed. The statue looked at her with
blood-red eyes, which said to her : " If thou

wouldst overcome thine enemies, make thyself
heartless and implacable." From that moment
her mind was made up. She must meet the
priestess of Isis, paralyse her with fear, even kill
her if necessary, with a poisoned look of hatred.
How could this encounter be effected?

On returning to Pompeii, Hedonia summoned
the old slave who had served as her agent in
many secret enterprises, ordering him to spy
into the doings and habits of the priestess of
Isis. He returned at night and informed the
patrician that she went every day to the garden
of Isis, where she spent long hours in prayer
and meditation, close to a so-called tombstone,
erected in memory of Ombricius Rufus.

"The wretch!" exclaimed Hedonia Metella.
"She wishes to kill him, and me with him, by
means of her magic charms. This will make a
fresh charge against the followers of Isis. But
I must surprise her. . . . I must see this
priestess . . . face to face. . . . To-morrow I will
go to the garden of Isis and thou shalt accompany me."

Hedonia Metella had regained her wonted
composure and strength. True, she suspected
that the prophetess was in possession of some
unknown power, but at all events she would
find herself confronted with definite facts.
This was no longer the Invisible, enveloping
her with intangible enemies. Now she knew

where her enemy was, and how to attack her.

The struggle had begun . . . a struggle to the death . . . between Herself and the Other.

.   .   .   .   .   .

The day following, Alcyone had requested Helvidia not to accompany her to the lotus fountain. An old man-servant was to bring her back to Pompeii at nightfall. She sat beneath the mimosa, near the *stela* at the edge of the spring, and gazed long into the peaceful water. The flowers were almost all dead ; a single lotus, however, still appeared on the surface, though it seemed to have no strength to unfold its petals. The sun was setting behind a clump of olive trees, and everything around was bathed in a golden light—the ruins of the temple of Ceres surrounded with oleanders, the chapel of Persephone in the midst of a grove of cypresses, the wide-spreading leaves of the water-plants on the surface of the fountain, and the transparent foliage of the mimosa, reflected in the stagnant water. Alcyone's heart was filled with sorrow and darkness, a sadness that came like a black veil between herself and the world without. In vain for several days past she had invoked Ombricius, hoping that he would answer the appeal of her heart, and return to the spot which had been sanctified by their oath of love. The final links that bound them were now

broken.   She sank to the foot of the *stela* and
closed her eyes.   Hot tears began to stream
down her cheeks; death would have been to her
a welcome relief.   A feeling of peace succeeded
these gloomy thoughts, to be followed in its
turn by one of unrest and pain.   Although she
kept her eyes shut, a dense shadow seemed to
spread around and press heavily upon her.   The
sensation became almost intolerable.

Suddenly she heard a rustling sound in the
reeds, and, turning round, uttered a faint cry.
A tall, stately woman, clad in a folding grey
stola and wearing a black veil, stood watching
her with stern glance, her arms folded over her
breast.   Her hair seemed to form a sombre halo
over her brow, which was crowned with a diadem.   Alcyone recognised the harpy-winged
figure she had often seen in her dreams.   The
living woman, however, sinister and motionless,
was far more terrible to behold than her phan-
tasmal shadow, born of the dreamy vapourings
of the night.   Alcyone clung to the *stela* as the
bird, fascinated by the serpent, clings to the
branch.   Finally she gasped in stifled accents:

" What dost thou wish with me ? "

Enjoying the fear she had inspired in the
prophetess, Hedonia stood there without uttering a word.   Alcyone spoke again in tones of
mingled despair and energy :

" Who art thou ? "

" One thou didst not expect to see here," said the patrician, in a deep, piercing voice. Hedonia Metella is my name; thou must know it, but let me tell thee that I too am a priestess, the priestess of Hecate. Beware of thyself; I am not ignorant of the crime thou art meditating."

" What have I done to thee ? " said Alcyone, clinging more closely to the cold marble.

" What hast thou done to me ? Thou knowest well what thou hast done, evil sorceress as thou art. With baneful thoughts and the froward rites of thy accursed religion, thou art matching thyself against me, seeking to destroy my work and bring it to naught. Thou art plotting against my life, and the life of those dear to me."

" Thou liest ! " said Alcyone. " What crime have I committed ? "

Hedonia walked up to the priestess with the step of a tigress, leaning against the *stela* her pallid face, to which hate had now given an olive hue.

" What means this false tomb on which I read the words : ' Here lies Ombricius Rufus ' ? Liar as thou art, thou hast invented this image in order to torture his soul in this tomb and bring about his death. This is the sacrilegious altar of thy criminal incantations."

At these insulting words Alcyone regained her dignity.

"This empty tomb," she said, "has been erected to the faithless disciple by his masters; such is the Pythagorean custom; there is no magic in it.   As for myself, I come here every day to think of him who once loved me, and whom I have never ceased to love.   I summon him to return to the light of Isis.   It is not his death I desire, but rather his salvation, for it is through thy charms that he has fallen into the darkness of evil."

"Charms?   It is thou who hast worked charms on him.   Long enough was the poor tribune thy slave.   Why didst thou not keep him; I would never have disputed his possession with thee. He only needed to see me twice to be mine. Now that he has become consul and a man of influence through my aid, thou wishest to tear him from me by thy spells, but thou shalt not succeed, cunning though thou art.   Ombricius Rufus belongs to me as long as he lives; he is my conquest, my sceptre, and my diadem. Practise thine art on other victims; know that I will never permit thee to touch my prey.   I will have this pretended tombstone broken to pieces by my slaves.   But first, I will over-throw the image of this ill-omened Genius, with which thou art meditating the death of my spouse!"

A domineering look in her passionate eyes, Hedonia was on the point of laying violent

hands on the small statue, as though, by breaking
the symbol, she would at the same time destroy
the power of the prophetess. The latter, however, with a haughty gesture, placed herself in
the way.

"Thou shalt not touch the image of my protecting Genius without crushing me at the same
time!"

"Wretch!" exclaimed Hedonia, giving way
to her adder-like wrath, "wilt thou brave me,
not knowing that both thy friends and thyself
are already destined to ruin? Knowest thou
not that thou art in my power? Obey and
depart, sorceress as thou art, or I will kill thee
with this weapon which has been consecrated to
Hecate and kissed by the lips of Ombricius!"

The dagger, slumbering beneath her veil on
the breast of the priestess of Hecate, now flashed
in her raised hand. Before such a threat
Hedonia was certain that the virgin would falter
and give way. She glared at her victim with
eyes full of patrician scorn and rival hatred.
Alcyone, however, stood proudly erect before
the glittering steel in a transport of prophetic
exaltation. The look she gave her was so intense
that it bewildered and astonished the priestess
of Hecate, as though it had been another dagger,
sharper and brighter than her own.

"Die! . . . for him . . . and at thy hands?
Well, I am willing to do so! But thou art not

aware that in that case thou wilt lose him.
Once thou hast shed my blood he will love me
again.   Thou art in possession only of his body,
whilst I have possessed his soul!   Is it a crown
of immortality thou wishest to give me?   Be it
so, I will take it."

Alcyone had calmly taken up the laurel wreath
hanging from the *stela*, whilst Hedonia stepped
backwards.

"Strike!" continued the prophetess.

Hedonia, terrified, continued to retreat backwards, when Alcyone tore open her robe with a
sudden movement, laying bare her snow-white
bosom.

"Strike here, strike!" she continued, "then
he will be saved by my blood.   Strike this virgin
breast, which has been torn with anguish for his
sake on many a lonely night.   Thou hast held
him close pressed to thy breast, but I, the Seer,
possess him in another fashion.   I am under
the protection of a Genius; I am Victory beyond
the grave!"

Step by step Hedonia had retreated before
the piercing glances of Alcyone's eyes.   Holding
her powerless weapon in her hand, the discomfited
magician appeared to be defending herself against
the impetuous virgin who, wreath in hand, advanced as the other gave way.   Both women
reached the entrance to the sloping path on the
farther side of the pond.   Here Hedonia suddenly

turned her back to the priestess, and, with a howl of baffled rage, fled like a vanquished fury through the garden.

On reaching the gate she found her slaves awaiting her with the litter. As she was mounting it she met Memnones, who, entering the garden, gave her a wondering glance. The priest saw fear in the distorted features of the woman, and in her eyes a relentless thirst for vengeance.

.   .   .   .   .   .

A presentiment of impending danger had brought Memnones in haste to the garden of Isis ; his meeting with the patrician confirmed his worst fears. He found Alcyone with her hands tightly clasped round the statue of Anteros. At the call of Memnones, she threw herself into his arms. In her eyes was an expression of savage triumph. The blood was coursing through her veins and her whole body seemed on fire.

" What did that wretched woman do to thee ? " said Memnones. "What did she want with thee ? "

" To kill me," replied Alcyone ; " but I drove her away . . . I drove her away !"

She almost shrieked out the words, which died away in a feeble sigh. The excessive strain had overcome her power of resistance, and suddenly she sank in a faint into the arms of the priest. Memnones bore her tenderly to the grotto behind the pond. He deposited his precious burden on the fine sand, and sat down himself on a large stone, resting the head of the prophetess on his knees. Long she remained motionless, sunk in a kind of utter prostration, whilst Memnones smoothed down her golden locks, from which the vital fluid escaped in tiny sparks. When she finally came out of her lethargy, day had given place to night; and stars, like eyes in the vault of heaven, pierced the azure sky beyond the delicate foliage of the mimosa. Alcyone raised her head and knelt in the sand. Frequently she passed her hands over her face, as though consciousness had not yet returned to her. She looked in turn with the utmost wonder at Memnones, the *stela*, and the sky above. As she recognised them an expression of despair and desolation was depicted in her eyes.

"Where hast thou been ? What is the matter with thee, Alcyone?" said Memnones.

Raising her hand, she said softly :

"Anteros is keeping watch in his golden light above, but here everything is dark; I have no one any longer to love me."

"What! Do I not love thee?" said Memnones, opening his arms to her.

Alcyone rose to her feet, and fixed her eyes on her adopted father. She recognised in his face an expression of infinite grief, like to her own,

the sorrow of being no longer loved. There
came to her the memory of all he had been to her,
as she stood there motionless for a few moments.
Then, opening her arms, she allowed herself to
fall on the breast of the old man, uttering one
of those cries, wrung from the heart, which cannot be expressed in words. The gesture and cry
combined annihilated the gulf that had separated them for the past four years. Alcyone
seemed to be melting away in a sea of sobs. By
degrees, however, she grew calm again in the
tender, loving embrace of the priest. Long
and silently they gazed into each other's eyes,
through a double mist of tears.

Every barrier between them had now fallen
away. Their souls were at last exposed, melting
into one another in the infinity of their grief.
This fusion filled them with perfect happiness.
Nothing on earth or in heaven could be more
divine than this silence, these looks of love.
Perfect self-oblivion in such pure affection had
destroyed every obstacle. Through their beings
there passed a vibration of the Soul of the world,
a ray from the heart of Isis.

CHAPTER XVIII

ONE August morning of the year 833 after the foundation of Rome (79 A.D.), a fresh disaster fell like a thunderbolt on the city of Pompeii.

The elective assembly had just met in the forum to nominate a new body of ediles. The decurions, distinguished by their broad purple stripes, were in the centre of the square, addressing the crowds circled around them in support of their candidates. Scriveners, register in hand, called aloud on the voters. The forum was swarming with noisy freedmen, artisans, and workmen of every description. Suddenly there appeared before the senators, in the centre of the forum, a legate from Cæsar, wearing a white, red-bordered toga, his head covered with black crape—a sign which ushered in bad news. In his hand he held an olive branch, in which was intertwined a veil of the same funereal colour. What was he about to announce? The death of the Emperor or of some member of the Imperial family? A suspension of the Circus games to punish Pompeii for her repeated gladiatorial quarrels, or the exile of some famous citizen? What scourge was about to fall on them all or on some one member? A feeling of anxious curiosity, a mixture of terror, pity, and cruelty, such as takes hold of all crowds on the approach of a great disaster, now ran through this mass of human beings. At last silence fell on the people, and Cæsar's envoy spoke as follows:

" Greeting to the illustrious city of Pompeii, in the name of the Emperor and of the Roman Senate. Titus Cæsar, Vespasian's successor, anxious to promote the prosperity and happiness of this city, has heard that it is being preyed upon by dangerous men, who pervert its morals and threaten the Roman people with anarchy by means of foreign cults and ceremonies and doctrines hostile to the Empire. In order to protect the city against its enemies and also in his own defence, Cæsar has summoned before the court Marcus Helvidius, the duumvir, and his wife, Memnones of Alexandria, priest of Isis, and Alcyone, a prophetess, under the triple accusation of conspiracy against the people of Rome, sacrilege against the Emperor and magical incantations. He has delegated his authority as judge at the trial to Ombricius Rufus, consul, who will make a triumphal entry into the city in three days, and judge the case at the court of Pompeii."

A few shouts of "Long life and glory to

Augustus Cæsar!"—raised by hired Hedonians
—followed this proclamation, but the great
majority of those who filled the square received
it in gloomy silence. Everybody seemed filled
with consternation. The accusation of a duumvir,
the first magistrate of the city, was a serious
matter, almost an outrage on the community.
Besides, Helvidius was greatly respected for his
affable disposition, his love of justice, and his
generosity. The prophetess was loved for her
purity of life and kindliness of heart. She had
healed many who were sick. The common
people called her the Vestal, whilst artists gave
her the name of the Dove of Isis. Consequently
a murmur of pity ran through the motley crowd
at the sad news.

Lentulus, however, the duumvir colleague of
the accused, came forward to reassure the people.
He gave a long, crafty speech, full of clever
flattery and ending with the words : " Do not
imagine that Titus Cæsar has any grievances
against this city, or that he hates the prisoners.
The charges brought against them are serious,
and judgment will be pronounced here. The
accused will defend themselves, and if they are
innocent Cæsar himself will load them with
praise and honour and punish their traducers.
The illustrious Ombricius Rufus is coming here
not only in the full flush of victory and enjoying
the confidence of Cæsar, but in joyful triumph.

To celebrate his victory over the Britons, he will give in Pompeii two great shows in the theatre and three gladiatorial fights in the Circus. Prepare to receive him with due honour."

The promise of a triumphal festival and public games possessed so great an attraction for the people that the speech was welcomed with shouts of joy; so fickle, too, is the crowd that the passing sympathy felt for the duumvir and the followers of Isis was speedily drowned in the noise and tumult caused by the expectation of fresh rejoicings.

For months past Memnones had foreseen the fatal blow, for he had been kept informed of Hedonia's schemes and plottings in Rome, and the intrigues of the Hedonians in Pompeii. He urged Helvidius to avoid disaster by exiling himself from Pompeii with his small group of followers, in the trireme which had long been ready, and continuing the sacred work in some other town of Greece or Egypt, far from the suspicious eye of Cæsar and the treacherous patrician who had sworn to ruin them all. Helvidius thought differently, and replied that the hour of the great struggle had come, that he must withstand the blow and brave the enemy face to face, even at the peril of his life. He relied on his eloquence, the prestige of the prophetess, and, in spite of everything, on the justice of Cæsar. His opinion prevailed.

When Alcyone heard that Ombricius was returning in triumph to judge her friends and
herself, she thought of nothing but one thing—
that she would see him again, would meet him
face to face. This one idea awoke the invincible hope of the lover and all the pride of
the priestess. At once she conceived the desire
to make one final attempt to bring her former
fiancé, now a powerful consul, back to the light
of truth by the might of her love. No sooner
had this desire entered that burning virgin heart
than it became a radiant certainty.

Hedonia, relying on the favour of Cæsar and
the victories of Ombricius, was living like a queen
in her palace at Pompeii, engaged with Lentulus
and the Hedonian brotherhood in preparing the
triumphant reception of the consul, shortly to be
followed by her marriage to him. But there was
an ever-gnawing worm present to destroy her
happiness. Could she forget her shameful rout
in the garden of Isis, the bared bosom of the prophetess defying her dagger, the look of triumph on
the face of the virgin as she drove her away like
a thief, and the laurel wreath brandished against
her as a sign of victory ? Though a delicate,
refined woman, so far as voluptuousness and the
art of living were concerned, Hedonia was virile
in action. Now, what man clings to most is confidence in himself; though stripped of all else,
with faith he can again overcome the world.

Though he were to hold the world in his hand, had
he not faith in his own powers it would crumble
away into dust. This faith is the strongest of all
forces ; it is the sinew and the marrow of courage,
the fortress of the will. The wicked know this
as well as the good, consequently they are incapable of pardoning those who make them doubt
their own powers. It was for this reason that
Hedonia Metella, whilst absolutely certain of
Ombricius, could not forgive the prophetess.
Hers must be a brilliant revenge—the humiliation
of her rival and the destruction of the followers
of Isis. Then only would the outraged Roman
patrician become once more in her own eyes the
invincible Hedonia Metella. Accordingly, she
was drawing up beforehand, with the help of
Lentulus, the order of the trial, the points of
accusation, and a list of witnesses.

Meanwhile Ombricius was making his way
from Rome to Pompeii, with a guard consisting
of a cohort of legionaries. Cheers and acclamations rent the air, flowers were thrown at him as
he passed. He was now nearing the summit of
his desires, and yet he had never been so tortured
with anguish. Hedonia had imposed on him the
rôle of judge of the followers of Isis, a character
utterly repellent to him, for Memnones, his former
master, in spite of everything, inspired in him a
feeling of respect. Their condemnation, he well
knew, was the condition of his marriage with the

patrician. But then, could he decide to become the murderer of Alcyone ? Ever since the
mysterious scene of the kiss of Anteros he had
nourished a feeling of bitter resentment against
her. None the less, however strongly he might
accuse the priest of deceit and imposture, and
the prophetess of treachery, she remained a being
apart in his eyes, strange and holy. What would
be his feelings in her presence ? How, in this
trial inspired by hatred and vengeance, could he
reconcile his dignity as consul and judge with the
tyrannical will of Hedonia Metella and the pity
due to a virgin—perhaps altogether innocent ?

When, however, Ombricius was received with
great pomp and ceremony at the gate of Pompeii
by the senate of the city, the flamens of Jupiter,
and by Hedonia herself at the head of the priestesses ; when at night he found himself in the
patrician's reception room, listening to the flatteries
of the Hedonian party ; when he saw the torches
of his approaching marriage shine like glowing
rays of fire in the large dark eyes of Hedonia herself—then his fears and scruples all disappeared.
She who now poured into the same goblet the
wine of pleasure and ambition regained all her
influence over him. Strange feelings entered
the heart of the young consul, for the intoxicating
nectar he was drinking in long draughts from the
eyes and lips and voice of Hedonia flowed through
his veins like some subtle liquid which hardened

him, covering his breast with armour that would be proof against all the attacks of Isis.

. . . . . .

The trial had lasted a week, the witnesses had been heard and the prisoners cross-examined. The day had now arrived on which judgment was to be pronounced.

The public court of Pompeii consisted of three large arcades, facing the temple of Jupiter, at the farther end of the large rectangular forum. Beneath each arcade rose a massive curule chair, made of marble. In the centre one, the highest, sat the consul, Ombricius Rufus, as judge; on his right sat Lentulus, the duumvir; and on the left was a decurion, who acted as clerk of the court and controlled the proceedings. Behind the consul, a bust of Cæsar, of white marble, stood prominently out from an immense pile of arms, consisting of shields, javelins, and bronze eagles, insignia of the legions. On the square facing the judge, there had been erected a kind of wooden platform, on which were the four prisoners—Helvidius and his wife, Memnones and Alcyone. These were separated from the tumultuous mob covering the square by lictors and legionaries, grouped in a semicircle. The witnesses from the different towns, even from Pompeii, were unable to demonstrate that the prisoners had committed a crime or broken the law in any way. Lentulus, however, now began to make treacherous insinuations against Helvidius and Memnones. He accused his colleague of having, in his many travels, detached several towns in Italy and Sicily from Rome, by instigating the senators in them to set up an aristocratic government, and he affirmed that Helvidius had even aspired to become king. His speech ended with a virulent attack on the priest of Isis.

"As for thee, Memnones," he said, "thou art nothing else than a tool of the conspirator Helvidius. Thou hast introduced into this city the worship of a false goddess, the Egyptian Isis, with the object of turning the people aside from the gods of their country. Thou hast dabbled in magic, along with thy prophetess, who has foretold the future, cured the sick in the name of evil spirits, and cast baneful spells on her enemies. In a word, you have all refused to sacrifice to the divinity of Augustus, to the living Cæsar now eigning over the world. For all these crimes we expect the consul to condemn you according to the law. We demand that the fatal trireme which has carried revolt to the coasts of Italy be given up to us ; that its armament and treasures be delivered to the Emperor, and that the hulk of the accursed vessel, polluted by witchcraft, be broken into pieces and burnt on the beach by the citizens of Pompeii."

Helvidius rose to his feet and refuted these charges one after another, except the one dealing with the refusal to sacrifice to Cæsar, which he passed over in silence. He ended with the following words, a fearless affirmation of his thoughts, his plans and hopes :

" I have not opposed Cæsar, but have rather defended the liberties of these towns and their ancient traditions. In each city there ought to be a chosen body of free men, who will teach true dignity and liberty to the people. In these days of cowardice and falsehood, vice and corruption, you create none but slaves of Cæsar or of the people. We initiates are working to forward the time when honours and dignities shall be bestowed according to the worth of a nation's soul ; we furnish an instance of this in our association, in which each soul is free, though acting in accordance with its rank. For this divine dream, this eternal truth, we are ready to live or to die."

" Thou wouldst be king ! " exclaimed Lentulus.

" Yea, a king in spirit ! " replied the accused, in haughty, thrilling accents.

Memnones rose in his turn, and in grave tones said :

" I know not if we be guilty according to the laws of the Roman empire and religion ; we are not by those divine laws inscribed in the heart of man. We only proclaim the truth revealed to each of us in the secret places of human consciousness and on the summits of meditation. This

eternal truth, the oldest in the world, has always
been concealed from the masses of the people; it
is the truth of initiates in every age. It may
be divined by enthusiasm, won by sacrifice, and
proved by action. The order we desire to establish
on earth is nothing but the mirror of the sublime
hierarchy reigning in the forces of the invisible
universe and the world of spirits into which we
enter. We are advancing towards an age when
the gods will be understood in their essence, blending in the light of Isis, the Soul of the world."

"In speaking thus," said Ombricius, "thou
blasphemest against the gods of the State,
acknowledging thyself to be guilty."

Memnones continued :

"There was a time when thou, who speakest
from thy lofty estate, wert thyself tired of these
gods of stone and brass, the instruments of
tyrannical rule. Thirsting after truth and hoping in the light, thou didst come to us, calling
us thy masters, Ombricius Rufus. Claiming to
judge us, thou condemnest thyself to bitter
remorse. We are not afraid of thee ; it is thou
who tremblest before us. In past times we
caused the living gods to speak in thy presence,
the Spirit, clothed in light and fire. Wilt thou
deny that thou hast seen this Spirit? Darest thou
affirm, in presence of this people, that thou didst
not believe in the prophetess here, that she did
not give thee truthful testimony ?"

Ombricius had assumed his sternest and most haughty expression, though moved against his will as he listened to the voice of his former master. For the first time since the trial began he found courage to look at Alcyone, whose eyes had assumed their trance-like brilliancy. Evdently he was hesitating.

There was a stir in the crowd, and Hedonia Metella appeared, coming from the temple of Augustus, and accompanied by the priestesses of the temple. Dressed as a high priestess, in a purple *stola*, a diadem on her brow, and a band of violet gauze round her head, she advanced right to the centre of the semicircle, facing the tribunal.

"I come here as witness against the accused," said Hedonia. "A month ago I found Alcyone the priestess kneeling before an imitation tombstone erected to the memory of Ombricius Rufus, the consul. The *stela* may be seen by any one in the garden of Isis, bearing the name of the alleged deceased. To avenge herself, she was invoking the aid of her evil spirits, beseeching them to kill the consul, whom she dreaded as her judge."

Whispering murmurs ran through the crowd. Alcyone stood upright and said in clear, distinct tones:

"Never! Not his death, but mine own was I demanding of God. Close by the *stela*, erected by his masters to the faithless disciple, I was offering myself as a sacrifice that he might be saved!"

A murmur of admiration arose from another group. Encouraged by this exhibition of sympathy, Alcyone, in obedience to a sudden inspiration, left the platform, mounted the three steps leading to the tribunal, and kneeling at the consul's feet, held up to him, in suppliant gesture, the lotus flower in her hand. Her gentle voice was heard like a sigh, penetrating to the outer edge of the crowd:

"Remember, Ombricius Rufus!"

The Hedonians, noticing an uncertain look in the consul's face, and afraid lest their cause be compromised, shouted out in one body:

"She is guilty! Her crime has been proved! To the gibbet with the witch!"

Seeing that his liberty of decision was menaced, Ombricius rose to his feet, and, with outstretched arm as though protecting the suppliant woman, he shouted to the people:

"Silence! Let all await the sentence!"

Hedonia Metella, seeing that her victory was being contested, and that Alcyone was regaining lost ground in the mind of her judge, sprang up, a look of scornful pride in her face, as she continued:

"Nor is this all. Look at this cunning, treacherous woman, now endeavouring to deceive her judge with tears and supplications.

Like a Fury she threatened me with death on the pretended tomb of her former love!"

"Thou liest!" exclaimed Alcyone, erect as a lily. "It was thou who wert bent on slaying me with thy dagger. . . . In witness of the truth of what I now affirm, I call upon the gods and my divine protector, upon him who saved me from thee, my Genius, Anteros!"

On hearing this name, Ombricius saw once more in mental vision the scene of the kiss of Anteros. His passionate love for the priestess and his mad jealousy against the intangible lover were now aroused, leaving him in a state of terrible uncertainty. So strong was this impression that, for several seconds, he imagined he saw the chapel of Persephone above the head of the prophetess, who was now defying her rival. No longer did Anteros appear in the guise of a shepherd with his crook, or an Eros bearing a torch; he now resembled a youthful warrior, like another Harmodius, holding in his hand a sword, surrounded by a branch of myrtle.

The consul, terrified, withdrew a step, leaning for support on the curule chair.

Taking advantage of this occurrence, Hedonia addressed herself to the people, and said:

"See, she would bewitch my spouse by invoking her evil Genius!"

In presence of this new situation, which

brought into manifestation the secrets of the
soul and laid bare the deepest motives of the
will; before this scene which brought into view
two rivals in love, contending for a judge,
terrified and harassed; before all this pomp and
splendour which changed the tribunal into a
theatre, the passions of the multitude seemed
to have been unchained, like the roaring sea.
One section cried aloud, "Long live the
prophetess!" another, "Long live Hedonia
Metella!" whilst others applauded Ombricius
Rufus.   The patrician, conscious that some
striking deed or word was needed to attract the
mob to her side and cause the scales of human
justice to incline in her favour, had a sudden
inspiration in her turn.   Rushing to the tribunal,
she seized the consul by the shoulder, as though
to deliver him from the fiendish possession, then,
placing on his head a wreath of gold which she
held in her hand, she exclaimed :

"May Jupiter protect the consul and the
justice of Cæsar!"

Shouts of applause rose from the square,
repeating the words and mingling with them
the cry, "Death to the followers of Isis!"   The
protests of the few were drowned beneath the
increasing uproar.   From that moment there was
neither judge nor court, witness nor auditor, in
that maddened human crowd ; only a band of
motionless lovers surrounded by an ocean of

foaming passions. At a touch of Hedonia, who
held him triumphantly in her arms, Ombricius
felt his fear disappear. No longer did he see
the prophetess or his former masters; he only
heard the roar of the thousand-headed monster,
and felt the thrill which came from the patrician's
arm taking possession of his heart and brain.
Hedonia whispered something in his ear. When
the uproar had calmed down, the consul, amid
deathlike silence, uttered the sentence:

"The followers of Isis are guilty. Let them
be removed to the prison of the Curia. Cæsar
will decide as to their fate."

Amidst the outcry following this verdict
Alcyone remained motionless. Ombricius no
longer saw her, but Hedonia was looking at her,
a gleam of triumph in her eyes. With priestly
gesture, Alcyone crossed her hands over her
breast. Her face had assumed a ghastly aspect,
and her eyes had again lost their light. No one
saw the frequent thrills which ran over her
whole frame. Six lictors surrounded Memnones,
Helvidius and his wife, and led them away to
the subterranean prison of the Curia. Two
others brutally seized hold of the prophetess by
her arms. Inert and motionless, she offered no
resistance. Just at this moment a band of
men, women, and children ran up, exclaiming,
"Do not harm the priestess who healed us of our
infirmities; she is sacred!" An old priest of

Apollo, who had witnessed the whole scene of the trial and condemnation, intervened, and said in a tone understood by both the consul and Hedonia:

" Let this virgin be taken to the temple of Apollo. She is a Pythoness. I will take her under my protection, and I forbid any one to touch her. If Cæsar claims her, Apollo will restore her to him."

No one dared utter a word of protest. The lictors released Alcyone, and the prophetess, with face white as the robe she wore, and pressing with both hands the lotus flower to her breast, walked slowly, amid a silent respectful crowd, in the direction of the temple of Apollo, facing the Curia.

CHAPTER XIX

THE LOTUS FLOWER

In a dark cell in the temple of Apollo the old priest was standing before the prophetess, seated on a straw-mattress.

"Stay here," said the old man. "No one will disturb thee. We know that a god speaks through thee. Rest and fear nothing, we will protect thee."

Alcyone bowed her head in token of assent, and, in her gratitude, held out both her arms. Then she fell on to the couch quite tired out. The priest left her there, after placing on the table some bread and a bowl of milk.

A creature of dreams and inspirations, Memnones' adopted daughter had hitherto lived by impulse. The flying hours had brought her the intoxication of joy or the torture of sorrow, without her knowing the reason. Her wonderful dreams had transported her from earth to heaven, flinging her back into the depths of the infernal regions, without her understanding the law governing these changes. She had allowed herself to be hurled down from the heights of

bliss to extreme grief, just as the vessel, tossed
on the waves, rolls from storm to calm and from
calm to storm.   A terrible shock had now come
upon her ; a cold sweat covered her whole frame.
In the light of this catastrophe, which had also
befallen those dear to her, she began to reflect
on her destiny, and, for the first time, caught a
glimpse of her life as a whole.

Such is the power of that great revealer,
Grief, that it enables a man to behold in a flash
what he had never before seen in the whole of
his life.   Alcyone accordingly asked herself, for
the first time, what strange influence had brought
her, the child of Samothrace, to the temple of
Isis on the banks of the Nile, and from there to
that voluptuous city of Pompeii on the coast of
Italy.   The whole experience of her life as a
prophetess was condensed in that inner, sublime
light, into which she had sometimes been plunged,
casting transcendent looks on mankind and into
the world of spirits.   Had not the might of this
light been concentrated in the glorious vision of
Horus-Anteros ?   Now she knew that the Genius
of her sleep was this Horus, the pure lover of
her youth and childhood who had appeared before her and mysteriously disappeared in the
Isle of Reeds.   What else was the prophetess
ordered to do by Memnones except to bring into
the world the new truth, by the light of Isis
and the love of Anteros ?   And now, overcome

by a baneful love, she had given her heart to
this fatal Roman ; to him alone had she wished
to offer all the wealth of her soul. The wretched
man, however, in his pride, had allied himself
with the powers of darkness, and been won
over by a queen, delighting in luxury and of
overweening ambition. He had spurned all
Alcyone's gifts ; she had no longer any power
over him. It was the Other, the proud, sensual
woman, who now held him in her clutches. In
obedience to the whisper of that infamous mouth,
he had pronounced the criminal sentence, sharp
as the blow of an axe, condemning the prophetess
and her friends to chains and exile, perhaps even
to death !

Everything was crumbling away at once—her
love and her home, her family and country,
temple and god. She was alone . . . alone !

A feeling of faintness came over her with
these reflections, and she sank, face downwards,
on to the couch of the cell. A long-drawn moan
escaped her lips, and her teeth closed upon the
rough mattress, as though she were bent on
suffocating herself.

Finally she recovered, and, feeling considerably
calmer, her thoughts travelled in another direction. Yes, she was alone, stricken to the earth
and apparently powerless. But in her solitude
she felt welling up within her a new power of
sovereign incalculable import—her will. She

no longer loved Ombricius, who had ceased to
exist for her.   The enslaved consul had nothing
of the free tribune she had loved formerly ; he
was not the same person.   He resembled his
mask of old no more than a ravenous wolf
resembles a handsome youth.   The prophetess,
however, must avenge Isis, save her followers,
and bring the truth into manifestation by striking with its dazzling rays the accursed couple.
   Now she had the power to do this, for her
will had become all-powerful, a force sufficient to
break chains, or dash walls to the ground.   To
attain this, she must be willing to die ; only
from the grave-broken doors would a torrent of
light flash on the guilty pair and the ruined city,
saving the followers of Isis for some new work.
Determined on death, Alcyone sank on to her
knees and swore to offer herself up as a sacrifice.
Then rising to her feet, she called upon the two
powers in which she believed—Divine Truth and
her Genius ; and, in the dim light of the temple,
she uttered these two cries, arousing the echoes
from every side : " Isis ! Anteros ! . . . Light !
Justice ! "

.   .   .   .   .   .

   It was the day appointed for the marriage of
the consul and the patrician.   The city of Pompeii had taken on a festival air.   Feastings and
dances had lasted throughout the night, and were
about to recommence, for the rejoicings were to

continue three days, and included such attractions as combats in the Circus and theatrical performances. The names of Ombricius Rufus and Hedonia Metella, interlaced in each other, could be read on the public notices above verdant arches.

Followed by a long procession, they entered the temple of Jupiter. On leaving it, they mounted sixteen steps leading to the temple over against the forum, and there sat down on two chairs resembling thrones.

Here the consular balcony had been erected, ornamented with palm branches, eagles, and trophies for the ceremony of the triumph which had been conferred on the consul by the Senate. Ombricius, with haughty, fierce glance, wearing a red mantle and crowned with laurel leaves, was resplendent in gold and bronze. Hedonia, in a purple *stola*, radiant with joy, her mauve-coloured veil flung back over her shoulders, was seated by his side, in the middle of the daïs. The Senate were grouped around, the priests and the flamens of Jupiter flanking both sides of the staircase. In the square below stood a cohort of legionaries, a human wall indicating the triumphal path by a double palisade of javelins. The forum was swarming with people.

Every time the trumpeters, standing behind the consul, made the square resound with their loud flourishes, a small group mounted the stairs, depositing their offerings at the feet of the consul and his wife.

Legionary soldiers brought shields from Britain, shouting out their war-cry as they piled them on the top of one another. Gladiators flung before the tribune their long swords, their nets and visors. A procession of patrician women placed before the couple caskets of cedar-wood, filled with Syrian silks, and tripods in which Oriental perfumes were burning. The grape-gatherers, men and women with faun-like gestures, came from the neighbouring country, carrying baskets of fruit, cornucopias, and bundles of thyrsus. Decked with vine leaves, they sang of the new Bacchus, victor over the barbarians, and of his Ariadne. Finally Lentulus, in the name of the Senate, offered a small golden statue of Victory "to the deliverer of Pompeii." With a gracious smile, Hedonia Metella received it in her hands and placed it on the top of the consular throne.

"Long live the deliverer of Pompeii! Long live Hedonia Metella!"

Whilst the clamorous plaudits were resounding throughout the forum, Ombricius rose to his feet briefly to thank the Senate, people, and city which had welcomed him so heartily. The words, however, froze on his lips, for his fascinated eyes had caught sight of an unexpected procession leaving the temple of Apollo and coming towards him from the other end of the square. The crowd respectfully stood aside to afford free passage.

It was a procession of women, clad in white. These priestesses of Apollo bore in their hands branches of laurels, surrounded with fillets. As they came they sang a solemn Doric melopœia. At their head was the old priest, preceded by a white-robed virgin of ghastly pallor. She advanced with slow, measured steps, and seemed to be guiding the procession. A thrill ran through the frame of Ombricius, who recognised the prophetess, Alcyone. Hedonia too had risen and stood there amazed at the sight. The crowd, which a minute before had been in a state of mad excitement, had suddenly become silent, and were now strangely moved, as though in the presence of some mighty power.

Alcyone, tranquil and steadfast as Destiny, mounted the temple steps, followed by the priests and priestesses. When within a few steps of the daïs she halted in front of the triumphal couple, surrounded with palms and trophies and tripods filled with burning incense. Gazing in turn at the consul and his wife, the senate on the daïs, the priests marshalled on the steps, and the people at her feet, she said in gentle, penetrating tones:

"Ombricius Rufus, consul of Rome, and Hedonia Metella, his bride; you priests, soldiers, and dwellers in Pompeii, give heed for the last time to the prophetess who has come from the shores of Egypt to bring you the ray of Isis."

Priests and senators bent forward, overcome by a feeling of uneasy curiosity. A sympathetic murmur ran through the crowd, like the ripple of a zephyr on the surface of a stagnant pool. Hedonia Metella had, however, now regained possession over herself. With a foreboding of impending misfortune, she raised her powerful voice and said :

"Do you, flamens of Jupiter and priests of Apollo, impose silence on this woman, speaking here against the law, and take her back to the prison where she ought now to be lying. The court of Cæsar has condemned her; she is a priestess no longer."

The priest of Apollo, raising on high his laurel branch, answered :

"One may not silence a Pythoness, consecrated to her god. Thou shalt listen to her, yea, and in silence to the end, daughter of Metellus and spouse of a consul ; and all the people shall be present, for these are her dying words ! "

Not a priest opened his mouth ; not a senator moved. The immense crowd stood motionless, with bated breath. Alcyone, who appeared not to have noticed the interruption, continued in familiar, almost childish tones, which the swelling waves of an inner ocean gradually brought up from the depths of her consciousness :

"Five years ago my father Memnones and myself came as envoys from the sages of Egypt to bring a ray of sacred light into this land. At the marriage of the intrepid Helvidius and the noble Helvidia I met this man, Ombricius Rufus, who besought me to open for him the world of light, to which I had the key. I promised to do so, and he plighted his troth to me near the lotus-fountain . . . and I loved him." (At this point Alcyone's expression was one of wonder and amaze. She bowed her head as though looking intently into the depths of an abyss.) "Oh, I had no hopes of becoming his wife, like this woman, before all the people and amid scenes of imperial pomp and glory. My ambition was to guide him in the sacred barque to the haven of Isis. . . . He would have come back . . . different . . . a hero . . . a demi-god . . . to this city . . . filled with divine thoughts . . . with garlands of fire and swords of light . . . and I should have remained unknown, in the temple . . . his veiled, his hidden love . . . his prophetess! This was naught but a virgin's dream. Ombricius, thou hast preferred to follow the powerful patrician. She has made thee consul by enveloping thee with a mantle of darkness. Into thine heart she has poured the poison of falsehood and hatred, defiling thy hands with the blood of thy rival. In order to still the voice of Isis, she has closed the temple of the goddess and flung her disciples into chains. Beware, Hedonia Metella! Thy victims' chains shall be broken by fire. Their prison walls shall fall, crushing thee beneath their ruins. The barque of Isis, the trireme thou wouldst burn, shall escape thy destroying hands and set sail to other shores. . . . Do thou also beware, Ombricius Rufus, for in thy very wedding chamber thy Bacchante will be transformed into a Fury!"

"Thou art a Fury thyself!" exclaimed Hedonia Metella, losing all self-control. "Priests of Jupiter, will you be so cowardly as to see me defiled with the foaming, venomous slime of her hate? Quick! thrust a gag into her mouth!"

The priests, however, paid no heed to the consul's wife. Dumb with amaze, they hung on every word of the prophetess. Continuing in sweeter and more doleful tones, she said:

"Be not alarmed, Hedonia; I will do nothing to hinder thy marriage. But I, too, Ombricius, must bring thee a wedding present. Others have given thee weapons and perfumes and trophies; I bring thee a flower. This lotus bloom thou once didst bid me keep is thy soul. . . . I have kept watch over it as my only treasure. . . . This flower has been my love, my passion and my glory. For it, I forgot all— Greece, Egypt, my father, even Isis herself. . . . For it, I have languished and burned with passion; for it, I have lived and now go to my death. As I

promised, I return it to thee. And now . . . this
soul for which I have given all, this soul I wished
to bear away to Heaven like a torch of light . . .
is here ! . . . But . . . see ! . . . It is dead ! "

With a gesture eloquent of despair, Alcyone
extended her hand into the empty air. Suddenly she sank down on to the steps, her face
of a wax-like pallor, as her fingers clasped the
withered flower. The consul drew nigh and
leaned over the body. He touched her hair ;
cold drops of sweat were trickling down. Then
he placed his hand on her heart, which was feebly
beating. In accents of despair, he called aloud :
" Alcyone ! Alcyone ! "

He seemed to understand for the first time
the full significance of this name. The priest
of Apollo also bent over the prostrate form
to feel the heart of the prophetess. After a
moment's interval he stood erect and, turning
to face the square, said in solemn accents :
" She is dead ! "

The crowd immediately made a rush in the
direction of the stairs. All wished to see the
sacred body of the prophetess, to look on that
face from which the soul had now fled.

At this moment the ears of all present were
deafened by a frightful sound—the rolling of
subterranean thunder. It shook the ground
with the noise of thousands of war-chariots and
the crash of the thunder-bolt in the clouds. This

lasted for several seconds, then everything became quiet once again.   Not a house had fallen, but for a few moments the forum had resembled a storm-tossed sea, and the temples around had looked like ships driven before the gale.   From a thousand mouths arose the horrified cry : *terræ motus!* Sixteen years before, the city had been devastated by an earthquake, consequently at this fresh indication of coming disasters a panic of fright had seized upon this human ant-hill. Senators and priests, people and soldiers jostled one another like the ebbing tide as they fled in every direction, filling the air with groans and curses.

Ombricius had stayed on his knees by the side of the dead Alcyone, his left hand laid on the clammy brow of the priestess, his right pressed against her heart, which had ceased to beat. Hedonia Metella was standing there, silently gazing on the scene.   Her hand clutched the vacant throne convulsively as she looked on, paralysed for the first time in her life by a fear stronger than her own will.   When the awful thunder beneath the earth had passed and she saw the people fleeing, she descended a few steps, and, seizing Ombricius by the arm, which she shook vigorously, said :

"Wretch! wilt thou remain here or follow me?"

Ombricius rose, passed his hand over his brow, and, with a startled look in his face, he murmured:

"Yes, let us go!"

The consul and his wife hastily descended the temple steps. Amid the general panic no one troubled about them. They hurriedly mounted the palanquin and were borne away by the Libyan slaves.

A solitary group of flamens and senators remained by the body of Alcyone on the steps of the temple of Jupiter. In their midst stood the priest of Apollo, who spoke:

"You have condemned a true prophetess, one protected by the gods. Let this city see to the funeral of Alcyone. Erect in her honour a royal funeral pile, surpassing any that princess ever had. So will Pompeii atone for its misdeeds and avert divine vengeance."

"Yes," said a senator, "let us raise to her a queenly pile to assuage the people, who, in their fear and rage, might turn against us."

"To appease the anger of the gods," said a priest of Jupiter.

"To honour a nobler soul than ours," said the priest of Apollo.

That evening, in the deserted forum of Pompeii, a solemn procession made its way—priests of Apollo, followed by weeping priestesses, bearing funeral torches. On a bier covered with flowers the lifeless body of the prophetess was carried away to the temple of Isis, where it was laid out in state.

BOOK IV

LIGHT

Lux Victrix.

" Æternumque adytis effert penetralibus ignem."
—VIRGIL.

" La philosophie n'est qu'un retour conscient et réfléchi aux données de l'intuition."—BERGSON.

CHAPTER XX

The burnished gold of the twilight lit up the cornices of the temple of Jupiter, and the large square of Pompeii was almost deserted, when twelve lictors, accompanied by a troop of legionaries, conducted the three condemned prisoners into the subterranean vault beneath the forum. The prison was entered by a low door opening on to a narrow staircase inside the *curia*. The jailor's dark lantern lit up the steps. Memnones, with impassive countenance, was the first to descend; Helvidius followed him. Before entering the darkness of the prison a glance of defiance shone in his eyes as he turned round to look at the setting sun. Helvidia followed, a veil round her head, unable to restrain a sigh as she set her foot on the damp soil of the pit. Legionaries, with drawn swords, brought up the procession. They traversed several dark dismal-looking dungeons, and finally came to a wide vaulted cellar. Through a grated window in the roof a feeble ray of light made its way.

"Here the condemned prisoners," said the jailor, "are to await the orders of Cæsar."

Then with his attendants he disappeared, a heavy door closed noisily, and the prisoners remained alone in subterranean darkness.

The dim light from the roof showed them a couple of straw mattresses, a table containing a few cakes of rye, a large pitcher full of water, and terra-cotta plates.

Clinging to her husband's arm, Helvidia, dumb with terror, looked in despair at the pale light from the air-hole, as though her last hopes were dying away. By this light the priest of Isis and the disciple of Pythagoras gazed at one another. Worn out by the fatigue of the day and half crushed by their unhappy lot, they yet read in each other's eyes not the lassitude and weariness born of despair, but rather energy for the final struggle and defiance of death. They understood and clasped each other's hands.

"Let us sleep now," said Helvidius; "to-morrow we will make an attempt at escape."

Memnones flung himself upon his wretched couch, Helvidius sat on the other, whilst Helvidia stretched herself with a groan by his side on the straw. Utterly exhausted, she fell asleep, but the two men lay there, staring into the darkness, reviewing the whole of their past lives and seeking to fathom the destiny in store for them.

His powerlessness added a feeling of profound

bitterness to the sadness of Memnones. Was not this dark cell, presage of an ignominious end, the supreme irony of destiny against a life wholly dedicated to the search for truth? Had he not sacrificed all to the desire to penetrate behind the veil of Nature into the world of spirits right to the centre of all life? At the outset the invisible powers had favoured him by giving him his adopted daughter, Alcyone the prophetess. She had become his illumination, his torch, and his hope. By her help and in her company he had entered the world of the Beyond, but just as the initiate was about to attain to the divine source he had been blinded by the illumination issuing from it. Horus-Anteros the disciple, the rival he had formerly repulsed, and who had become the Genius of Alcyone, had said to him : "Thou shalt go no further!" Since then Memnones had been living in the shadow of darkness. He had waited and suffered, finally accepting a new disciple, Ombricius, who had become another rival. He had loved him so well that he had promised him Alcyone as his bride. And now the ambitious youth had become the destroyer of them both and everything seemed lost. What would become of Alcyone, separated from himself? Was she to perish in wretchedness and misery, or was he to die without seeing her again? Was this the terrible Nemesis that Sabaccas had pre-

dicted for her on the sands of Egypt? Was
this what the spirit was exacting of him in order
that he might attain to the final initiation?   So
that he might mount to God, must he renounce
all that was most divine and sweet—the possession of the soul he loved?   Before such
a thought he seemed to feel eternal darkness
closing in upon him.

Suddenly, in obedience to a fresh impulse
coming from the inmost depths of his being,
Memnones rose to his feet and said with all the
energy born of that inner voice which calls forth
unknown forces:

"Be it so, I will make the renunciation . . .
but grant that I may see my Alcyone once more
victorious, in the light of Isis, as I see her now
. . . . and may the guilty receive their due
punishment!   Light, Justice, Truth!   When
these three rays unite into one, then becomes
manifest the glory of God!"

In the other corner of the prison, Helvidius
too lay plunged in thought.   The darkness
weighed no less heavily on him, nor were his
reflections less painful, but he did not suffer so
much.   Younger and more energetic, he had
retained power to rebel.   Rebellion, the final
resource of the slave and the prisoner, though it
be silent and unmanifest, is action all the same,
the roar and groan of a hope that cannot be
quenched.   Helvidius was one of those men who

have come into the world with light both in
heart and in mind. The profound learning of
Memnones was not his, though he possessed, in
a measure, its very essence, instilled into his inmost feelings and thoughts, and shining forth in
his slightest actions. His dream and aspiration
was the free city, not knowledge of the great
mystery—free, though not after the style of the
cities of Greece in which implacable oligarchies
and raging demagogies strove for power, nor as
in Rome where the might of a tyrannical Senate
had finally become concentrated within the hands
of an all-powerful Cæsar. What Helvidius
wished was a city free because it held a select body
of initiates, setting up around them a hierarchical
chain of souls, according to their worth or stage
of evolution. A fantastic dream, they said,
perhaps a premature one, but then was it not
appointed for man by the laws of the universe
and of human consciousness? Such a faith had
been that of Pythagoras; now it was his own.

To fulfil this dream he had had the trireme
built, and carried the new gospel to the towns
of Magna Græcia, after inviting Memnones and
Alcyone to Pompeii. In this belief he had won
the heart of Julia Helconia, who had become
his wife Helvidia. Alas! what had been the
result? In spite of his eloquence and his earnest
efforts, he and his party were falling into the
hands of Cæsar, and the blow had been struck

by the very man on whom he had founded his brightest hopes, Ombricius Rufus, the faithless disciple who had been converted into an enemy. The duumvir's fortune would help to fill the coffers of the emperor, whilst he himself, with his wife and his friend, might be put to death at any moment, under the charge of conspiracy. Helvidius could not think without a groan of how his young children would fare, his two sons who had been left at home under the care of freedmen.

And yet something told him that he would not perish in that squalid prison, that some power mightier than his own would burst open the dungeon doors. Then, thinking of the great Stoics whom Nero had put to death, Helvidius rose to his feet and uttered to himself the following prayer:

"Sovereign God, who reignest over my soul, I have lived for Light and Liberty. If I am to die, grant that my blood may be shed, in the light of day, before the whole people, as an offering to Jupiter the Deliverer!"

Peace thus entered their troubled souls, and Memnones and Helvidius sank into a deep sleep. Helvidia, starting up from a nightmare, heard through the darkness nothing louder than the sinister flight of a bat and the intermittent moaning of the wind through the window of the vault.

.   .   .   .   .   .

The prisoners awoke late, aroused by the sound of ceaseless steps and mingled voices in the forum. Had the people assembled spontaneously in order to set them free ? For a moment that was what they believed; they were speedily undeceived, however, for the air was rent with cries of "Long live the consul! Glory to Hedonia Metella!" Then they understood that the fatal couple were celebrating their marriage, building up their triumph on the downfall of the poor prisoners. Fascinated by the murmurs of the crowd thronging above their heads, they stood beneath the window, trying to guess what was taking place on the square. Their over-excited imagination pictured a glorious scene—the couple mounting the sixteen steps of the temple of Jupiter. From the prolonged cheers and frenzied shouts of the masses, they recognised that Ombricius and Hedonia had left the sanctuary. After a time, a dull feeling of anguish came over them, overwhelmed by the waves of that human ocean, ever ready to plunge into the most abject servitude before the apotheosis of evil.

When the hymn of the priests of Apollo sounded forth, they imagined that these latter also were submitting to their insolent conquerors, for they knew not that Alcyone was at their head, about to breathe out her life at the feet of the consul in one final cry of love and devotion. Then followed profound silence,

strange and prolonged, to be succeeded in turn
by a mighty clap of thunder and the rumbling
of an earthquake.   For a moment the prisoners
imagined that the vault of the cell along with
the forum would crash down upon their heads.
The terrified crowds were now flying in all
directions, and presently a voice was heard,
calling through the window :

"Memnones, Helvidius, are you there?"

"Yes, we are here!" replied Helvidius, who
had recognised the voice of Calvus.   "What is
the matter?"

"Alcyone is dead. . . . The Senate have
decreed a funeral pile in her honour. . . . The
people are on the point of revolt. . . . Hope on!
We wish to——"

The rough voice of the legionaries, guarding
the *curia*, cut short the communications of
Calvus, whom they drove away.   On hearing the
fatal news, however, Memnones had tottered
and fallen to the ground.   With some difficulty
Helvidius and his wife dragged him to his couch,
where he lay motionless.   In his deep despair
and stupor his lips could utter nothing but the
syllables of that beloved name, summing up as
they did the immensity of his love and of the
loss he had sustained :

"Alcyone is dead!   Alcyone!"

"Courage!" said Helvidius, "her soul is now
set free to aid us left behind to fight for the

truth. Remember the earthquake; Nemesis is at hand. Wait."

More gloomy and heavy than the first was the captives' second night. Memnones sank into that profound slumber which sometimes comes upon those who are patiently waiting for death. Towards morning he had a more beautiful and living dream than any that had yet come to him. A shining white light appeared at the upper door of the prison and descended the stairs. As it drew near the priest recognised Horus-Anteros, in the shape of Hermes, caduceus in hand. His body shone like a silver shield, and his face reflected the glory of the sun. He said:

"Peace! Alcyone is still sleeping. Soon she will awake in joy and bliss beneath my sceptre. Thou wilt see us both in the solar radiance. Now rise to work! Escape in the trireme. Avoid Eleusis where the torch of Isis is dying out; proceed in the direction of the north!"

Memnones awoke, relieved by this wonderful dream, and feeling as though he were coming from a bath of light, whose warm soothing waves still rippled over his revived limbs. It was night, but a faint gleam of light entered by the window. Filled with renewed strength, the priest drew near Helvidius, who was asleep on his pallet, in sitting posture, leaning against the wall. Vigorously he shook the duumvir, who shortly opened his eyes. Helvidia was sunk in slumber, her head reclining on her husband's shoulder.

"Hast thou seen nothing?" asked Memnones.

"A few minutes ago," said Helvidius, still half asleep, "I thought I saw a youthful Hermes pointing with his caduceus to our trireme."

"And thou?" asked Memnones of Helvidia, who had just raised her tired head from her husband's shoulder.

"I saw a Genius leave this place," she said. "With his sceptre of light he traced out a path over the sea."

"Courage!" said Memnones, "I too saw him. It is Anteros, the Genius of Alcyone and our guide, and he spoke to me. Soon we shall be free to begin again a new life!"

Thereupon the three prisoners stood up in the cell and embraced one another as though they had just met after a long journey. They seemed to form an unbreakable chain. The pale dawn entered through the window, and the doors of the prison still remained closed against them; all the same, everything had changed, for their souls had been revived with celestial beams. The walls separating their bodies had crumbled to dust; the barriers that kept their souls apart had melted into thin air. The mighty universe lay open before them beneath the foaming billows of light that welled up from their enraptured hearts.

CHAPTER XXI

THE FUNERAL PILE

THE consul and his wife had slunk into their splendid palace like thieves amid a crowd of terrified slaves. The tragic death of the priestess weighed heavily on the minds of all; it was a sinister omen, big with dreadful misfortunes close at hand. Not a man in Pompeii but trembled at the threat of Destiny; the most wretched and terror-stricken of all was Ombricius himself. Certain events produce in the mind an effect resembling that caused by a mighty cataclysm. A veritable upheaval of the poles of existence, they prove to man that he has no real power, that there is a power which is higher than his and opposed to it. The consul, who a short time before had appeared all-powerful, now had the appearance of a wild beast which, after an earthquake, has lost his den and is prowling anxiously around for his lair. Hedonia followed him, troubled and dismayed. As though to conceal himself from the eyes of all, he returned home and went straight to the *lararium*, the chapel of his wife's household gods, and there he sat down amid the statues of the ancestors of the

Metella family.   These draped figures seemed to look down in scorn at him.   Hedonia sank down by his side and, flinging her arms round his neck, whispered in his ears :

"What is the matter with thee, Ombricius ? Wake up, forget this nightmare.   Hast thou ceased to be consul because of the earthquake ? This priestess, who is now dead, was thy evil genius.   Our enemies are vanquished.   Leave these stupid people to weep and lament ; to-morrow we shall be the masters."

"Masters of what ? " stammered Ombricius, as though speaking in a dream.

"Of Pompeii and Rome ; of the whole world."

"True.   But Pompeii is no longer ours.   Rome is not Rome any more, and the world is no longer the world."

Ombricius still saw Alcyone dying at his feet, the withered flower in her hand, which moved convulsively.

He was listening again to those terrible words : "Here is thy soul . . . it is dead ! "   He saw the people rushing about the streets, and an empty space all around.   It seemed to him that the world, too, had lost its soul.

Hedonia continued, her burning words mingled with caresses :

"Art thou no longer Ombricius, my virgin Cæsar who has now become my spouse ?   Art thou my Bacchus no more ?   Remember the

days of Rome and Baiæ. . . . Come, let us give
ourselves up to love. . . . To-morrow we shall
be younger and stronger than ever ! "

Mechanically Ombricius rose to his feet and
allowed himself to be led away. Though Hedonia
still had her arms round him, he imagined himself
to be trampling through blood, and that breath
which had once filled him with the intoxication
of delight now seemed to emanate from some
wild beast. Seeing the triumphal bed in a room
all covered with oriental carpets, he shuddered
all over and placed his hand to his heart. He
imagined he saw the temple of Isis changed into
a "chapelle ardente," and Alcyone's corpse, transparent as alabaster in its rigid beauty, laid out on
a couch in the middle. This corpse, more precious than any living thing, attracted him with
irresistible might. . . . Then this inner vision faded
away, and he saw once more the purple bed in the
room which now seemed to him a place of infamy,
the den of an assassin, red with the blood of
the just and innocent. Hedonia herself appeared
to be one of the chimera-faced spectres, with its
ghastly smile and lewd, wanton eyes distilling
deadly poison.

"Leave me," he said suddenly, with a look of
horror in his face ; "I must be alone."

He appeared like one possessed. Hedonia, in
astonishment, left him, seeing that she had no
power over him at that time. Ombricius retired

to the *lararium* and sat there with a lamp on the ground in front of him, for he could not endure to be alone in the darkness. Finally he sank into a kind of half sleep; at one moment he saw Alcyone come up from a spring, as with a smile she raised to heaven a flower of light; then, again, he saw her expire at his feet, with the cry, "Thy soul is dead!" Thereupon, Ombricius rose to his feet and drew his sword to prove to himself that he was indeed alive, only to sink back on to his bronze seat, his heart all cold and chill as though the hand of death lay on him.

Hedonia, too, spent a sleepless night on her lonely couch. For the first time Ombricius had opposed her; the spectre of Alcyone was keeping him back from his wife. Hedonia had torn her lover from the living priestess; was this latter, now dead, about to take him back from his lawful wife? Impossible! But what was the meaning of this phantom gliding between them like a veil? Was Hedonia about to lose the man she had drilled for her work, the weapon she had forged for herself, the sceptre she had won by her magic, the future Cæsar for whom she was weaving a mantle of purple on the cunningly wrought warp of her whole existence? For the future their destinies were one; if Ombricius fell, she would fall also. No, this could not be; it should not take place. Hecate would not abandon them, for Hecate was Hedonia Metella, with all her feminine charm and masculine will.   At all costs, however, the demon-possessed consul must be taken away from Pompeii before Alcyone's funeral procession took place.   Hedonia turned over on her couch and lay with her burning cheek pressed against the dagger of Hecate.   The cold steel relieved her, as, unable to sleep, she lay there motionless, meditating with all her powers of concentration.

.   .   .   .   .   .

The following day Ombricius wrote a letter to Cæsar and gave a few orders to the centurions guarding the city, for rumours of rebellion were now in the air.   Then he sat down once more, deep in thought.

"What can this formidable power be," he reflected, "rising up behind the corpse of the priestess and hurling itself upon me ?   Is there a God, and if so, can he be with the followers of Isis? Are they right, or am I ?   The side which proves itself strongest will be right.   But how can I attack this invisible power which has paralysed my will and is inciting the people against me ?"

Raising his eyes, he observed Hedonia Metella standing before him.   She wore a travelling mantle, a dark veil wrapped round her head, and covering her face, so that she could not be recognised.   Her arms were crossed, and a smile of bitter scorn was on her lips.

" What thoughts are thine ?   Wilt thou spend

the whole day hiding here like a terrified slave
when we should be up and at our foes? If thou
art too cowardly to be the husband of Hedonia
Metella, remember, at least, that thy duty calls
thee to rule over this city. Dost thou hear
those shouts in the distance? It is the crowd
clamouring against us."

" It is thou who hast brought the tempest
about our ears with this trial thou hast instituted,"
said Ombricius.

" Ungrateful coward ! " continued Hedonia,
" it was I who made thee consul ! But for me,
what would have become of thee? Whatever
thou doest now, our destinies are united for
ever. Thy power is mine and my crimes are
thine. We must overcome or perish together."

" Thou speakest truth," said Ombricius, with
bowed head.

Walking up to him, she placed both hands on
his shoulders. Her hastily tied locks fell in disorder about her neck, whilst a look of eager desire
shone in her eyes which a secret anguish had
endowed with a new charm. At this moment
she resembled a guilty shade from Acheron, promising her lover unheard-of delights in the dark
bowers of some deep inferno. She whispered :

" We will wait till the storm is over and
escape for a few days. Come with me to my
retreat at Baiæ ; there I am a sorceress, able to
restore thee to thine own self once again ! "

"Be it so!" said Ombricius, rising.

He could see no other escape from the anguish with which he was torn. Hedonia had already hurried him to the door, where the litter and the attendant Libyans were waiting. Here a mighty uproar greeted them; crowds of the populace were rushing up the street, exclaiming:

"The procession! The funeral procession!"

In a neighbouring thoroughfare could be heard the dull sound of hurrying men and women, mingled with the plaintive strains of a melopœia chanted by the priests. A bare-armed, sinewy blacksmith strode along waving a lighted torch and shouting aloud:

"This torch is to light the funeral pile of Alcyone."

Hedonia turned pale and Ombricius stood still, as though struck by lightning. An inner voice was hammering into his brain these words:

"What! A whole city is in mourning for Alcyone; a stranger bears her torch, whilst I whom she loved, for whom she died, may not behold her funeral pile?"

An irresistible force impelled him forward. Hurriedly flinging the words at Hedonia, " I must go with the rest . . . wait for me!" he plunged into the crowd, as a swimmer flings himself into a river.

Maddened with anger and dismay, the pat-

rician ran after the consul. Seizing him by
the arm, she exclaimed :

"No, no, Ombricius ! Our lives are in danger!"

He thrust her aside, saying :

"I must go ! I must go !"

Twice she attempted to stop him, but in vain.
Then, concealed behind her veil, she resigned
herself to follow him, for she too was impelled
forward by the surging crowd and the fascination
of death, whose dreadful mystery attracts the
spirit in spite of the repugnance felt by the body.

After passing the gate of Herculaneum, a
strange sight burst upon their astonished gaze.
From this elevation the road leading to the tombs
descends obliquely in the direction of the sea.
The mortuary, extending like a triumphal path
from the gate of every city in times of antiquity,
was a specially imposing and magnificent one in
Pompeii. Even in these modern days it may
be seen, scarcely injured by the flight of time.
Two rows of gravestones, small temples, pyramids,
and square or round mausoleums formed a wide,
descending street. These monuments, erected
to perpetuate the lives of those who had passed
away, with their bas-reliefs and urns, their
crypts and lamps, surpassed the dwellings of the
living in grandeur and splendour. The road,
lined with cypresses, gradually widened into a
small wood consisting of a clump of these funereal trees, resembling black obelisks. Mount

Vesuvius and the sea formed the background of the picture.

On this occasion a long procession of men and women dressed in black was making its way along the road. They were surrounded by an immense crowd. A lofty funeral pile on a raised platform showed itself like a pyramid in front of the wood of cypresses. Torches were burning at its four corners. Stretched out on the top of the funeral pile the body of Alcyone lay all draped in white, on a bed of asbestos. From the distance it resembled an immaculate flower, offered up as a sacrifice or a precious perfume about to burst into flame. Priests of Apollo, standing in a circle round this altar, were chanting a funeral hymn.

Even more affecting than the spectacle in itself was the silence of the people and the feeling of sorrow and sadness that weighed them down. The death of the priestess, followed by the earthquake, had stirred to unknown depths the consciences of these servile and sensual citizens. They dimly felt their unworthiness, and trembled at the reflection that they had allowed the noblest being living in their midst to die in this fashion. In accordance with the old superstition that a victim offering himself as a voluntary sacrifice can save a guilty nation from divine wrath, they now filled the air with their supplications, beseeching the departed

priestess to avert punishment from them.   The
dead Alcyone seemed mutely to protest and say
in answer : "O ! City, already dead, I was the
only living soul in thy midst.   I wished to save
thee, but thou wert not willing.   Woe be to thee!"

This at all events was what Ombricius imagined
he heard, in the secret of his heart, as he looked
at Alcyone.   A feeling of terrible anguish had
come upon Hedonia, and this feeling grew more
and more intense from the unwonted appearance
of the surrounding atmosphere.   A yellow mist
was hovering above Vesuvius, gradually enveloping the gulf and causing the light of the sun to
be dimmed.   The air was heavy and stifling.

"Here are the Libyans with our litter," said
Hedonia.   "Thou hast seen all thou didst wish
to see.   Now let us go."

Ombricius, however, forcing his way through
the crowd, soon reached the foot of the
funeral pile.   Dismayed and bewildered, he
looked up at the frail delicate profile of the dead
girl, whose head was hidden beneath a mass of
white roses.   Scarcely any portion of her body
was visible save her waxen blue-veined feet and
a tress of dark golden hair.   Suddenly the hymns
ceased and the priests flung simultaneously their
torches at the four corners of the structure.
The flames curled upwards, licking with hungry
tongues the body which was speedily enveloped
in fire and smoke.

Then the crowd, hitherto silent, rushed forward. Men, women, and children flung into the flames necklaces and ornaments, pearls and precious silks. Hedonia once more seized Ombricius by the arm and said to him:

"Come with me!"

But the consul stood there, rooted to the ground. On seeing the body of Alcyone disappear in the flames he seemed to feel an iron hand plunge into his breast and snatch up his heart, which it flung all quivering and throbbing into the fire. . . . In its place remained an immense void. The living Fury, who had taken his arm in an endeavour to tear him away from the dead girl, was the murderer of the poor victim.

And now the crowd, motionless with terror, was gazing at another spectacle. A column of black smoke was ascending from Vesuvius, splitting up into several branches like a gigantic pine. Shortly afterwards, a series of convulsions shook the ground and a raging wind sprang up. The volcano was shaken with horrible thunder-claps, followed by a mighty eruption. Priests, procession, and people scattered in every direction, like a flock of sheep dispersed by a storm. In a few moments the whole place was deserted. Ombricius and Hedonia alone remained at the foot of the funeral pile, which continued to burn. The smoke ascended to meet that coming from the volcano, like the incense of a sacrifice.

"Thou art ruining us," said Hedonia, in suppliant tones. "Let us take the road leading to Stabiæ and make for the shore. . . . There is still time!"

But Ombricius could not remove his eyes from the funeral pile, which was now nothing more than a pyramid of burning ashes, on which the body of Alcyone appeared, like an incandescent mass.

"I will, I must see her for the last time!" said the consul, stirring up the ruins with an extinguished torch.

"Come at once!" exclaimed Hedonia. "She is nothing more than dust and ashes."

"Dust and ashes? Impossible! She was all flame and life. Thou art darkness, but she was light. Thou art slavery; she was freedom."

Hedonia interrupted him with a haughty, scornful look as she said :

"The fire is dying out and the funeral pile crumbling to the ground. . . . Alcyone is dead!"

"Dead? It may be so. All the same, I love her still; thee I hate!"

Total darkness followed these words. A shower of hot ashes and stones fell on the accursed couple, whose sombre love was flaming forth into livid hatred. The sky was nothing more than a black catafalque and the earth a surface of grey ashes, distinguished at intervals by the aid of the lightning-flashes which formed a wreath of flame round the volcano. Crashes of thunder pealed forth unceasingly.

" Dost thou still love her?" continued Hedonia, in the midst of the tempest. "Then stay with her, wretch as thou art! I looked upon thee as a Cæsar, thou art nothing more than a feeble worm. Farewell!"

" No, by Hecate," said Ombricius, " thou shalt die with me!"

As she was already in flight he ran after and seized her in his turn. With a sudden movement she plunged the dagger of Hecate into his throat, at the very spot where he had struck Cecina. He retained his hold of her, and both rolled into the ashes beneath a rain of fire.

As she fell Hedonia gave a final cry :

" Cæsar! The Empire!"

Through the tempest of ashes and thick darkness, filling eye and mouth, they heard a superhuman voice call out through the depths of space :

" A Soul is worth more than an Empire!"

CHAPTER XXII

THE DREAM OF MEMNONES

A column of smoke, forerunner of the coming
eruption, had just appeared on the top of Vesuvius; the sky was already growing dark, and
the maddened populace was spreading over the
beach, amid the wails of women, the shrill cries
of children, and the shouts of men. Just at this
moment the fishermen on the shore saw the
white trireme, with its yellow sails, which had
been lying motionless a short distance to sea,
suddenly set sail and make for the open bay
amidst a shower of ashes. This was the trireme of Helvidius disappearing in the gathering
darkness.

On the morning of this day the legionaries,
terrified by the subterranean shocks, had
abandoned the *curia*. The prisoners' friends
broke down the dungeon door; Memnones, the
duumvir and his wife were set at liberty. Helvidius at once gathered together his small band
of followers. For weeks past he had had his
dearest treasures transported on board the vessel.
On this occasion he took with him the most

precious of them all—a bronze urn, in which had been placed the burning coals of the hearth and the living fire from the domestic altar, where the final perfumes had been burning during the last prayer. This fire, carefully kept alight, was to glow beneath the ashes until the day when a new home should be founded in another city. Memnones took with him only one thing—a small palm-wood box, containing the books of Hermes. The image of the prophetess remained graven on his heart.

The exiles, grouped on the deck round the hierophant and the disciples of Pythagoras, were all fully resigned to the perilous voyage. They knew they were leaving a city fated to perish, to continue elsewhere the work of life. In their eyes the prediction of the prophetess was now being accomplished. Fire and ashes were raining down on the voluptuous city, in which injustice had erected its tribunal. The smoke, which the volcano's mouth was now belching forth, had already covered the face of the heavens. The black ashes, mixed with pumice-stone, fell in heavy masses on both travellers and sailors. The sea hissed and foamed, and seemed as though bent on becoming reabsorbed in itself, threatening, in its convulsive pitchings and plungings, to capsize the fugitive vessel. With the exception of Memnones and Helvidius, who stood by the pilot, all went below into the cabins. The ship made slow progress, though the darkness was lit up by bursts of flame on the sides of Vesuvius. Squalls and whirlwinds followed each other in rapid succession. Every few moments the cloud would open, pierced by long streaks of flame, like fiery arrows, casting their reflection in the pitchy waters. It was a veritable passing of Erebus, for on every hand the abyss opened its mouth, and death came very near the exiles with each lightning-flash, each yawning of the inky depths. Driven ahead by the tempest, the ship was flung on to the island of Capri ; but just as it grazed the stupendous reef of its precipitous rocks the skies cleared, and the sun appeared once more as from behind a yellow pall. Memnones looked back. The whole of the Bay of Naples now resembled a deep cavern, the black smoke and sulphurous fumes issuing from which formed a gigantic vault. Away in the distance could be seen the fiery cone of Vesuvius, down whose sides a stream of red lava poured over Herculaneum into the sea.

This was the last act of the drama. The sudden eruption of the volcano ended in the total destruction of Herculaneum and the disappearance of Pompeii.

The ship, wafted gently along by a light breeze from the south, now turned her prow to the north, and her sails began to fill. Now that

the danger was over and Cape Miseno rounded,
Memnones was overcome with a feeling of deep
sadness. His tears now flowed for the first time
since the day on which he had held the weeping
prophetess in his arms in the garden of Isis.
He was not now sorrowing for the death of
Alcyone and the loss of a disciple alone. In the
downfall of the past and the uncertainty of the
future he no longer thought of himself. He wept
for the ruined cities and their unfortunate inhabitants ; the whole of mankind and its innumerable
ills ; the sorrows of a world which progresses
only by means of disasters and cataclysms.

Wrapt in his mantle, Memnones lay on a roll
of twisted cord in the open cabin of the prow.
He fell asleep, longing never to wake again, but
as morning was approaching a divine dream
visited him, the most beautiful he had ever had.

He saw Pompeii once again, now a stone-
covered desert. The black cone of Vesuvius was
silent, like an extinct volcano. The path leading to the tombs resembled a field of snow by
moonlight; its monuments, covered with grey
ashes, had all the appearance of an army of
ghosts. Above all this desolation and silence
rose the funeral pile of the prophetess, like an
incandescent torch. In the air above was a
glorious vision . . . a divine couple, Anteros—
Alcyone, clasped in each other's arms. Alcyone
gave Memnones a look of infinite tenderness,

laying her phantom hand on the hierophant's head ; Anteros touched the master's heart with his flaming torch. Then Memnones felt his heart glow with superhuman love, and the divine couple disappeared in the heavens, like a meteor flashing through the azure vault on a warm summer night along the shore of the Mediterranean.

From every direction—from tombs, mountains, cities, country, sea—a populace of souls, alone, in pairs or in groups, resembling thousands of swallows meeting in one mighty swarm before emigrating to some distant land, came hovering about the funeral pile.   In the air the swarm resembled a serpent of light rising higher and higher in ever increasing spirals.   It was making its way to a distant sun, formed of thousands of elect spirits, of such as no longer incarnate on earth, being, as Hermes calls them, "masters of life, lords of time and space."

The funeral pile of Alcyone, the nuptial couch of her heavenly marriage, the only living object in the dead city, all plunged in darkness, still shone and crackled with ruddy flames throughout the night.   It seemed to protest against universal death, and to summon earth to renewed life with its flame of love, a very torch of sacrifice.

In the deep blue of the sky Memnones perceived another spiral issuing like a delicate ray from the distant dazzling sun, to which life was given by the elect spirits, the Lords of Heaven and Earth. This spiral described an immense curve consisting of numerous orbs; it descended to earth as the other ascended to heaven. It was the spiral of souls attracted towards incarnation by the flames of terrestrial love, in which the fire of desire is so strangely mingled with that of sacrifice. As the spiral drew near the earth it widened out into a vast circle, like the mouth of a watering-pot. Its colour passed gradually from a luminous white to a deep red. Like innumerable moths, fire-flies, and bats these soul-sparks were seen to glide beneath the roofs of the busy cities, or into cabins on lonely shores, disappearing in the darkness. All were mysteriously attracted by eager embraces of loving couples to submit to the trial of rebirth.

A wonderful vision of the incarnation and liberation of souls! Were not the descending and ascending spirals, the moving of the Spirit throughout the universe, the ebb and flow of life, the out-breathing and in-breathing of God? For a moment Memnones felt that he had been plunged into the source of the great All. He found himself in the centre, so to speak, of a boundless sphere, from which rays of light flashed in every direction. This Light, which was a Sound, pierced him through and through; and this Sound, which was the Word, said: "Creation! Sacrifice! Love!"

Then the initiate of Isis awoke. It was still dark. The ship was speeding lightly over the waves as the pilot sang a proud, melancholy chant.

Memnones was conscious of a degree of peace and strength hitherto unknown. The Soul of the world had spoken to him in the silence of the night, and the voice of Light was still saying within him: "It is time that men remembered their origin and their end. Woe to him who forgets heaven for earth or earth for heaven. Life receives consecration only by eternity; eternity is won only by life."

Now he felt able to transmute his life into love, and his love into action. Because he had renounced all, he had become a master.

The fusion of Alcyone with her Genius had revealed to him the essence of things. Like a fire-brand snatched from the divine mystery, he bore away this torch far from the ruined city of Pompeii. In like fashion did Virgil's Æneas carry off a flaming brand from the smoking altar of the crumbling city of Troy:

" Æternumque adytis effert penetralibus ignem."

Not, however, from a mortal city or an altar of stone had Memnones received his light. It was from the sun of souls, the heart of God, that it had come down into his own heart . . . a living fire, an eternal ray, able to give light to millions of souls!

CHAPTER XXIII

THE BARQUE OF ISIS

THE sun had not yet risen, and a fresh breeze was coming from the sea, when Helvidius and his wife, taking their two sons by .the hand, came up from the interior of the trireme on to the deck. Memnones joined them, and they all seated themselves close to the large bronze urn which contained the hot ashes of the domestic altar. Helvidius and Helvidia dared not look at each other, for fear they would read in each other's eyes the anguish of the past month and the terrors of the previous evening. Sadly they watched the innumerable waves rippling over the surface of the boundless sea, their only home for the present. They were astonished to behold the clear limpid sky, which appeared to know nothing of the disaster that had befallen Herculaneum and Pompeii. Memnones kept his dream within the depths of his own heart, as the mother-of-pearl shell contains its immaculate treasure within its secret embrace, in the bosom of the peaceful sea, far, far below the storms of the surface. Finally Helvidia, who had placed her cold hands on the burning urn, broke the silence and said with tears in her eyes :

"It is still warm. The fire is alive beneath the ashes."

Helvidius, in his turn, touched the bronze, then pointing to the palm-wood box which Memnones was carrying under his arm, the one containing the books of Hermes, he said :

" We are taking with us the sacred fire of the hearth and the holy tradition ; with these a new city can be founded."

"Cities crumble into dust," said Memnones, " Empires pass away, but the Barque of Isis sails on and on."

" Look, mother ! Kingfishers !" exclaimed the elder of the two sons of Helvidius.

Helvidia followed the flight of the blue birds as they sped past the trireme and disappeared in silver spangles within the opal zone of the horizon, away to the north, as though to indicate to the exiles the direction they must take.

" Happy birds !" said Helvidia. " But where is our Kingfisher, our Alcyone ? "

She raised her hands to her face and wept.

Memnones turned pale. A quiver ran through his whole frame, but he mastered himself, and, gently placing his hands on the young wife's head, he murmured :

" Be not anxious, Helvidia ; Alcyone is far from here, in a world of splendour and gladness, but she will always be with us as Victory, hovering above our lives ! "

And now the coast of Italy had disappeared in the mist. Dawn now showed her rosy countenance in the mauve-coloured sky. A sudden gust of wind bent the mast and shook the trireme on her keel. The children rolled over on to the deck, and the terrified mother gave a cry of alarm as she snatched up the younger boy who was weeping bitterly.

Finally the sun rose above the waves. Half his golden disc pierced the haze, and a thousand streaks of fire shone over the translucent azure of the Mediterranean. Once again a heavy wave set the vessel rolling from side to side.

"The ship is going to sink!" said the little son of Helvidius, clinging to his mother.

His elder brother, however, exclaimed with a merry laugh :

" *Fluctuat nec mergitur !* She tosses about, but does not sink ! "

Then in childish, treble tones he added :

" The sun ! The sun ! "

His tiny hand pointed in triumph to the King-

Star, whose beams shone with all the colours of the rainbow through the gushing foam of the waves.

Thereupon all rose to their feet to greet the source of universal life.

THE END

Ibis Press Books
Age-Old Wisdom for the New Age World!

Ancient Pagan Symbols
Elisabeth Goldsmith

". . . a good resource for symbols of various ancient religions. There is a decent amount of explanation for each symbol, with plenty of illustrations to make the ideas tangible. A considerable amount of research went into this volume."
—*Goat and Candle Book Reviews*

Illustrated with symbols from many great pagan traditions, including Egyptian, Greek, Roman, Nordic, Phoenician, Syrian, and many more. Includes an index for easy referral.
$18.95 • Paper • 288 pp. • 4 ½ x 6 ½ • Frontispiece plus 18 plates with 48 illustrations • ISBN 0-89254-072-9

Asteroid Goddesses
The Mythology, Psychology,
and Astrology of the Re-emerging Feminine
Demetra George and Douglas Bloch

• New edition of a classic first published in 1986, now with updated ephemerides of 16 asteroids for 1930-2050

"Astrologers interested in having an in-depth knowledge of the key asteroids and those who wish to understand better the role that the goddess myths of these four (Ceres, Pallas Athena, Juno and Vesta) as they relate to the changing social values over the past decades will find this book to be the most useful in print. This new edition has a greatly improved ephemeris. . . Those new to the work will find it a rich resource. Older readers like myself will appreciate the improved quality of the printed work."—*The Hermit's Lantern* 10, no. 110
$22.95 • 368 pp. • Paper • 5 ½" x 8 ½" •
22 Illustrations • ISBN 0-89254-082-6

The Cloud Upon the Sanctuary
Karl von Eckartshausen
Translated and annotated by Isabelle de Steiger

• One of the most important, non-mainstream mystical works of the Romantic era.
• Beautifully written inspirational work that helps us reclaim access to our innate spirituality.

In *The Cloud upon the Sanctuary*, Eckartshausen lays out his unique understanding of the Way of Regeneration in Christ and the concept of the "Interior Church"—that mystical body of true believers linked by spiritual experience rather than by doctrine. Foreword by Edward Dunning, editor of *A. E. Waite: Selected Masonic Papers* details Eckartshausen's influence on the Golden Dawn magical order. Preface by J. W. Brodie-Innes; Introduction by A. E. Waite
    $16.95 • 192 pp. • Paper • 5" x 7" • ISBN 0-89254-084-2

The Blazing Star and the Jewish Kabbala
William B. Greene

"Originally published in 1872, *The Blazing Star And The Jewish Kabbalah* by William B. Greene a seminal study of the Kabbalah in terms of its applications beyond the realm of Judeo-Christian mysticism, as well as its role in the western mystery tradition including Rosicrucianism and Freemasonry. Exploring the symbolisms of Kabbalah with a meticulous and scholarly dissection, [it] transcends the century in which it was written and continues to be a relevant and enduring contribution to Metaphysical Studies with its astute insights and thoughtful explanations."—*The Bookwatch*. Foreword by R. A. Gilbert
    $14.95 • 112 pp. • Paper • 5 ½" x 7 ½" • ISBN 0-89254-086-9

The Book of the Mysteries
of the Heavens and the Earth
E. A. Wallis Budge Foreword by R. A. Gilbert

• Long out-of-print translation of the Ethiopic texts formerly thought to be *The Book of Enoch.*
• Essential for serious scholars of esoterica and religion.
• Budge, one of the foremost scholars of ancient Egyptian and Assyrian language, history, and religion, brings clarity to this rare text.

The continuing fascination with Gnostic Christianity has stimulated the translation of a vast range of Gnostic texts with both popular and critical commentaries. But the later texts of the Coptic Church remain virtually unknown outside a small circle of scholars, even more so in their Ethiopic versions. One exception is *The Book of Enoch*, but Enoch does not stand alone. Associated with it is an even stranger and more complex apocalyptic work, The *Book of the Mysteries of the Heavens and the Earth*, which is believed to have been revealed by the Archangel Gabriel in the 15th century. It was introduced to the Western public in 1935 by Wallis Budge. This edition includes an interpretation of St. John's apocalyptic vision, a discourse on the Godhead and the Trinity and a discourse on the birth of Enoch. A new foreword by R. A. Gilbert explains why this book is of particular interest to all students of the occult and Enochian magic.

$18.95 • 192 pp. • Paper • 5" x 7" • ISBN 0-89254-087-7

Count Michael Maier:
Life and Writings
J. B. Craven
Foreword by R. A. Gilbert

"First published in 1914, the photo-mechanically reproduced edition of *Count Michael Maier: Life And Writings* by J. B. Craven analyzes all of the works about alchemy created by Count Michael Maier (1568-1622). Offering a biography of this alchemical pioneer, his pursuit for the formula that would transmute lead into gold, his views of alchemy as both science and a metaphor for spiritual attainment, and so much more, *Count Michael Maier: Life and Writings* is an amazing compilation that sublimely captivates a creative passion that transcends its century of origin. . . ."—*The Bookwatch*

$16.95 • 192 pp. • Paper • 5 ½" x 8 ½" • ISBN 0-89254-083-4

The Diamond Sutra
The Prajna Paramita
William Gemmell, translator

First published in 1912, William Gemmell's translation of *The Diamond Sutra* was one of the first books to introduce general Western readers to Buddhism. *The Diamond Sutra*, a sacred Buddhist text, recounts the Buddha's discourse to one of his disciples. It discusses fundamental Buddhist practices, including the eight articles that Buddhist monks are permitted to possess; begging for alms; how food is to be consumed; and the monastic vows. Gemmell's fully annotated translation presents important information from the Asia experts of his day and still-relevant parallels between Buddhist principles and Western spirituality. One of the best general introductions to Buddhism.

$16.95 • Paper • 160 pp. • 5 x 7 ½ • ISBN 0-89254-075-3

The Mystic Thesaurus
Willis F. Whitehead

During the 1920s, Willis F. Whitehead, was Supreme Grand Vizier, Ancient Order of Oriental Magic. In *The Mystic Thesaurus*, he shares the secrets and tools he worked with in a lifetime of practicing magic. Readers will learn the hidden meaning of the symbolism of the zodiac, the significance of alphabets and tarot cards, the mystery of numbers, and how to make and use a magic mirror to establish contact with astral beings! With a sampling of the work of the famous magician Henry Cornelius Agrippa, *The Mystic Thesaurus* is a primer that any student of the occult will want in their library.

$14.95 • Paper • 96 pp. • 5 ½ x 7 ½ • ISBN 0-89254-069-9

Dionysius the Areopagite on the Divine Names and the Mystical Theology
Translated by C. E. Rolt
New preface by Golden Dawn expert Alan Armstrong

The Divine Names and *The Mystical Theology* were written by a theologian who professed to be St. Paul's Athenian convert, Dionysius. Rolt, however, places him in the time of Proclus, in the 5th century A.D. These works of Neo-Platonic Christian mysticism had an important influence on the early church and other Western esoteric orders and continue to be essential in the serious study of theology. Within these writings are the doctrine of the Super-Essential Godhead and its relation to creation, a discussion on the nature of evil, and a guide to the path of contemplation.

$16.95 • Paper • 240 pages • 5 ½ x 8 ½ •
ISBN: 0-89254-095-8

The Eleusinian Mysteries and Rites
Dudley Wright

The Eleusinian rites emerged from the Greek myth of the goddess Demeter and her daughter Persephone to bring forth abundance from the earth. Yet strikingly similar rituals and legends appear in the doctrines of Freemasonry, Buddhism, the early Church, and other religions and spiritual traditions. In *The Eleusinian Mysteries and Rites*, Dudley Wright explains the core mythology of Demeter and the many stories born of her myth. He includes an examination of the Ritual of the Mysteries, when and how they are carried out, the rites of initiation and their mystical significance. Examination of the myth of Demeter and her daughter Persephone sheds light on the spiritual lives of many ancient peoples. Includes an index.

$16.95 • Paper • 112 pp. • 4 ½ x 7 ½ • ISBN 0-89254-070-2

Important Symbols
In Their Hebrew, Pagan, and Christian Forms
Adelaide S. Hall

Important Symbols presents an extensive compilation of the symbols of ancient cultures, describing the context and usage of each symbol around the world and throughout time. Adelaide Hall groups the symbols into categories, each comprising a chapter of the book. Chapters including "The Halo and the Crown," "Fabulous Creatures," "Architectural Forms," "Military Emblems," "Plants and Blossoms," "Angelic Personages," "Animals," and more open with short explanations and include dictionary style listings of symbols and their meanings. The book is fully indexed for easy reference and includes a bibliography.

$14.95 • Paper • 112 pp. • 5 ½ x 7 ½ • ISBN 0-89254-074-5

Paradoxes of the Highest Science
With Footnotes by a Master of the Wisdom
Eliphas Levi
Introduction by R. A. Gilbert

Paradoxes of the Highest Science first appeared in 1883 in Calcutta as a pamphlet in the Theosophical Miscellanies series. In it, Levi makes an appeal for a balance between science and religion, Levi addresses seven paradoxical statements, including, "Religion is magic sanctioned by authority," "liberty is obedience to the Law," and "reason is God." Included in this edition are the extensive and illuminating footnotes that were added to Levi's text. Some of these are by the anonymous translator, and some by the "Eminent Occultist" who seems to have been Madame Blavatsky herself. Levi could have asked for no better commentator on his work.

$14.95 • 208 pp. • Paper • 5 ½" x 7 ½" • ISBN 0-89254-085-0

With the Adepts
An Adventure among the Rosicrucians Franz Hartmann
Introduction by R. A. Gilbert

Hartmann skillfully weaves the actual beliefs and practices of the ancient Rosicrucians into a tale that includes magic and an alchemical laboratory, unexpected revelations, recollections of past lives, the Rosicrucian view of women and spirituality, the alchemical laboratory, and the higher life. Includes an Appendix about the establishment of a Rosicrucian institution in Switzerland.

$18.95 • Paper • 208 pp. • 5 ½ x 8 ½ • ISBN 0-89254-076-1

Rassa Shastra
Inayat Khan on the Mysteries of Love, Sex, and Marriage
Hazrat Inayat Khan

"This new edition of a book long out of print is welcome in today's world as a greater understanding of some of Islam's mysteries is necessary. Although some of his views (sex is only for "generative" goals) may seem dated, the book is excellent reading and highly recommended."—*The Unicorn*

There are spiritual ideals and moral perspective in relating and Khan covers these aspects in topics such as: types of lovers; the character of the beloved; beauty; passion; marriage; monogamy; perversion; prostitution; attraction and repulsion; sex; courtship; and chivalry.

$14.95 • Paper • 96 pp. • 5 ½ x 7 ½ • ISBN: 0-89254-071-0

Symbols of Revelation
Frederick Carter

This book reveals Frederick Carter's wholly original interpretation of the dragon as a central force in St. John's apocalyptic vision in the Book of Revelation. Weaving the biblical story together with zodiacal and astrological references and their ancient meanings, this book reexamines the vision from a new point of view and asks: Was it prophetic, an allegorical teaching, or an account of a mystical experience? By illustrating the zodiacal and astrological references, and their ancient meaning, Carter gives us the celestial sphere to help us explore threads that make up the fabric in the vision.

$14.95 • Paper • 96 pp. • 5 x 7 •
4 line drawings by the author • ISBN 0-89254-068-0

Theurgy, or the Hermetic Practice
A Treatise on Spiritual Alchemy
E. J. Langford Garstin
Foreword by Edward Dunning

• A thorough introduction to the path of spiritual alchemy.
• Interpretation of alchemical symbolism makes it of great
value to modern readers.

Theurgy means "the science or art of divine works." In
alchemy, this process is called the "Great Work," which is
the purification an exaltation of our "lower" nature by the
proper application of esoteric principles, so that it may
become united with its higher counterparts, whereby we
may attain spiritual, and ultimately divine, consciousness.
Drawing on the teachings of the Egyptian, Greek, and
Hebrew mystery schools and quoting extensively from
important alchemical writers, Garstin details this process of
purification. Students who are curious about alchemy but
daunted by the body of its literature and its strange allegories
will find this book to be an excellent introduction. Garstin
discusses source alchemical works and clearly explains what
their esoteric symbolism means. With the information in
this book, students of alchemy can then proceed to make
a more informed exploration of the alchemic, works and
other writings of the Western Mystery Tradition.

$12.95 • Paper • 160 pages • 5 ½ x 8 ½ •
ISBN: 0-89254-091-5

Forthcoming in July 2004

The Book of Formation, or Sepher Yetzirah

Attributed to Rabbi Akiba ben Joseph
Translated by Knut Stenring,
Introduced and edited by A. E. Waite
Foreword by R. A. Gilbert

The Sepher Yetzirah, or Book of Formation, although very short, is probably the most important of the Kabalistic texts. Its secrets were passed on in the Hebrew oral tradition until it was written down in the 2nd century B.C.E. It lays out the principles of Kabalistic cosmology and the Tree of Life, how humankind (the microcosm) reflects the Divine (the macrocosm). It also sets forth the Hebrew doctrine of Logos—the creation of the world in numbers, letters, and sound. As such, it is a seminal text for all serious magicians. Stenring has made a word-for-word translation from several texts, choosing only those parts which he believed to be authentic. He reveals the text's secrets in his diagrams, tables, and extensive notes. His "Master Key to the Theoretical and Practical Kabala" is a diagram of the correspondences between the English and Hebrew alphabets and is not found in other translations of the Sepher Yetzirah. Also unique in this translation is Stenring's assignment of certain tarot cards to the paths on the Tree of Life. Several authors have done this before, but Stenring asserts that he arrived at his correspondences on his own. The introduction by Waite surveys the historical background of the Sepher Yetzirah translations and the import of this foundational Kabbalistic text. Gilbert's Foreword provides background information on Waite's interest and involvement with Stenring's translation.

$14.95 • Paper • 96 pages • 6 x 9 • Line art and foldout •
ISBN: 0-89254-094-X

Forthcoming in August 2004

The House of the Hidden Places and The Book of the Master
W. Marsham Adams
Foreword by R. A. Gilbert

• Combines two classics on Ancient Egypt into one volume.
• Source work gives clues to the mysteries of the Great Pyramid at Giza and the Ancient Egyptian religion—of interests to all students of the Western Mystery Tradition.

In *The House of the Hidden Places*, first published in 1895, Adams clear lays out evidence that the Great Pyramid at Giza corresponds architectural the initiation ritual detailed in the Egyptian Book of the Dead (which Adams preferred to call what he felt was its rightful title, The Book of ti Master). *The House of the Hidden Places* was the first book to go beyond the current speculations on the astronomical purpose of the pyramid to reveal its deeper meaning. *The Book of the Master*, first published in 1898, is an in-depth exploration of the religious beliefs of the Ancient Egyptians. His penetrating study revealed startling insights for his day, pointing to the origins of Christian theology as well as those of humanity itself. Long before Dr. Leakey discovered proof of our African origins, Adams theorized, based on his Egyptian studies, that civilization began in Africa, rather than Asia, which was the accepted theory in his time.

$24.95 • Paper • 512 pages • 5 ½ x 8 ½ • Illustrations and one foldout • ISBN: 0-89254-092-3